# Revenge Among the Stars

## by

## Vicky Burkholder

**Revenge Among the Stars**

Cover Art by *Debbie Taylor*

The Wild Rose Press, Inc.
PO Box 708
Adams Basin, NY 14410-0708
Visit us at www.thewildrosepress.com

Publishing History:
Previously published as ebook, 2008, and as paperback at Ellora's Cave, 2013
First Fantasy Rose Edition, 2019
Print ISBN 978-1-5092-2800-3
Digital ISBN 978-1-5092-2801-0

Published in the United States of America

Ali hated hiding—only cowards hung back. An action that went against everything she'd learned at the academy. She'd been trained to fight in combat and held the rank of a Battle Captain. BC's did not hide and wait. But neither did they go into a skirmish without a plan.

She forced back her grief for Sean. There would be time later for tears, for the chance to mourn her brother and friends. She needed a plan.

Ali studied the activity again. She couldn't go to the camp or back to the ship. She had enough air for an hour, maybe two, but with her emergency systems off, she would get extremely cold quickly. As she watched, the occupants in the ship nearest the camp started harvesting the asteroids tethered to the home 'roid. It wouldn't take them long to get to her hiding spot.

Another body, this one larger and wearing a standard gray-issue jumpsuit common to most miners, tumbled past her. She didn't want to know whom— didn't want to think. But the bodies gave her a gruesome idea. She thrust slightly toward some drifting debris and forced her body to go limp, pretending to join her friends on their last journey. After all, what was one more body floating around?

## Dedication

Dedicated to my own hero, my husband,
and in memory of my father,
who taught me to look to the stars and beyond

Chapter One

Aleksia Matthews loved her job. Not many people could say the same, so she was doubly blessed. As a geologist and assayer for the Amalgamated Worlds, she traveled throughout the rim worlds, all paid for by the miners and companies who contracted her. But having her brother Sean with her made the time feel like a permanent vacation.

The assayer ship she shared with her brother shone like a silver teardrop in the near distance. Small by modern standards and well out-of-date, it got them where they needed to go. Only Sean's expertise with the antiquated systems kept them running. They knew they should update to a newer one, but the ship had been their home for a long time and held precious memories of their parents for both of them. Neither she nor Sean could give up the connection yet. Their parents had been well thought of in both government and private circles, and their deaths at the hands of pirates had shocked and saddened many—none more so than Sean and Aleksia.

Several times on their travels, she and Sean had come across camps decimated by the thugs. Every time they did, they sent the coordinates to the security forces in the quadrant. Several months ago, she'd started keeping track of the camps. If anyone ever asked, she'd be able to tell them exactly where, when, and who had been hit. So far, though, no one had asked.

She and Sean had been lucky, but luck could be fickle at best. Hopefully the new security systems they'd installed would give them an edge. That and her charts. She had figured out the basics of a pattern to the attacks, but didn't have enough data accumulated, yet. She'd rather not run across any more pirated sites, but if she did, she'd add the information to what she already had. Sean didn't know what she'd been working on, and she didn't plan to tell him—at least, not until she had a blueprint formalized. She would be going after the pirates. And they would pay for what they'd done to her family.

Ali swallowed the sudden lump in her throat and went back to work. She bumped the switch in her helmet with her chin to turn on her mike. She needed something to take her mind off her thoughts. "Hey, Sean, you there?"

"Of course. What can I do for you? You're not done yet, are you?"

"Not quite. But it's too quiet out here. I could use some conversation or music or something."

She winced when Sean started singing an old song he knew she hated. Although he had a good voice, he sang deliberately off-key. She grinned as an idea came to her concerning Sean and his fiancée. "Sean, don't you dare. Stop right now, or I'll tell Susan where you were last week."

The song cut off in mid lyrics. "You wouldn't."

"Try me." Ali jabbed her tester through the flaky surface on the rock. "How 'bout some trivia?"

"Not while I'm rewiring this damned console."

"Again? You just did that two weeks ago."

"Yeah, and it shorted out again this morning. Ali, I know we said we'd never get rid of the old girl, but I think we need to give some serious thought to at least getting a second one—hopefully one with working systems."

"We can talk about it when I get in. Mom and Dad always said the ship would bring us luck. She has so far. I'd really hate to give up on her. I'll let you alone to work on her."

"No prob. You about done?"

"Yeah. Probably another twenty minutes. See you then."

She and Sean were making a name for themselves. They were honest and charged decent rates. In addition, thanks to their expertise with Ki crystals, especially the rare red ones, they were in demand. The crystals' power and strength made them a desired commodity, and the rarity made those who found a source extremely rich. Find a pocket of red, and you were set for life and beyond. As in old times, the draw of riches brought the miners.

Two prospectors had managed to capture a large rock half a kilometer across, but virtually worthless in mineral wealth. In the fatalistic manner of most miners, they had thrown caution to the wind, hollowed out a portion of the worthless rock, and set up camp. They'd spent their last credits on a cheap anchoring system and pulled in a dozen of the smaller rocks circling nearby and hired Ali and Sean to examine them.

Ali checked her test samples and let out a low whistle. She hit the mike button. "Sean?"

"What you got?"

She could just imagine her brother, his head

probably stuck inside an access panel, a lock of dark chestnut hair falling over his eyes. She kept threatening to take a pair of scissors to his unruly locks, but he laughed at her. He said Susan loved it that way, so it stayed.

"The info should be downloading into Posi now. I'm afraid we'll have to tell them they don't have nuclears or even much in the way of precious minerals." Ali bit her lip as she tried to rein in her excitement.

"Come on, Ali, this is me. I know you. You have a hallelujah tone in your voice. I can hear it even over your mike. What's up?"

Although disappointed she hadn't been able to pull one over on Sean, his comment didn't surprise her. Five years her senior, he'd taken over after their parents' deaths and knew her almost better than she knew herself. They were close before the tragedy and had grown even closer afterward.

"Take a look at the raw data and you'll see. I think the gods of luckless miners must be smiling on this group." She waited a moment and grinned as Sean's excited voice came back.

"Does this mean what I think it does?"

Ali heard a thud and then rich swearing. He'd probably dropped the access panel on his foot—again. Her brother was a genius when it came to electronics and business, but grace and agility certainly weren't two of Sean's stronger assets. She bit back a laugh.

"Yep. At least three of these rocks are almost pure Ki crystals, including a tiny bit of red. These guys are going to be so freakin' rich they'll never be able to spend it in several lifetimes. And our cut should be more than enough to get us those upgrades to the ship with some cash left over. Why don't you go ahead and tell them?"

"I'll wait until you're here so we can tell them together," Sean said.

Ali hesitated just a second, but it was enough.

"I don't understand you sometimes, Ali. I can see you not wanting to share bad news, but this... God, they'll love you forever." Disappointment and sadness tinged Sean's voice.

She knew he was waiting for her to say something—anything. She didn't.

"Relax. I'll take care of them. Come on in. You're getting close on air."

"Be there in a few." Ali turned her mike off and activated her jets. Since she'd gone into business with him, she'd insisted he handle the clients as well as the business end while she handled the physical end of their enterprise. She knew Sean didn't understand her reluctance to meet with their clients. How could he when she didn't understand it herself?

When she'd awakened in the med-center almost ten years ago, he'd been there. He'd been with her through rehab as they rebuilt her body, but nobody could rebuild the part of her mind that refused to remember who'd attacked her. Sean had even understood—and backed her—when she decided to switch from a straight science track at the academy to the military-science track, standing proudly when she graduated at the top of her class with honors in hand-to-hand combat techniques. What he didn't understand—and she couldn't explain—was her continued reluctance almost a decade later to meet anyone. Oh, she went out—

usually with old acquaintances, and even dated on rare occasions, but strangers always made her uncomfortable.

Ali pushed off from the asteroid and jetted to the ship. A few minutes later, she cycled through the airlock and entered the hold. Smaller than most as far as holds went, they had everything neatly labeled and stowed as efficiently as possible. The floor-to-ceiling racks ringing the outer walls currently held samples from several dozen miners. After this stop, they'd head to Delphi station to unload at the assayer's office.

The draw of wealth brought men and women of all sorts to the rim worlds just as the gold rushes of ancient times had taken those desiring to be rich to California and Alaska. Unfortunately, just like those old miners, many of the new ones weren't prepared for the rigors of mining in space and were lured to their deaths. For every miner who found the rich life, a hundred others failed—many of them fatally. Space did not forgive mistakes.

Ali pulled off her gloves and helmet, ran her hand through her hair, and grimaced. Sweat-plastered curls stuck to her head, as if she hadn't washed it in days—although it had only been hours since her shower.

"First things first," she muttered. "Posi?" She called to their Portable Systems Intelligence. Their artificial intelligence, Posi, ran the ship as well as her and Sean. Their mother had programmed the AI and still had some of her protection protocols in place, even though Sean had tried to get rid of them on numerous occasions. Unfortunately, due to the age of the ship and the system limitations, they couldn't do much.

"Yes, Aleksia?" Posi's deep maternal voice echoed

in the room.

"My suit is in desperate need of a thorough check." Ali stripped out of the offending suit and hung it in the diagnostic locker. "It smells like a Denebian blood worm died in there. I think the filters are malfunctioning."

"Hook the suit up and go get yourself cleaned up. I'm sending a servo to your cabin with a tray."

"Thanks, Posi. You're a doll." Ali hooked the diagnostic outlet to her suit and sealed the locker. Sean caught up with her, while Ali was on her way to her cabin.

"Whew. What died in here?" Sean pinched his nose and grinned at her.

Ali punched him lightly on the chin. "Not funny. My suit's filters must be malfunctioning. It's worse than usual."

Sean palmed open her cabin door. "Get thee to a shower—quickly, please."

Ali laughed when he ushered her into the cabin. Her laughter dissolved when she caught his next words.

"Oh, and put on something nice 'cause we're going to a party, and no excuses."

The door swished shut. She rushed over and hit the open button, but it refused to budge. "Posi, unlock this door. Now."

"No can do, Aleksia. Sean's orders."

"And I know as well as you do, you override orders all the time. Now open this door."

"Sorry, Aleksia."

Ali stripped out of the thin under-suit she wore, all the while cursing her brother.

"If your mother heard the garbage spewing from

your mouth, she'd be ashamed of you," Posi said.

Ali winced at the censure in Posi's voice and sighed. "I know, Posi. But he shouldn't have done that. I've got a good mind just to stay in my room." A sudden blast of frigid air from her vents disavowed her of any such ideas.

"All right. All right. I get the picture." Maybe she could fake a headache. As soon as she thought it, she discarded the idea. Ali rarely got sick. Sean would never buy such an excuse. "Shower. Hot." She stepped into the tiny cubicle.

A real water shower on board a small ship like this one showed a certain level of decadence, but her mother wouldn't do without one, and Ali thanked her every time she took one. She leaned her head against the wall and let the water slide over her.

"I can do this. It's just a couple of miners. No big deal. And Sean will be there. It's perfectly safe." She took a deep breath and let it out slowly. She needed to get over this ridiculous fear and move on with her life. A few short minutes later, her allotted time ended, and the water shut off. She shook the wetness out of her hair. The system would recover as much of the precious moisture as possible, and she didn't like to waste a drop.

She quickly toweled off and picked out a pair of dark blue trousers and a lighter tunic trimmed to match the pants and embossed with gold embroidery. A pair of soft, black demi-boots completed the outfit. She ran her hand through her hair, fluffing out the natural curls, finishing just as she heard a tentative knock at her door.

"Ali? You ready?"

"Open up, Posi," Ali said. "I'm ready." When the

door opened, Sean's hand holding a single pale peach rose came into view. "Oh, Sean." She gently took the flower and sniffed its delicate fragrance, her former anger almost, but not totally, forgotten. "Where did you get a rose? It's beautiful."

"You're welcome. As to where I got it, let's just say I pulled in some favors, plus I've been experimenting with some of these in hydroponics."

"It works. The scent is perfect." She inhaled deeply. "What about the find?"

"I sent your results on a priority beam. It seems our prospectors' little find is quite pure. Their claim is the richest ever filed in this sector, and they gave us a bonus. Am I forgiven?"

Sean wore soft gray slacks and a dark green shirt that showed off his eyes. Her brother was an extremely handsome man, she thought. But then, she could be just a little prejudiced.

"No. But thank you."

"You're welcome. Let's go. We have a party to attend."

\*\*\*\*

And what a party they had. Ali had to admit when she fell into her bunk several hours later she'd had a good time. The miners she'd been so afraid of had turned out to be twin sisters, their mates, and multiple children. When they'd arrived, Ali had held back, letting Sean go into the group first, but when a tiny blond-haired, blue-eyed child toddled up to her and took her hand, she couldn't help but unbend. The adorable little boy, the youngest of several, stayed with her until he fell asleep, and she laid him in his makeshift crib.

The family had managed to put together a good spread of fresh food, surprising her. When she saw their hydroponics farm area, the extent of its bounty in the barren 'roid astounded her. They'd had fresh melons, apples, pineapples, and even the huge, sweet rainbow fruits she was particularly fond of, as well as a salad they claimed contained every vegetable available in the sector. One of the women had even baked a multi-tiered, rich chocolate cake in an oven cobbled together with scrap parts from the engine room. Once they'd eaten their fill, the older family members had pulled out some antique but well-maintained instruments and played some remarkably good music. They'd danced and sang and told stories until none of them had any voices left. Ali had been surprised by how much she'd enjoyed the entire evening. She fell asleep with the memory of laughter and music in her mind.

\*\*\*\*

Aleksia's ears popped, and she grabbed the side of her bunk as gravity disappeared. Ingrained habit took over even before she knew what had awakened her, and she pushed off toward the shower cubicle and safety. Hands shaking, she sealed the door and jabbed at a small button on one side of the frame. Another door slid open to reveal a narrow space she slipped into. Her parents had drilled her and her brother in emergency procedures from the time she could crawl. They'd told her, "Safety first, then figure out the problem."

"Posi, emergency encapsulate." Ali waited for a count of three seconds but nothing happened. She hit another button, and the emergency environmental suit surrounded her. The readouts in her helmet all showed green. "Posi? Are you on?"

The AI didn't answer.

Ali attempted to control her panic and touched a second button on the wall while waiting for the telltale light on her helmet display to tell her Posi's backup had transferred to her suit. For the time being, she'd keep the file in storage. Her suit didn't have enough power to run too much info, and she didn't know what she'd need. She disconnected her suit from the ship, floated back into her cabin and punched up the system display on her terminal. A troop of pirates swarmed over the small ship. She counted at least a dozen with more coming from two dark ships flanking hers.

Sean. Where could he be? He'd been on the bridge when she went to bed. Where was her brother? Then she saw him lying on the bridge.

Pain ripped through her chest, denial holding her immobile for a precious second. She grabbed her sidearm and spun toward her door, then stopped as her mother's words echoed in her mind— "Assess first, then kick their bloody asses."

Going in half-cocked and angry might get her a few of the pirates. *It would most certainly get her dead.* If she wanted justice for Sean, she needed to stay alive. Ali slipped back into the hidden space and touched a series of buttons on the wall. She waited in the dark, certain the raiders could hear her heart beating. After what seemed like an eternity, but actually was less than a couple of minutes, she hand-cranked the emergency hatch open and peeked outside. No one appeared on her side of the ship, so she slipped out.

Once her path cleared, she activated her jets and shot into open space, steering toward the dark side of one of the half-dozen asteroids surrounding her ship.

She crouched in the shadows on one of the smaller asteroids, praying she hadn't been seen, and risked a quick look.

Besides the ships, she could see figures in dark suits moving from them to the nearby miners' camp and then to the asteroid farthest away from her. All six were still anchored to the largest central one, their legal mining operations beacons still flashing. She and Sean had space-anchored above the miners' camp.

A plume of white vapor—escaping air and moisture—flowed from the far side of her ship, proof the ship's hull had been compromised. Bodies, visible in the lights from the other ships, tumbled from the camps' airlocks.

A tiny body floated past her position. She bit her lip until she tasted blood. The features were unrecognizable, but she knew. Oh gods, she knew—the little baby she'd bounced on her lap a few hours ago during her visit to the camp. She lowered her head, and the mike toggled on.

"The woman. His sister works with him. Find her. She has to be on the ship."

She clenched her jaw. They were looking for her. She turned off her telltales and systems and considered her options. There weren't many.

Ali hated hiding—only cowards hung back. An action that went against everything she'd learned at the academy. She'd been trained to fight in combat and held the rank of a Battle Captain. BC's did not hide and wait. But neither did they go into a skirmish without a plan.

She forced back her grief for Sean. There would be time later for tears, for the chance to mourn her brother and friends. She needed a plan.

Ali studied the activity again. She couldn't go to the camp or back to the ship. She had enough air for an hour, maybe two, but with her emergency systems off, she would get extremely cold quickly. As she watched, the occupants in the ship nearest the camp started harvesting the asteroids tethered to the home 'roid. It wouldn't take them long to get to her hiding spot.

Another body, this one larger and wearing a standard gray-issue jumpsuit common to most miners, tumbled past her. She didn't want to know who—didn't want to think. But the bodies gave her a gruesome idea. She thrust slightly toward some drifting debris and forced her body to go limp, pretending to join her friends on their last journey. After all, what was one more body floating around?

Chapter Two

Jason Cole studied the remains of what had once been a family's living quarters. Not much remained intact. He tramped through the destruction looking for something—anything to help him nail down who'd done this. A patch of bright blue cloth stuck out from under a broken chair, and he bent to pick the scrap up. Instead of a piece of material, he held a child's doll. The implications weren't lost on him. He kicked aside the chair with more vehemence than necessary to clear the path.

"Jason?" The voice in his helmet belonged to his AI, Sami.

"What?"

"Your vitals took a huge spike. Is everything okay?"

He stared at the toy in his hand. "Oh yeah. Everything's just great. Except we were too late—again."

"No survivors?"

Jason sighed and gently laid the doll on top of an undamaged chair. "Not down here. You got anything on your sweeps out there?"

"Just debris. Wait. I might have something."

Jason headed back toward the camp's access. Nothing of use could be found here, so he'd better be ready for whatever Sami had discovered.

"Sami?" He climbed the ladder and exited through the broken airlock.

"I've got a warm body. The ones I managed to gather were all drifting away from the damage, but this one is in the ship."

"That doesn't sound right. An injured pirate? Can't be anyone else. They don't leave survivors. You said the body still registered as warm?"

"Yes, but barely. I'm reading borderline on all systems, and unlike the others this one's in a suit."

"Maybe we got our first break. I'm on my way." Jason climbed into his jets and powered them on. A few minutes later he cycled into the airlock on his ship. "Where is it?"

"Coming up on the ship now. My sensors can't detect anything within. Either they've got some really sophisticated shielding, which is unlikely for a ship so old, or there's nothing left alive."

Jason settled his helmet back on his head. "But maybe not beyond saving. Give me an emergency exit."

The airlock swooshed open, yanking him out into the vacuum of space. He got his bearings and aimed for the huge hole in the side of the little ship.

To combat the stygian darkness inside, he turned on a hand light to add to the lights on his helmet. The light showed a short, empty corridor to his left. Jason turned right and thought he caught a glimpse of bright yellow floating at the edge of his light. He shrugged out of his jets and thrust toward the object. As he drew closer, he could see an emergency suit with someone inside. He checked the gauges on the air supply. Empty. But for how long? He took several deep breaths and unhooked his supply, attached the hose to the suit, and towed the body to the breach.

"Sami? I have the body. No life signs. The systems are off, and the air is exhausted. I've temped it with mine."

"You've got one minute to get your butt back here. I'm in as close as I can get."

Sami's locks winked at him from a short distance away. He shoved the body through the breach, keeping one hand on the suit so it wouldn't float away. Once he exited, he grabbed his jets, gathered the bundle into his arms, and kicked off from the ship straight into Sami's lock. The door slammed shut, and the emergency air flooded in. Almost before the inner door opened, he'd removed his gloves and helmet. Sami had a med-cart waiting for him. He dumped his now heavy burden on the cart and removed the helmet. The vision almost made him pause, but years of training kicked in.

He stripped the suit off the woman and yanked the diagnostic canopy over her.

"She's in!" Jason rushed the cart toward the cabin that also served as his sickbay. Lights flickered as the displays came on-line.

"Get the cart hooked into my systems as soon as you can. Remotes aren't going to work well enough," Sami said. "Wish Dex had my avatar finished."

"Dex should have the upgrades ready in two weeks. We'll pick him up next time we're at the Web," Jason said. He hated to admit it, but he missed Sami's avatar too. The android was handy to have around—especially at times like this. And unlike humans, didn't demand his time or attention.

Jason positioned the head of the cart against the front wall and hooked in the leads. "Ready."

He studied the overhead display, nodding when the flat-lined heart rate spiked, and then settled to a steady beat. "What do you think, Sami? Did we get to her in time?"

"Brain activity is good. All vitals are looking good. Do you want her awake or asleep?"

Jason cocked his head. "Asleep for now. I'd like to check over her ship. I wonder why the pirates left it more-or-less intact. Why leave this one behind? More importantly, who is this woman, and why is she still alive? And how did she escape? Or did she? Could she be one of them? In all these months, they've never left more than pieces of ships too small to even sell for salvage, and they've never left anyone alive. Why now? And why her?"

"Maybe they saw us coming?"

Jason snorted. "They were long gone by the time we got here. Keep her asleep until I get back. Then we'll try for some answers."

"No problem." A fine mist flooded the unit.

Jason took a minute to study the woman inside. She had some lean height to her with curves in all the right places and the pale skin marking her as a spacer, but not the roughened features of most miners or grubbers. Her short, white-blonde hair curled softly around her face—the length also marked her as a spacer—short hair required less water, less time. It looked as if her nose had been broken sometime in the past, and her chin looked too angular for her to be called a classic beauty, but he thought her face beautiful anyway. He fingered his own nose and wondered why she hadn't had hers fixed like he had.

"While you're looking, do an ID scan on her and

17

her ship. Let's see if we can find out who she is. How's she doing?"

"I already did the ship—there's nothing there. The ship's ID has been wiped clean."

"Odd. Okay. See what you can find out about her. I'd like to talk to her—find out her occupation and her reason for being out here. How about her health?"

"She has a touch of minor frostbite, and I've detected higher than normal levels of CO2 in her bloodstream, consistent with her systems being down. I contacted Doc at the Web and got his input. I've already started the remedies. Are you leaving, or are you just going to stand there and stare at your slumbering beauty?"

Jason jerked his head. "Okay, okay. I'm going. Slave driver."

"One of us has to keep things moving."

He grumbled but got out a fresh air pack and locked on his helmet. A few minutes later he returned to the scuttled ship. He did a check on the systems, but nothing remained. No wonder they couldn't ID the ship. The pirates had trashed the bridge. The breach had been in the hold so he didn't bother going there. Amidship he found four small cabins and a gathering area. Had there been others on this ship? If so, where were they?

The first two cabins were empty, almost like guest cabins. Nothing more than the basics. The third one was a mess. Personal items floated around, mixing with data cubes and bedding. He snagged several of the items and studied them. Men's things. Maybe a married couple? There was nothing feminine about anything here. If married, they didn't share quarters. He grabbed the data cubes and stowed them in a bag to take back to his ship.

The rest he ignored.

He closed the door on the room and floated to the last one. The door wouldn't open, and there was nothing to brace against to force it, no way to get a grip.

"Sami? A ship this old, where would the controls to the door release be?"

"Should be one meter up from the floor and one centimeter to the right of the opening."

Jason removed a small laser torch from his tool belt and aimed the beam at the spot Sami indicated. He sliced through the paneling, exposing the catch. He ripped the wires out then shoved at the door. The opening widened centimeter by centimeter until he had enough room to slip through.

Unlike the other cabin, very few things floated around. He snagged a silky shirt and smiled. The woman couldn't be a grubber if she wore stuff like this. Although she had the looks, he didn't think she belonged to the Magdalene Guild.

He studied the cabin. So, who and what was she? He opened a few drawers. Everything had been stowed neatly, in a specific manner he knew intimately. He hesitated, his hand on the drawer under the washbasin. "Comb and brush on the right, oral hygiene in the middle, scissors and clips on the left." He opened the drawer. The interior looked exactly like he thought it would.

"Sami?"

"Yes?"

"Have you found out who our guest is yet?"

"I'm waiting for the data to come in. There's an ion storm disrupting communications with the Web. Why?"

"Check her out with IMF. Unless I miss my guess,

she's had some training, maybe even graduated."

"Interplanetary Military? Interesting. I'll let you know as soon as I get through."

Jason continued through the room, confiscating any data cubes he found and packing a small bag for the woman. He went through the rest of the ship but found nothing of substance.

"Jason?"

"Yes?"

"Comm's back up, and you've got an urgent summons from Ulric. We're wanted at the Web."

"Damn. Can you put him off? I'd like to do some more checking around here."

"No can do, Boss. He sounded rather adamant. Big job on the board—he wants everyone in."

Jason sighed. "Okay. Set non-salvage buoys in the area. I'll tag the ship as private until we can figure out who the owner is, although I'm certain it's the woman we have with us. We can drop her off at the station."

"You're not taking her to the Web?"

He pursed his lips. "No. If Ulric's got something big cooking, he might not appreciate us bringing in a floater. Plus, I don't think she'd be happy if we took her so far."

"Travel time is less than two days, Boss."

"I know. Call it a hunch. There's a station outside the asteroid field. We'll drop her off there and alert whoever's in charge there's a possibility pirates are raiding nearby. Tell Ulric we're on our way." He paused. "Let's make the tags official. There might be a bounty or award for her. As long as I'm taking the time, I might as well make the trip worth my while."

"Aye, sir. If I may, why a mild warning about the

pirates instead of something stronger?"

"Although they trashed the camp, they left the ship mostly intact, and the woman is alive. The pirates don't do that. My guess is probably some locals trying to look like they're big badasses. Either way, local security needs to know." Jason finished his work and cycled back into his ship. "Is she still out?"

"Yes. Doc said it might not be a good idea to bring her out in unfamiliar surroundings—especially if she came from that ship."

"Agreed. Did you alert medical on the station?"

"Yes. They'll meet you at our docking station. She'll be in sleep mode for another two hours."

"What did you find out about her?"

"Her name is Aleksia Matthews, and you were right, she's IMF, currently on reserve status. Works as a freelance assayer. Parents are both deceased, has one brother, Sean, who works with her. Her uncle, Rod Matthews, is station manager for this quadrant. There's more, but I'll let you see the file for yourself when you have time."

Jason stood over the medical cart and stared down at the woman. "Hello, Aleksia Matthews. I can't wait to hear the story you have for me."

He laid his hand on the canopy. "What's our ETA?"

"Docking now. Medical is ready for her. I've sent her uncle the files of what we found and where the ship is. He's going to send out a team to bring the ship in. Docking complete, Jason."

Jason unhooked the cart from the wall, activated the portable controls, and guided it to the hatch. Two med-techs stood outside waiting for him. He turned the cart over to them.

"My AI sent his report to you. I'll be back in a few days to pick up my equipment."

"Don't worry, Mr. Cole, we'll take good care of her. We've known Ali for a long time. Any idea what happened to her brother?"

"No. I didn't find anyone else." A low buzz came from the com-button behind his left ear. "Okay, Sami, I'm coming," he whispered.

He watched the techs take the woman away and then ducked back into his ship. A minute later, he slid into his seat on the bridge, and the station faded into the distance.

"Did Ulric give you any details on the emergency?"

"No. Just that we need to get our butts back there ASAP."

**** 

"You can't stop me, Uncle Rod. Those pirates murdered everyone at the camp and laughed while they did so. They should be spaced." Ali spread her hands on Commander Matthews' desk and tried to rein in her temper. "Why can't you understand what this means to me? Sean is dead, and you're acting like he's just another statistic, like Mom and Dad. They were your family too. This gang is terrorizing every mining camp in this belt. Nobody is safe from them."

Ali didn't remember much beyond drifting with the debris. She'd woken up in the station's sickbay, thanks to some passerby. According to her uncle, he'd been a drifter looking for a quick reward. The commander had paid him a hundred credits, and the man had disappeared, most likely to drink his profits away. Or so he'd told her. She wondered though. She'd seen a bounty hunter credit on the monitor with her name on it, but her uncle had quickly deleted the page, shrugging it off as a miscommunication.

Her ship had been stripped and damaged almost beyond repair. Sean's body hadn't been found, but that didn't matter. He was dead. He had to be. When she'd last seen him over the view screen in her cabin, his handsome face had been a bloody mess. And as far as she knew nobody had ever survived a raid, except her, and from what she'd seen of Sean, he couldn't have either. At first, she'd wished her savior had left her to die along with the others, but then her anger had kicked in. She would bring those murderers to justice or die trying.

She'd tried to get her uncle to rescind her reserve status and make her an official part of the hunt. But almost a week later, he still refused to help her. She'd rather go after the pirates officially, but if she couldn't, she still intended to stop them.

Her uncle had complained he couldn't send someone whose diapers he'd changed after one of the most ruthless gangs in the quadrant. In her mind, his reasons didn't make any difference. She couldn't sit around and do nothing while they got away with murder.

Rod Matthews shook his head and frowned at her. "Do you hear yourself, Leksi? Nobody knows better than I do what they're capable of." He indicated his cloned arm, the result of a botched attempt to chase another set of pirates down.

Ali winced. He always brought up his arm when he didn't want to do something. The reconstructed limb couldn't be distinguished from his other arm, and nobody else would know the difference, but he made sure they did. Only a few people knew he'd lost his arm while asleep on duty in the cargo bay of the IMF ship he'd been on. The injury had put him on the fast track to promotion—something that should never have happened. She knew his superiors had been on his back about the raids, but they hadn't sent anyone to help. She could help, but he refused to let her.

Ali sighed and sank into a nearby chair. "I'm going to find them, Uncle Rod."

She kept private her vow to make them pay for what they'd done to her and to her family. First her parents and now Sean. All gone.

He leaned forward in his chair, brown eyes focused on hers. "What can you do that I haven't already done? You'll end up dead. I promised your parents if anything ever happened to them, I'd take care of you. How can I if you're out there chasing these killers?"

"You don't have to worry about me, Uncle Rod. I've put out a net summons. With the right partner, I can follow them—perhaps even find their base of operations. Sooner or later, they'll make a mistake and I intend to be there when they do."

"A mercenary? They're nothing more than criminals themselves."

"Not exactly a mercenary—a bounty hunter." Too tense to sit still, Ali jumped up and paced the small office. She thought about the fast raid on her ship. They'd come out of nowhere. And the alarms had been curiously silent. Laughing, handsome Sean never had a chance. Nor had the miners. She should have fought, but at least this way, she'd have a chance to get them.

The story sounded the same all over the asteroid belt. The pirates came in fast and hard, took everything worth taking, and left no witnesses. The raids were happening more and more often. She'd made a chart of the raids and had the beginnings of a pattern. Rod had refused to even consider her analysis, but she believed in her data. She had to.

Her uncle's eyes followed her short path. She hated the detached look he sometimes got. It meant her mother, Lynette, filled his mind. With her pale hair and golden eyes, Ali physically resembled her mother, but she had her father's temperament. Sean had gotten their father's dark hair and green eyes, but their mother's sweet temper and fun-loving attitude. Ali clenched her jaw against a wave of grief for her missing family. They were gone and she'd never see them again.

Sometimes her uncle slipped and called Ali by her mother's name. While flattering, at the same time the slip gave her a chill, and the lapses were getting worse. If she didn't know better, she'd say he'd taken some kind of drug, but that couldn't be possible. The telltale all active IMF personnel wore on their wrists would turn red, and his glowed a healthy green.

She faced him, her hands clenched at her sides. "I have to do this, Uncle Rod."

"You're not turning vigilante on me. That's against every regulation you swore to uphold. Why can't you wait until I get some extra help? Headquarters is supposed to be sending me some more people in a few weeks."

Ali clenched her jaw until it hurt. She forced herself to relax. "In a few weeks, this entire quadrant could be overrun. We need to move fast."

Her uncle shook his head. "I've got everyone I can spare out looking for them, but this is a big area. Even with help, you can't go running after them. What makes you think someone you can trust will answer your summons? You'd be alone out there with a total stranger, parsecs away from any assistance. After he's done with you, he'll probably hand you over to the pirates and join them himself."

"What if *he* turns out to be a woman? Would you feel better then?" Ali teased her uncle. Sometimes he had the most outdated ideas about her and her abilities. Yes, he wanted to protect her, but she had her limits.

"Have you had any women apply?"

"Well, no. But it doesn't mean one couldn't."

"Any smart woman wouldn't. What if your would-be partner is already one of the pirates? As far as we know, you're the only person who ever survived one of the raids. Why can't you stay here, where you're safe? I can protect you here."

Ali stared out the porthole at the bustling activity outside the station. Small, boxy shuttles moved passengers and supplies from a wide variety of ships docked nearby. Were the pirates in one of them? Did those baby killers walk through the station's corridors? Her uncle wanted her to be safe, but how could she be while the enemy still ran free?

The entire IMF hadn't been able to stop them. In her opinion, they hadn't even tried. After all, the rim planets didn't hold much influence. They were too far from the seat of power in the Abboo system. But the recent discovery of Ki crystals in the asteroid belts brought a lot of attention—most of it unwelcome. The locals tried to protect themselves but had no training, so

26

she had to try. She owed as much to her family and friends.

"Uncle Rod, you know I'm not stupid. I've already turned down several applicants because I didn't like them. I won't pick just anyone, but I can't sit around and do nothing. You know I can take care of myself."

"I haven't forgotten, Leksi, but you're only fooling yourself. You're well trained—and I'll even admit, you're one of the best I've ever seen—but these are cold-blooded killers. You're lucky you didn't see their faces so you can't ID them."

She chewed her lip. She hadn't told her uncle—hadn't told anyone—but she had seen the pirates' faces. She had the data wafers to back her up, thanks to the specially shielded security cameras Sean had installed. They'd destroyed everything else on the ship but had missed the cameras—thank the stars. Fortunately, since her uncle had the ship towed in, she'd been able to retrieve the data after medical had released her. Nobody questioned her wanting to see the damage. In fact, many of the people on the repair crew had offered her their sympathy and given her space when she asked to see the bridge. She'd been able to sit at the helm and download the data without anyone being wiser. She'd watched the playback of the raid until she saw it vividly in her sleep, and she knew their voices intimately. If she told her uncle, he'd come up with some excuse to keep her from doing what she had to do. The data cube and her charts reinforced her plan to track them down. The problem came down to time, and if her suspicions proved true, they had run out of the commodity.

"I'll be careful, Uncle Rod," she said with more confidence than she felt. "I won't fall into a trap."

"Your plan is so full of holes it could hold a battle cruiser with room to spare. And that ridiculous reward you're offering, you're wasting good money. Where'd you get so much credit? I thought probate had stalled everything from your parents' estate."

"I have my sources—mostly from private funds." Let him think she had other backers. Coming up with the credits had taken all of her savings and most of the trust fund left by her parents. If bringing the pirates to justice took everything she owned, she'd give it all up and more.

"What's to keep your hired help from taking the credits and leaving you stranded—or worse?" Her uncle continued his argument.

His concern touched Ali, but his arguments were getting tiresome. "He can't collect without my authorization."

Rod shifted his eyes from hers. "You know we've tried getting the pirates. The odds are against us. If I left here, who would protect the station? A dead commander isn't any good to anybody."

Ali knew her uncle couldn't handle the job, but she didn't want to hurt his feelings. He fit the shoes of a bureaucrat, not a fighter.

"Uncle Rod, you know I don't blame you. You're only one man with many responsibilities. You don't have the time or the resources to track down the pirates." She smiled. "I think you have a hard time staying here when you could be out there looking for them. Since that's not an option, I need someone who knows this quadrant inside out, from the asteroid fields to the planets. Someone who thinks like the raiders and can help me track them down. Someone who's honest and well-trained and can live by his wits."

"You're talking nonsense. Nobody like that exists."

"Oh, he exists." She headed for the door.

Her uncle laughed, a short derisive sound. "You've read too many fantasy stories. I told your parents they would regret indulging you. This isn't one of your silly novels where the good guys always win and everybody lives happily ever after. This is deadly serious," he warned. "What you're planning is too dangerous, and I won't let you go. If nothing else, I'll throw you in the brig until you come to your senses."

Only Ali's training kept her face from showing her shock. "You can't stop me, Uncle Rod, and if you try, I'll disappear. We both know I'm quite capable of doing so. I'm going to do this with or without your approval. I'd rather have your support, but the choice is mine."

She closed the door before he had a chance to answer. She'd heard enough of his doubts—especially when they mimicked her own.

****

Rod looked up as an elegantly dressed man entered his office. Sweat beaded on his forehead when he queried, "What do you want?"

"Our little Leksi is becoming a problem. I'm beginning to wonder if you can handle her."

The stylus in Rod's hand snapped in half, and he looked at the pieces in surprise. "I'll handle her. Leksi will listen to me. Give me time."

"Time is what we don't have. The final ships will be ready in less than a week."

"Then nobody will be able to stop us. We'll have everything we need," Rod said.

The man glared at Rod. "Take care of Leksi, or I will."

"I will." He stared hungrily at the palm-sized packet the man tossed onto Rod's desk. "I promise."

"Make sure you do." He strode out as Rod grabbed the packet and tore it open.

Chapter Three

Deep in thought, Ali wandered the corridors of the space station, not paying attention to her surroundings. The station filled up more than usual as word of the marauders got around. Miners were relocating their families to the station and banding together to protect their claims. She'd been lucky to get one of the last single apartments, but the place sat so far out on the ring, it almost belonged in another quadrant. Her uncle had offered her a room in his apartment, but she preferred her solitude—especially with the way they'd been arguing lately. Usually, she lived on the ship, only renting rooms with Sean when they were in port.

She stepped into a doorway as a large, noisy family passed by. Each one carried multiple bags and packs— probably all they owned in the world. They were complaining about the crowded conditions, and she bit back a laugh. Even crowded with refugees, the station had more amenities than any of the mining camps. A merchant district with restaurants, clubs, and shops where you could buy anything from the latest clothing styles to foods shipped in from any of the amalgamated worlds, took up some of the station. The designers had even gone to the trouble of choosing the best colors, textures, and scenes to decorate the corridors in order to achieve optimum social tranquility. If you couldn't be on a planet, you wanted to be here.

As she passed by one of the many grocers in the merchant section, a display of newly arrived fresh fruit caught her eye, and her stomach grumbled, reminding her she hadn't eaten in a while. Ali turned to head into the market and crashed into a man carrying an armful of bags. His packages went flying. Alex fought to keep her balance, but despite her efforts, gravity won, and she landed on one of the bags with an ominous squish.

"Are you all right?" The man reached down to help Ali up.

"Yes. I'm fine." After a second's hesitation, Ali accepted his hand and rose to her feet. She looked around at the scattered merchandise and at the bag she had landed on. Thick, iridescent orange goo oozed from a break in the bag, and an uncomfortable dampness spread across the seat of her jumpsuit.

The man looked from the ruined bag to the bright stain and grinned.

Ali frowned as she followed his gaze. "Let me guess—Altarian rainbows."

The huge, spherical, sweet fruit cost dearly, and it looked like she'd squashed more than one. And cleaning the stain out of any material had proven to be impossible for even the most dedicated cleaner. She looked from her suit to the man and stopped. Their gazes locked, and the silence grew. Even with the influx of new people, Ali knew most of the personnel on the station, and she'd never seen this hunk. Nor did he look like a typical asteroid miner. But he looked at her as if he knew her. She shivered in spite of the warmth of the station and backed up a step to give herself breathing room. She didn't like it when people got too close to her.

He looked away, breaking the spell binding them. "I'm sorry. How careless of me. Are you all right?"

"I'm fine, just wet and stained." Ali hoped her voice didn't shake. She picked at the wet blotch on her suit in an effort to keep her hands from trembling as she studied the stranger.

He wore his coal black hair cropped close like most spacers, and had clear sky-blue eyes ringed with a darker hue. He also had long, thick lashes that ought to be illegal on a man. Rather than the typical station jumpsuit, he wore a deep blue vest over a creamy shirt that fit as though molded on him. His dark pants matched the vest and fit like the shirt, leaving nothing to the imagination. Knee-high black boots completed the outfit, but she felt as if something were missing. He reminded her of a hero in the fantasy stories she liked to read. He looked like he ought to be wearing a set of pearl-handled guns, slung low on his hips. The dark shadow of a beard on his jaw gave his face a mysterious, sensual look, setting her heart to beating faster than normal.

"I guess I'd better go change. I'm a mess." She picked at her suit.

"You're a little iridescent, but you look fine to me." His voice flowed over her like hot lava.

As she tried to compose herself, Ali studied him further. Despite his seemingly relaxed manner, the subtle movement of his eyes told her he saw everything going on around them.

While he seemed pleasant enough, she couldn't tell what lay under the veneer. Who was he? Where did he come from? His arrival had to be logged in on the station database. She'd have to check the records for new arrivals. Sometimes there were advantages to being the niece of the station manager.

"Will you let me pay for the damages?" he asked. "If I remember correctly, rainbows don't wash out. I have to stop by station security, but I could see you to your place first."

Ali eyed him, wondering what business he had with her uncle. "No, but thanks. I can't even say for sure who ran into whom, and I'm the one who squashed your fruit. What about the rest of your stuff? Is it all right?"

With her help, he gathered his scattered supplies and checked them. He chucked the smashed bag in the nearest refuse chute. "Everything else seems all right. If you're sure you're okay, I'll be on my way."

Ali watched him stroll down the corridor until he disappeared around a corner. Shamelessly, she followed. Since she knew his destination, she took a seldom-used maintenance corridor to her uncle's office. She slipped in through a side entrance but remained out of sight. The office door stood open, and she could hear every word being spoken.

"Commander, I hope you can help me. I'm looking for A.K. Andrews. I understand he's staying here."

Ali bit her lip. She'd used the name A.K. Andrews on her net summons—a combination of her initials and her mother's maiden name—but she hadn't given any location. What could the strange man want with her? She listened as Rod asked what the man wanted with Andrews.

"This is about a job he advertised on the net," the stranger said.

The summons had specified she be contacted

through her advocates. She'd made no mention of the station. How had the man traced her here? Now he intrigued her even more than before. Only someone extremely cunning could have found her base. She made a quick decision and strolled into the office.

"Uncle Rod?" she announced as she entered. "I forgot to give you a copy of the salvage schedule for my ship." She met the stranger's eyes. "Oh, I'm sorry. I didn't realize you had someone in here." She stuck out her hand. "Hi. We weren't properly introduced before. I'm Aleksia Matthews—Ali to most people. And you're?"

\*\*\*\*

Jason had been aware of her in the outer office. He'd heard her come in and had caught the smell of crushed fruit. "Jason Cole. I'm looking for an A.K. Matthews. You wouldn't know him, would you?"

"I do. I'm him. The name is to protect my privacy. The job is still open, if you're qualified." She looked him over, making her scrutiny obvious.

Jason didn't like making mistakes. He'd have to check Sami's sources for where they went wrong. He bit back a smile as the woman studied him. His heart beat a little faster when he stared into her unusual eyes, and he forced himself to control unwanted emotions. He'd recognized her immediately in the corridor but held his tongue until he knew the situation. No one could forget a face like hers. Her short, white-blonde hair curled softly, framing a face delicate and strong— all at the same time. However, her eyes really intrigued him. They reminded him of rare amber—gold and brown and infinitely beautiful. He wondered if somewhere in her background, she had some Abboo blood. Though taller and slimmer than a pure Abboolian, her coloring reminded him of the original natives, before the Amalgamation of Planets took over and corrupted everything on the central planet.

Jason continued his scan. Her lips, soft and full, were made for kissing. As his eyes traveled lower, he noted the swell of her breasts and the gentle curve of her hips, and he thanked whatever lucky stars had guided him to that camp.

"Oh, I'm qualified, but"—he looked her up and down, raking her with his eyes—"are you? I won't take just anyone with me."

"That's not what the notice stipulates. Please don't tell me you're from one of those backward planets where they don't believe women can do this sort of work."

Jason thought about some of the women he'd worked with over the years and smiled. "Not at all. I've known some incredibly talented women, but I work alone."

"I'm afraid in this case, that's not possible. The notice specifies the reward is to help *me* locate and destroy the pirates. I intend to be there when it happens, or there's no deal."

He could tell from her face he'd played the arrogant bit just right. He'd gotten a rise out of her, made her unsure of who held the power. He didn't need some vigilante going off half-cocked, although he didn't think she fit the profile. He glanced at the commander then back at Ali, noting the glare on the man's face and the stubbornness apparent in her features. Undercurrents of tension flowed between the two. "This is no job for a neophyte. This isn't a training run we'll be on."

Ali raised an eyebrow, but her expression remained calm. "If you're aware of the situation, then you know the authorities haven't been able to track them down. I'm an IMF Captain with a full battle ranking, currently on reserve status. What makes you think you'll be able to keep up with me?"

Jason schooled his face. Thanks to Sami, he'd known about the rank. She'd finished first in her class, with top honors in physical training. According to her files, several of her instructors had noted she'd almost seemed driven to excel in hand-to-hand forms of combat. He also knew about an attack in her first year of college that had landed her, barely alive, in the hospital, and the people responsible had never been found. Fate had moved in an odd way. When he found her ship, he'd stumbled into the job Ulric had called him in for.

The agency had received an urgent request from one of the more honest IMF commanders for them to search for and help one A.K. Andrews in tracking the pirates. He couldn't go in as himself—a top IMF agent—but he could go undercover as a bounty hunter, especially since he'd already established that persona with the commander. A.K. had applied pressure through some high channels, and Jason needed to find out why.

He frowned at the challenge she presented. "You have no idea what you're getting into. If you're smart, you'll go home and leave this to the experts."

"My home is now little more than salvage, thanks to those thugs. I'm not afraid of the mission, only of what will happen if those murderers aren't caught. As far as the so-called experts are concerned, they haven't done squat. Maybe it's time someone with a brain took over," she gritted out.

Jason reasoned with her. "If you had half a brain, you'd be scared. Anyone would be. Why are you so bent on getting yourself killed?"

"I don't intend to end up dead. Any other information will be between me and my partner."

He decided to try a different tactic. He needed to find out if she could take attitude as well as dish it out. Someone who easily flew off the handle would be worse than useless—she could be dangerous. He could see the way she clenched her jaw and knew he had pressed her to the edge. "I agree with the commander. There has been a mistake. This has been a waste of my time."

"How do I know you won't betray me the first chance you get? I need someone I can trust—who's smart and can keep his wits about him in a fight and who knows his way around weapons and this quadrant." She smiled at his answering grin and then continued. "I also need someone who can take orders from me without argument. What I don't need is a gold digger who can't take me or my mission seriously."

"You're not asking for much are you?" Jason could tell the minute she'd gotten control of her anger. She held her temper well, a good thing in this line of work. Unfortunately, lying with a straight face also fit his job description—something he excelled at.

Ali shrugged. "The situation demands a lot. Both mine and my partner's survival depends on me hiring the best. You aren't the first person to apply for this job, and it isn't yours until I say so. Either way, I still have to go change. If you're interested in the position, meet me at the practice range in thirty minutes. I want to see if you're as good as you think you are."

Jason cocked his head to one side at the open challenge. "This isn't a game. What makes you so sure you can find the pirates?"

"What makes you think I can't?" she threw back at him. "You need either me or my money or you wouldn't be here. I know my capabilities, but I don't know yours. It's either that, or you're one of them and are here to kill me. You have thirty minutes to decide. I'm leaving at the end—"

"Leksi, you can't do this." The station manager broke in on the banter. "I swear, I'll throw you into the brig before I let you go off by yourself, or with him."

"You have no legal reason to hold me, Uncle Rod. Besides, didn't you tell me I'm the perfect bait? Once the pirates know I'm alive, nobody will be safe around me. They'll want to finish the job. I won't risk the lives of everyone on this station by staying here." She focused on Jason as she said the last statement. Mimicking Leksi's expression, he raised an eyebrow. "The practice range in thirty minutes. Good day, gentlemen."

Jason watched her go, his stomach clenched. Why did he have the sinking sentiment this case had just gotten a lot worse? "What did she mean by she's bait? Tell me you didn't let on to others she survived the raid."

The commander shrugged. "News gets around. She thinks she's invincible. She's going to get herself killed. Forget about her crazy scheme and go back to where you belong."

The man didn't say anything else, but the warning

came across loud and clear to Jason. He chose to ignore the implied threat. Staying close to the woman had just become his number one priority. In one statement, his entire reason for being on the station changed. This had been a trip to see who had posted the reward on the net, now it had become a bodyguard situation. And he knew for certain she wouldn't appreciate taking orders from him. "Why haven't any descriptions been posted with the authorities? Hell, she ought to have half a dozen agents around her."

"She can't ID them. When the pirates hit, she'd been asleep and barely escaped. I may have to tolerate you because you rescued her, but she is no longer your responsibility. She is under my protection now."

Jason pursed his lips. Somehow, her determination seemed too intense for someone who couldn't ID them. His instincts told him she knew more than she let on—a lot more. "Sounds to me she'd be safer if she left than sitting here waiting to be killed."

Rod's eyes narrowed. "As I said, she's under my personal protection, Cole. I am grateful to you for bringing her in, but Leksi is not leaving here with a bounty hunter."

Jason clenched his jaws against the insult. The work he did undercover as an Orion bounty hunter required he maintain a certain reputation, but sometimes the slurs rankled. Hunters—especially Orion Hunters—were sanctioned by the law, but barely tolerated by some IMF personnel. They performed an important duty, but there were drawbacks. Too many people wanted his hide. Being part of the well-known Orion Hunters helped—except for times like this when some self-important bureaucrat refused to acknowledge the service they provided. This idiot fit the description perfectly.

"If the lady wants to hire me, I'd say that's her business, not yours. She put out the bounty, not you."

Rod's gaze dropped down Cole's frame and back up again. "Leksi is special to me, and I won't let anyone take advantage of her. Don't force my hand, Cole. I have powerful friends."

Jason couldn't help throwing in a few of his own barbs. The man came across as a paper-pusher who'd probably crawl under his desk at the first sign of trouble. He didn't belong out here on the frontier. "Thanks for the advice, Matthews. Trouble is, her offer is rather attractive."

He strode out of the office.

Jason returned to his ship in order to do some quick research before his meeting with Aleksia Matthews. He had to figure out how to stop her before she got herself killed. "Sami?" he called to his AI when he got on board.

"Yes, Boss?"

"I need some research done on one Rod Matthews, current commander, this station and uncle to Aleksia Matthews. In addition, give me anything you can find on other relatives and close friends. I'm beginning to think there's a lot more to this family than what we know."

"Aye, Boss."

"Oh, and give me the body count from the last camp we found."

"Ten dead and Miss Matthews."

"Were all the bodies IDed?"

"Yes. And none of them were related to Miss

Matthews."

Jason grinned. Sometimes Sami knew what he wanted before he did. "Thanks, Sami." He paused. "Wait. None were related?"

"No."

"I understand both she and her brother lived on the ship."

"According to my records, local law enforcement did a full sweep of the area, and all bodies were retrieved."

"I suppose he could have been on a side trip?"

"He sent a message from the ship to the station quarter master less than fifteen minutes before they were hit."

"So he was on board." Jason sighed and shook his head. "His body probably got snagged on a rock. Put out a notice to keep a look out for one matching his description."

"Done. What are you going to do next, Boss?"

Jason grinned and went to change into recreation gear. "I'm going to find out how good our Battle Captain is in a fight."

Chapter Four

Ali palmed open the door to her room. Shades of dark green, cream, and gold highlighted the small but well-appointed efficiency cabin. A tiny catering area and sitting room occupied the front half of the room. The sleeping area, bathroom, and storage took up the second half. In addition to the daybed, a dinette set stood in front of the caterer, along with a couple of utility chairs and a desk, which sat against one wall. A screened foyer separated the entry from the rest of the room.

"Central Command, give me recreation, please." She called to the station AI as she shrugged out of her ruined clothes and dumped them in the disposal chute.

"Yes, ma'am."

She waited a few seconds for the computer to come back. "Request, please."

Ali slipped into a form-fitting black workout suit. "Request target arena one. Time, 1430 to 1600. Two players. Debit my personal account."

"Request approved. Debit entered. Do you wish your balance?"

"No. Command released."

She hurried to the practice arena. On her way there, she realized she didn't know anything about Jason beyond his name. She paused as she thought about him. He had an air about him that both attracted and repelled her. For years, she'd avoided people—especially men. Now, she could no longer afford to be afraid. It had taken this latest disaster for her to find her backbone again. Maybe something good could come out of this mess after all.

She arrived at the arena and signed in. The courts were almost empty. Only a few players stood around waiting their turns at various activities. She palmed open the door to the weapons arena.

"You're late, Miss Matthews." A low, mellow voice came from the shadows.

Ali jumped and then reined in her momentary panic. Her old life and the fears that went with it had ended. She took a deep breath and exhaled slowly. Jason's outfit, identical to hers, blended with the flat black walls of the court. Their gazes touched and locked. *Lust—that's all this is*, the rational part of her mind screamed. *He's an incredibly good-looking man and what you're experiencing is pure animal lust—nothing more.*

From the smoldering expression on his face, he returned the sentiment. That one look made her toes tingle, and the feeling traveled upward. She took a deep breath and gathered her scattered wits and glanced at her watch. "Actually, I'm exactly on time. Are you in a hurry?"

"Not at all. Shall we?"

Confused, Ali broke her gaze from his. "What?" She blushed as he pointed to the laser pistols in the cabinet by the door.

"Oh. Yes." For some unfathomable reason, disappointment speared Ali. She would need to be careful, if she had any hope of hiring him. Jason must

44

take her seriously, and she had to regain control of the situation. Somehow, she had allowed her emotions to get carried away—something she couldn't afford—not if she wanted this to work.

"I hope you're qualified for the job and willing to take it because time is of the essence." Ali really hoped he did have the qualifications.

Jason grinned. "The commander implied I should leave, but your mission intrigued me enough to risk his displeasure. I enjoy a good challenge."

Ali noted the way he moved with a natural ease, not an act meant to impress. So far, she liked what she saw, but she needed more. Unfortunately, he probably wouldn't be forthcoming with personal information. She knew almost nothing about him, but instinct told her she could trust him. She picked out one of the weapons from the rack. Like the others, the piece weighed little, as well as being balanced and shielded for safety. She watched as Jason picked out a second pistol and tested the weapon.

"Half-lights," Ali called out. The arena dimmed. "Run program Practice Weapons, Level 5, Random Pattern." The mid-level program would help her judge his skills. "You're red, I'm blue. Ready?"

Jason nodded and took up his stance. "Begin," he said.

Floating targets appeared and darted around the room while both Ali and Jason fired at them. A short fifteen minutes later, Ali hit the winning shot a fraction of a second before Jason.

He acknowledged her win with a short bow. "Now that we're warmed up, do you have anything harder?"

She'd watched him move during the match. He

knew his stuff, but how would he be in the field with her in charge?

"Next level," Ali called out. Again, they hit almost every target, but this time Jason had the edge. She didn't even bother to ask before calling out "Next level."

Ali enjoyed herself more than she wanted to admit. It had been a long time since anyone had given her a contest in the practice arena. Extremely aware of the man next to her—the way he moved with confidence and cunning told her more than words could. She began to admire him as an opponent.

By this time, they had a small audience in the viewing area above the arena. Their third game ended in a dead heat, something never done in station history. A round of applause startled them, but they took the kudos in stride and bowed to the gathering.

"What's the top level?" Jason asked.

"Ten. Are you up to a little challenge?"

He raised his eyebrow and nodded.

"Control, level ten, random pattern, maximum speed." She heard a concerted gasp from the audience. As far as she knew, no one else besides her had ever attempted this level at maximum speed. "Begin."

Thirty minutes later Jason squeezed off his final target a millisecond before Ali hit her target. The significantly larger crowd roared its approval.

"Game goes to red," the computer intoned. "High score will be amended."

"High score?" Jason asked as he looked at Ali. "Control, identify previous high score holder."

"Previous high score belonged to Aleksia Matthews."

"Seems like I've toppled you off your tower, Miss Matthews." Jason replaced his weapon in the rack and grinned at her.

"Actually, I should thank you. It's such a chore being on top all the time." Ali wiped a film of sweat from her face and grinned back at him.

He looked her over slowly from head to toe and back up again. "I do some of my best work from the top." He left no doubt as to his meaning.

Ali licked dry lips. The room had suddenly grown very warm. "I don't know about you, but I could use a shower and some food. Why don't we meet at Vito's Restaurant in, say, an hour?"

Jason smiled and raised his hand in a casual salute. "I'll see you there."

****

An hour later, cleaned and dressed in a soft, flowing emerald green tunic and pants, Ali hurried to Vito's Restaurant, one of her favorite places to eat at in the merchant's area. Although several other places specialized in foods from many different worlds, none matched the ambiance of Vito's.

Semi-private booths lined the walls offsetting the small tables scattered around the floor. A long, oval bar surrounded by high stools jutted out into the center of the large room. Decorated in shades of red, black, and white, the area came across as bright and inviting. The owner even had live waiters and waitresses instead of the usual robotic servers.

"Hey, Ali."

Ali glanced around. The owner, Angelo Vito, stood behind the bar, his ample girth threatening to burst the apron he wore. Although older than her parents had been, his hair remained coal black, and he had a twinkle in his eyes and a smile on his face for everyone. She joined him. "Hi, Angelo. How's the family?"

The older man shrugged. "Eh, same as always. My Mary Angelina had another baby last week, a girl this time."

"So how many grandchildren does that make now? Sixteen?"

"Twenty-two. You missed a few while you were at the academy." The smile left his face. "Hey, Ali, I heard about Sean. I'm so sorry. You need anything?"

Ali swallowed the sudden lump in her throat. "No, but thank you, Angelo." She looked around. "I'm meeting a friend here. Tall man, dark hair."

A brilliant smile replaced the frown on Angelo's face. "Ah, that one. I wondered who he might be meeting. He's in the back booth. Hey, he's a good-looking one. A keeper. Settle down and have babies, Ali. A person needs a family. You go join him, and I'll bring you a special meal, eh? Go. Go." He shooed her toward the booth.

Ali laughed at the old man and strolled to the back booth. Her easy movements belied the turmoil going on inside her. She noted Jason had changed, also. This time into buff pants, a dark brown shirt, and the same high boots. Comfortable warmth infused her as she slid into the seat opposite him. "Have you ordered yet?"

"No. What's good?"

A waiter showed up with a colorful salad, crusty bread, and two large glasses of Vegan ale. He looked Jason over and turned to Ali. "Your dinner will be ready shortly—our treat, Ali."

"Thank you, Dom. And thank your father for me."

Ali sniffed appreciatively at the bread, still warm from the ovens. She smiled at the question on Jason's face. "An old friend who thinks I can't take care of myself. You passed inspection or we'd be inundated with waiters, servers, and even kitchen staff. Trust me, whatever he brings is sure to be superb."

They made small talk while they waited for their dinner. When the food arrived, they weren't disappointed. Vito had prepared delicate pasta wraps stuffed with a mixture of crab and shrimp in a light creamy garlic sauce accompanied by sautéed asparagus.

Ali watched as Jason cut into the pasta and took a tentative bite. She grinned when his eyes closed and a satisfied sigh escaped. "Well?"

"Are these real shrimp?"

"Yep. Angelo has a special arrangement with a fishery on Delphi. He gets fresh deliveries of real seafood twice a week. Plus, he keeps small tanks for emergency purposes in the back. He grows the vegetables and greens on his own farms on a nearby anchored, hollowed out asteroid he terraformed. So do you like the food?"

"This is wonderful. I'd like to introduce him to a friend of mine. The two of them could probably corner the market on good food."

Ali smiled. "Well, at least we have similar tastes in food. That will make selecting supplies easier." She attacked her own dinner with relish. She blessed the older man for remembering one of her favorite meals. Jason inclined his head in agreement. "I'll select the supplies, at your expense of course."

He nodded toward two men sitting near the door, studiously avoiding looking at Ali and Jason. "Do you think we should send a bottle of the house beverage to our two chaperones?"

Ali recognized the men as two of the newest in station security. She'd been with her uncle when they were sworn in. They had a lot to learn, and she relished giving them their first lesson. "Of course. It would be only neighborly."

She motioned the waiter over and placed the order. A minute later, she and Jason laughed as the waiter delivered the order to the embarrassed operatives.

"You've got some convincing to do before I agree to take you with me on this mission, Mr. Cole."

"Call me Jason."

"May I ask what your background is? You shoot like you've had some IMF training."

"I'm an Orion Hunter."

Ali couldn't stop the disgust she felt before she thought about what having a hunter with her meant. Bounty hunters were easy to find. She'd already turned down several. But if he belonged to the Orion set, she knew Jason Cole's skills went way beyond an ordinary bounty hunter's expertise. "Where is your home base?"

"The Web on Orion Seven. Does that make a difference?"

Ali nodded once, not in answer to his question but in acceptance. The Orion Hunters were considered the best of the best. "Considering the job I have in mind, being an Orion Hunter is an asset. But I do have a question. I tried to hire one of you once before, and they turned me down. Why accept my contract now?"

Jason shrugged. "My boss doesn't give me his reasons for what he does. You're quick, Miss Matthews, and smart. Qualities that could save your life—or mine. Tell me about yourself."

****

He took a sip of his drink. How much would she tell him? And would her story match what he'd found out? He studied her face. She didn't give much away, more than likely due to her training, but he could recognize little telltales she couldn't completely suppress.

"I trained with IMF Security and served two years before going reserve and returning home. I graduated at the top of my class. I'm also a registered geologist, and was working with my brother when they…when…"

Ali faltered. Although her face remained calm, he could see the stark pain in her eyes. She gripped her glass to the point where he thought the stem would shatter. He might not know the specifics, but he knew intimately the kind of thoughts assaulting her. He gave her time to deal with them.

"We were testing a set of anchored asteroids for a small mining camp. The biggest one came back as worthless except for a habitat—which is what they used it for—and then I got to the smaller ones. Most of the rocks were industrial grade minerals, but I found a pocket of almost pure Ki crystals in one of them."

She gave him only the surface facts. Nothing he couldn't get from a public search. Though he understood her pain, Jason decided to press her a little. "How did you escape the pirates?"

Her voice wavered, a sign of her stress. "I was asleep in my cabin when they hit, but I managed to get to an emergency escape hatch. They breached the ship then stripped her clean—same with the camp. After that, they chunked the rocks, took the useful stuff and left the slag. The entire operation took less than an hour. When they got around to checking for survivors, I had drifted off with some of the debris. Just one more body floating around."

Ali grabbed for her drink, hiding behind the tall glass.

Jason looked at her in sympathy mixed with admiration. Most people wouldn't have had the courage or intelligence to do what she did. She'd kept her head and stayed alive. "You don't need to say anything else. I know the subject is painful." He didn't have to imagine what she hadn't said. He knew from firsthand experience. "How did you get back?"

"According to my uncle, some drifter found me and brought me in. Whoever he is, I hope to find him some day and thank him. He saved my life."

Ali took another long pull at her drink. "Uncle Rod had my ship towed in for me. She's not in good shape, but should be at least usable by the end of the week. *Fortune's Turn* isn't a luxury ship, but she'll do what's necessary. I'm no quitter, and with or without you, I'm going after the pirates."

"What about justice?"

Ali's eyes narrowed. "Where was justice when they attacked an unarmed ship? Where was justice when they slaughtered that family, including a baby? I stayed hidden and alive so I could bring them in, but I won't shed any tears if something happens along the way."

Jason listened to her words, knowing the emotions behind them all too well. "You talk a good line, Miss Matthews, but what about action? Do you honestly believe you could come face to face with a man and kill him?"

"Yes. Don't worry, Hunter. I won't freeze on you or back down."

Jason studied her. She hadn't hesitated. Her words rang true—at least as far as she knew right now. According to her file, she'd never seen more than minor action. This would be war and wouldn't be pretty. She came across as smart and skilled, but not foolish. "Do you believe you can track the pirates down and stop them—with my help?"

"Yes."

Jason blew out his breath at the confidence she showed. There was no *maybe* about any of her statements. That kind of conviction could be both an asset and a liability. Too much could make her reckless, which often translated to dead.

"I know what I'm up against, and I believe my plan will work. I know what the dangers are and the brutality of this gang. And I know I can't sit back and wait any longer." She met Jason's gaze. "There is a draft for fifty thousand amalgamated credits in the bank. If you become my partner and we succeed, it's yours."

Thanks to his training, Jason kept his astonishment from showing. Her ad had mentioned a reward, but this went beyond a mere reward. Fifty thousand credits would buy a small, private space station. Oddly, his boss, Ulric, hadn't told him the amount—with good reason. That much money bordered on a death contract. Did she only want vengeance? He hoped not. She didn't seem the type. She seemed serious, but maybe a little too eager. He wondered what secrets she held back.

"How do you know I'm not one of the pirates?"

Ali cocked her head. "If you were, I'd already be

dead. You'd never have stayed around this long in the open. To be honest, you're not the first person to apply for this job, but you are the first one I've considered hiring. I know you're good at what you do or you wouldn't be a Hunter. I also think you appreciate honesty. There are some things about the pirates only I know. If you become my partner, you'll know them too."

Jason leaned back in his seat, hands locked behind his head as he stared at her. She met his gaze with one of her own. Things had definitely taken a turn since he'd arrived. It remained to be seen if the turn landed on the side of good or not.

She had information on the pirates, possibly evidence. That meant double jeopardy, and that dolt of a commander couldn't begin to protect her. He'd come here to keep her from being killed and instead discovered she might have the key to solving the entire case. He had no choice—he had to agree.

"Okay, what do you know?"

"First of all, call me Ali, but not Leksi."

"I heard the commander call you that. A pet name?"

Ali frowned. "It's a name he and a friend of his use. I prefer Ali."

Jason watched Ali's face, noting the look of disgust when she mentioned the friend. He made a mental note to read Sami's findings very carefully. "Okay, Ali, let's get down to business. Tell me what you know and how you plan to locate the pirates."

She shook her head. "Tell me about yourself. If I'm going to trust you, you have to trust me."

He swallowed the last of his drink while he

considered her request. Though relatively empty, the restaurant had far too many people for his comfort. He needed her information, and she required his trust—something he neither gave lightly nor easily. It would be better if he could get her information and then drop her off at a safe spot.

His gut told him she had something important, but he'd been after the pirates far longer than she had. As a bounty hunter, he had the reputation of being ruthless. He'd let the reputation stand. According to Ulric, he had the authorization to hunt down the pirates and take care of them in any manner necessary.

He normally didn't go out on dead or alive jobs, but Ulric knew this one meant something special to him. Other agents had been assigned to the area to help with the search, but Jason had the lead. They needed the person running the organization. If she could give him that person, he'd do anything necessary to get the information—even if it meant lying to her.

Jason studied his empty glass while he decided how much to tell her. "I'm from this quadrant. I'm thirty-two years old and have no living relatives. I've earned a reputation that ensures my privacy, and I'm used to coming and going as I please, pretty strangers notwithstanding."

She gave him a brief nod. "I'd rather not talk here. If you've finished, what do you say we go for a walk?"

That fit with Jason's thoughts exactly. He slid out of the booth and waited for her. "If you're concerned about security, we could go to my ship."

Ali stared at him. "You have a ship docked here?"

"Yes. Why does that surprise you?"

"I don't know. I assumed you came by shuttle.

55

What airlock are you docked at?"

"Twelve-C." He led the way, followed closely by Ali. A few minutes later, they entered the ship. The neatness of the small ship appealed to her. Unlike Sean, who couldn't put away anything, here everything had been stowed in appropriate niches. The plain wall panels had been decorated with panoramas from various planetary sites. The space demonstrated a mixture of utility and comfort. The ship had a tiny galley, two cabins, a sickbay, a small cargo area, and the bridge, all very compact but not cramped.

"Sami, engage privacy mode," Jason said as he offered Ali a seat in the galley.

"Done," a light tenor voice answered.

Ali looked around. Her questioning gaze turned to Jason. "I'm assuming your AI?"

"Ali, let me introduce you to Sami, my System Automated Machine Intelligence. Sami, meet Aleksia Matthews, aka A.K. Andrews."

A tonal whistle as old as time came from the speakers in the ceiling. "A.K. Andrews? Boss, either my sensors need adjusting or she is very definitely not a man."

"Sami, behave yourself." Jason frowned.

"Aw, you never let me have any fun."

Ali could swear the voice actually sounded like he was pouting. As much as she liked her AI, Posi had little more than the most basic of personalities. She and Sean didn't have the money for upgrades. This one sounded almost human. Bounty hunters must make very good wages, she figured.

"Sami," Jason said, a warning in his tone.

"Okay. I am pleased to make your acquaintance,

Miss Matthews. Privacy mode is activated."

"Did anyone follow us?" Jason asked.

"One unfriendly—station security underling who got waylaid by a sudden malfunction of the sticky fields."

Jason chuckled. "Thanks, Sami. Sami can be a real pain at times." A fair imitation of a raspberry emanated from the speakers. "But he does keep things running well. What quarters are you staying in?"

"Why?"

"I assume you don't want the commander to know you're in here with me. I can have Sami show you are in your quarters."

"You can do that? No, don't tell me. I don't want to know. Private quarters, third ring, second level, number six east."

"Sami?"

"Done. She's taking a nap in her quarters."

"Thanks. Now, about your plan."

"Are you taking the job?"

"Are you offering?"

"Yes."

"Yes."

Chapter Five

Ali took a deep breath and exhaled. "Okay. If you look at the positions of the raids, the only pattern is the proximity to Xy-One and this station. Location doesn't give any clues either, as the raids were both planet-side and in the asteroids. On the surface, the raids appear random, with no connection."

"But you found one," Jason prompted.

"I believe so." Ali removed a data wafer from a pocket in her tunic. "Take a look at this."

Jason took the wafer, popped it in the reader, and scanned the data in the air in front of him.

"Look at the items stolen, as well as the placement. Ki crystals—an extremely potent energy source, especially the reds. Myethean polymers—a substance undetectable by any known means, and high grade nuclears." Ali swiped through several screens.

"What about all the electronics they stripped?"

"Inconsequential. I think they're more for red herring usage than anything. If you think about what they're doing, they're taking anything new and improved. Most of the stuff they stripped is outdated— useless on the black market. But not the other three."

Jason frowned as he concentrated on the data. He already knew everything she'd shown him. So how did it all connect?

"Okay, this is all basic stuff. Ki crystals are found

only in Abboo and this sector. The nuclears can be found in many places, but are most abundant in the asteroid belt, again in this sector. The polymer is manufactured on several worlds but is strictly regulated. How much did they take?" He knew he could access the information, but he wanted to see how much she knew.

Ali pointed to the file on amounts taken. "Enough to build a sizeable fleet, or a small station. In addition, I've managed to get a hold of several manufacturers' shipping records. There's been an abundance of legitimate shipments to Delphi Station on Xy-One, but the trail dead-ends there. Nobody knows anything about what happened to the shipments."

"You think they're stockpiling the supplies? Why? To build something or to corner the market?" Jason tapped his finger on his lips as he processed the new information. He'd have to get someone to look into it all.

Ali shrugged. "Who knows? Greed and power are the usual reasons. From what I can tell, it looks like they're trying to control the supply of Ki crystals. There are only two companies left in this sector who actively mine crystals, and all the smaller miners have either been killed or bought out."

She brought up another file. "One of the companies is Murphy Station, the other is Jones Base. Murphy's isn't in full production yet. They haven't filed any claims, so I don't think they have much or else they're keeping quiet until they're at full production. Jones, on the other hand, does."

"What if the pirates are from Murphy or Jones?"

Ali shook her head. "I know those people too well. They may be cutthroat businessmen, but sheer piracy isn't their style."

"So you think the pirates will hit Jones Base next."

"I'm sure. The problem is, Jones is heavily armed and under maximum security. They think they're ready for the pirates."

"So why not let them walk into Jones Base and into their security forces?"

"What would you say if I told you I've been on and off the base without anyone being the wiser?"

"I'd say they're not as secure as they think they are, and I'd wonder what you were about."

Ali laughed. "Oh, don't worry. I did it with the base commander's full knowledge. I led a Tiger Team searching out their weaknesses. His embarrassment when I showed up in his bedroom one night is still a sore spot. I'm not sure if his wife has stopped laughing yet. Good thing she knew my folks pretty well." She paused as Jason chuckled with her.

"Anyway, while they have corrected the errors I found, they're still not as secure as they could be. They have a terrain vulnerability they can't fix. The right hit in the right area would take them out. While I wouldn't shed any tears over losing the pirates, I don't want to see the guys from Jones hurt—and they would be."

Jason studied her data. "I've been on the trail of the pirates for almost a year. They show up, strike, and then vanish. And there're never any clues as to which direction they went."

"Not normally," Ali said and then quickly went on as if she'd revealed something. Jason thought hard about her words. "They knew exactly when to hit us. The miners had already filed a site claim. We were just confirming their find. The pirates breached both the ship and the camp and destroyed all the electronics they could find. What does that tell you?"

"They have spies who can tell them when the time is right, and they're near enough to all the sites to be able to get in and out quickly." Slender hope infused Jason for the first time in a long time. "What else do you know?"

"They wear shielded black suits but use regular band widths for communication. I guess they figure nobody will be listening in. I know I'd recognize voices and some other things. I'd like to visit some of the bases on the larger asteroids and even some of the cities on Xy-One, especially the ones ringing the northwest corridor. If we can whittle the number of pirates down, we can eventually destroy them."

"Why Xy-One and not the other planets? And why the northwest corridor?" Jason asked.

"Actually, it's a hunch. Before I turned my systems off, I heard one of the pirates say something about celebrating in New Nova. That's on Xy-One in the northwest."

An idea came to Jason, and he looked at Ali's data again. "Do you by any chance have the dates on the raids?"

Ali accessed the data. "Line chart okay?"

"Yes." He studied the data, growing more excited. "Look here. Do you see where the incidents rise here and here?" He pointed out the spikes on the chart.

"Yes. Do they mean something?"

"Maybe. Those dates correspond with the dry season in New Nova. The area is coming into the wet season. Let me think a minute." Jason stared at the table. He had an idea, but carrying it out would take some doing. They had to time this extremely carefully for it all to work. Their departure had to be discreetly planned, and had to throw her uncle and anyone else, off their trail. Nobody could get wind of their plans.

When Jason lifted his head, he found Ali staring at him. He admired her beauty. In addition to her looks, she had the wits, skills, and nerve to go after the pirates. He almost regretted he would have to leave her somewhere, but he'd deal with that when he had to. IMF or not, he didn't want to put her in any more danger than necessary. If he managed to get anyone alive, and if they survived to go to trial, he'd need her testimony. If anything happened to her, his boss would hold him responsible. With her out of the way, his neck would be the only one on the line. He had sworn to protect and serve, and protect her he would.

"We have to get a move on. First, you need to get off this ship and be seen about the station. We don't want the commander getting suspicious. You'll need funds."

Ali held up her hand to stop him. "I'll pay you a thousand credits a month for supplies and expenses for as long as needed. The rest stays in my account until the bureau receives my authorization to release the funds. This is how I protect myself. Agreed?"

"What about me? How do I get the credits if you end up dead?"

"I promise we'll figure out a way to protect your interests."

"If we don't, I may have to take payment out of your pretty hide."

Ali laughed. "And what happens if you do a lousy job? What about my interests?"

Jason stared at her, his breath hitching. "You can collect any way you please. But we need to do this in a roundabout way. I'll leave today for the asteroid belt. We'll use this ship instead of yours. This one's in good shape and has a few additions we may need. You can leave Wednesday on the public shuttle. Make sure people know you're heading for Delphi for a retreat. I'll meet you there."

"Why the separate schedules? And why Delphi? That's in the wrong direction from New Nova."

"Because shuttles don't go to Nova. You have to get a ground transport from Delphi. In addition, it would look suspicious for us to leave together. Everyone knows you're looking to hire someone to hunt the pirates down, and since it's probably common knowledge by now you're a witness, it would be safer if we weren't connected. It has to look like you've given up and are going to Delphi to get away from everything."

"Given up? Not many will believe that."

"Convince them. I'll put out I think you're on the crazy side and I'm leaving because of that. Most of all, your uncle has to believe us. You can *not* tell him the truth. Will you be able to lie to the commander?" Ali nodded, and Jason continued. "Pack only what you'll need for the trip. We'll be using a covered sled on planet, and they're not noted for their ample space."

When Ali didn't reply, Jason asked, "Are you getting cold feet?"

Ali smiled. "No. I'm thinking about what to tell Uncle Rod. I'm meeting him in a little while, so I'll set things in motion tonight." She tossed him a code key. "Use this on storage locker 976-A-5. My travel bag and start-up credits are stored there."

Jason chuckled. "I'll pick them up tonight. From now on, all conversations between us must be as casual acquaintances. Sami?"

"Yes, Boss?"

"What's the corridor look like?"

"Clear, Boss."

Ali raised her eyebrow. "Watch your six, Jason." She smiled, ducked out of the airlock, and headed for the public areas.

**** 

Jason turned on the monitor and watched Ali leave. "Did you have any trouble accessing the station systems, Sami?"

"No. They have a dumb system. I could pick its locks with my sensors closed. I've adjusted the records for her current location."

"Keep an eye on things, especially Miss Matthews. I want to know if anyone's trailing her."

"Oh? Let's see, heart rate accelerated, slight increase in respiration and perspiration. Hmm, if I didn't know better, I'd say you're smitten."

"Knock it off, Sami. She's our best hope of solving this case. I know she didn't tell me everything she knows, and I want to be sure she's alive to do so."

"Is it a good idea for her to be alone?"

Jason sighed. "I don't have much choice, but I'll keep as close as I can."

He accessed Ali's file and studied the contents. "There's something about her uncle that bothers me, but I don't know what it is. Did you find out anything about her family?"

"Ulric's supposed to be sending me the data ASAP,

but those ion storms are wreaking havoc with communications between here and Orion."

"Let me know when it gets in. There's more going on here than the raids. I don't like surprises. Oh, and send Ulric a copy of the data Miss Matthews gave me. He might be able to make more of it than we did."

"Aye."

"Do we have any adjunct personnel in this area?"

"Joey and Marty."

A huge grin broke out on Jason's face. "Joey's here? And Marty?"

"Thought you'd like that. Ulric set Joey up in a place on one of the larger asteroids. And Marty's on planet in New Nova. I'm to flash both all the info. Joey'll take point for the other agents and will give you details when you see her. You're all covered, Boss."

"Good." Jason left the ship and took the ramp to the second level of the merchant district. He strolled next to the railing overlooking the lower level, giving the appearance of a casual visitor. He stopped at a spot giving him a clear view of most of the area and leaned against the railing. From there he could keep an eye on Ali while still maintaining his distance.

She entered one of the shops. Jason straightened as three men also entered the establishment. He wouldn't have thought anything about them, but the store advertised as an elite clothing shop, and they were definitely not the types who belonged there. All three were unkempt and wearing plain gray standard issue jumpsuits.

"Sami," he whispered. "Check out a store called *Chez Chic*."

"Heads up, Boss." Jason heard Sami's voice over

the comm-tab he had behind his left ear. "Trouble in progress. Want me to notify the authorities?"

"Yes." Jason quickly made his way down to the shop, startling some shoppers on the way.

****

Ali studied the multi-hued gown in the mirrored dressing room. She'd come in for a jumpsuit to replace the one ruined by the crushed rainbow fruit, but the dress had caught her eye. The expensive price made her pause—especially with most of her funds tied up in the reward—but the beauty and draping drew her. While not a vain woman, she did like the way the gown looked on her. A filigree collar held the top up, while the back dipped almost to her hips.

It flared from the close-fitting top to a long, flowing skirt that shimmered in the light as she moved. The material had every shade of green from deep forest at the hem, while the kelly green bled into the pale grass-green bodice. She pirouetted to see the way the skirt flared out. Suddenly, the doors to the dressing room burst open, and two men crowded in followed by a third dragging the terrified clerk.

The larger of the first two grabbed Ali and pinned her to the wall. "Look at what we got here, Rafe." He licked his slobbering lips, and Ali struggled to control her panicked shudder. All three were unkempt and smelled like the only spot they'd visited of late was a bar. The long skirt hampered her movements, and she bided her time until she could take action without endangering herself or the clerk. The urge to scream almost overpowered her, but she fought it down.

"I don't think she likes me, Rafe," the man pinning her arms joked.

"Then we'll have to do something about that, won't we?" The third man cold-cocked the clerk, and the woman slid to the floor. Then the thug grabbed Ali's hand and squeezed painfully. "Make sure she's the right one," he ordered as he held out her hand. The second man pulled a portable verifier from his pocket and forced her hand into the slot. A few seconds later he nodded.

The first man yanked her arms behind her and bound them at the wrists and elbows. "Go make sure the place stays empty," he ordered the other two.

Ali's shoulders burned. She forced herself to stand still and considered her options. She thought she heard a commotion in the outer room and feared it might be another shopper.

"You've made some very important people nervous, and that's not a good thing." He slipped a thin-bladed knife from his boot and held the blade against the neckline of the dress. With one swift motion he slit the lacy collar. The top of the dress fell, leaving her naked from the hips up.

If she hadn't been so angry, she'd have laughed at the look on Rafe's face. His momentary lapse gave her the opportunity she'd been waiting for, and she used his slip to her advantage. With one swift movement, she brought her knee up, catching him in the groin. He dropped the knife as he doubled over, and she brought her knee up again, smashing his nose. With a howl of pain, he dropped face down on the floor, and Ali finished him off by kicking him once more on the back of his head. Exhaling in relief, she sat on him. He didn't move.

A minute later, her uncle knelt beside her. "Are

you hurt?"

Ali looked up at him. "I'm fine. However, I'd appreciate you getting these binders off me. Did you get the other two?"

"The bounty hunter already had them," he gritted out and clipped the binders.

Ali caught his gaze as she rubbed her arms. His glazed stare didn't come across as the look an uncle should give his niece. She grabbed a jacket off the rack by the door and covered up as Jason strolled in.

"If you'll excuse me, Commander, I'm going to leave this little party. This place is much too noisy for my tastes," Jason added. He nodded at Ali. "Miss Matthews, I'm glad to see you are unharmed."

"Wait." This seemed as good a time as any to put their plan into action. "Uncle Rod told me what you did." She smiled at her uncle and then turned back to Jason. "Thank you for saving my life." She lowered her voice to a whisper. "And thank you for helping me understand the dangers involved."

Ali glanced at the man on the floor. "If they can find me here, I'll never be able to get close to them, and I'm endangering everyone around me."

Jason gave her a quick, approving nod.

"You're finally getting some brains. Those pirates would kill you and anyone you have with you without a second thought. I'm not eager to die. If I were you, I'd make myself scarce for a while."

"I plan on doing that," she said. "I think I might go to one of the Delphi retreats."

Her uncle put his hand on her arm. "What are you talking about, Lynn, um, Leksi?"

Ali covered his hand with hers. She'd heard his slip

and added his obsession over her mother to her list of worries—something she didn't need right now. She knew he'd dated her mother once or twice, but that happened before she encountered his younger brother, Andrew. Once they met, there had never been anyone else for either.

"I planned to tell you later, Uncle Rod. I have to get away from here for a while, and the safest place is Delphi City. The retreats are exclusive and private. I'll be safe there, and I won't be putting anyone else in danger. Don't worry," she said as she smiled at him. "I won't join the sisterhood. I thought I'd go on Wednesday's shuttle." She couldn't seem to stop babbling. The adrenaline rush she'd gotten from the attack had her super-sensitive, and she needed to get out of the confining room.

"So soon?" Rod asked in dismay. "Are you sure about this?"

Jason stepped into the conversation. "If you're finished with me, Commander, I'd like to leave. I'm heading back to the inners on another job. Goodbye, Miss Matthews. I wish you luck." He turned and strode from the shop.

An inexplicable loneliness overcame Ali as she watched him leave, but she schooled her face to not show the emotion.

"I hate to see you go, Leksi," her uncle murmured, bringing her attention back to him.

"I know, but this is for the best. After talking with the hunter and now with this attack, I don't mind telling you I'm scared. All I can say is, I guess my crazy ideas came out of grief. If I leave now, you'll be safe. I'm endangering everyone." Ali sighed and smiled at her uncle. She experienced some guilt at her necessary deception. "I'm so tired of all this. I have to get away for a while. The retreats are what I need. They're the safest place for me until the pirates are caught."

"Promise me you'll be back soon?"

Ali smiled and nodded. He'd accepted her little ruse. "I promise. Are we still on for drinks later?"

"Of course. I'll meet you at Vito's at eight."

\*\*\*\*

After Ali left, Rod leaned over the thug still on the floor. He reached down, grabbed the man's head, and with one swift motion, snapped his neck. "No one touches Lynette." He strolled out of the room.

Chapter Six

At eight o'clock, Ali met her uncle at the restaurant. She'd taken extra care with her outfit, especially since the incident earlier. She'd chosen a high-necked gold tunic and pants trimmed in rust, and pulled her hair back with a matching ribbon. She slid into the seat opposite him.

"You know since I've decided to give up the hunt, I feel so much better. I'm sorry I made so many problems for you. Am I forgiven?" Ali implored in a light tone.

"Completely." He looked her over and smiled. "You're so beautiful. That color goes so well with your gold eyes." He frowned and studied the menu. "What would you like to order?"

"I'll just have dessert. I ate earlier."

Ali placed her order with the waiter and relaxed in her seat. She'd seen the look her uncle had given her followed by his confusion. She didn't understand his lapses but as her uncle and only living relative, she'd allow him some leeway.

"So, tell me about these new troops you have coming in a couple of weeks," she said, knowing the subject would give him a great deal to talk about.

She'd been right. The topic kept him focused for most of the evening.

Finally, he exhausted the subject of security and

71

they both grew quiet. Ali tried to figure out a graceful way to leave. "This has been wonderful, but I must get going. I've had a tiring day, and I have a lot to do tomorrow if I'm going on retreat in two days. I'm sorry." She yawned delicately to emphasize her words. "In fact, if you'll forgive me, I really need some sleep."

She leaned across the booth and kissed him lightly on the cheek and slipped out before he could say anything. A few minutes later she returned to her quarters. She leaned against the door.

"Computer, double security lock on these quarters."

"Yes, ma'am." The tinny, automated voice sounded nothing like the animated Sami in Cole's ship. Without bothering to bring up the lights, she crossed the small foyer to the sleeping area. She peeled off her clothes and tossed them across the chair next to the bed.

"Sami, I almost wish you were here. I could sure use someone to talk to," she said as she climbed into bed. She slid her hand under the pillow, probing for the knife she kept for extra security. The weapon had disappeared.

"Lights, one-quarter power."

"You shouldn't keep things like that under your pillow."

Ali went into a crouch, ready to fight. She struck out—and jerked back a fraction of a second before her hand connected with Jason's face as he stepped from the dark.

"Relax, Ali."

"Jason?" She barely controlled the adrenaline surging through her system. She took a deep breath and exhaled slowly.

Jason handed her the knife. "Are you all right?"

"I'm fine." Ali sat on the bed and wrapped the sheet around her, toga style. "You're lucky I didn't yell for security."

"I didn't think you would. You're not the type. Besides, I already took care of that."

Ali cocked her head and then smiled. "Oh. Hello, Sami."

"Hello, Ali." Sami's light tenor replaced the tinny station voice.

"So, what are you doing here?" She couldn't help but be aware of him standing just centimeters away from her and the thin sheet covering her.

Jason sat on the bed. "You're smart and alert, Ali, but if I'm going to trust you with my life, I had to be sure of you. You're good when you're safe, but how do you react when you're in danger? Or in the dark? You kept your head, but don't let your guard down too early."

Ali jumped, taking Jason by surprise. She rolled him onto his back, straddled him, and placed the knife at his throat. "As you can see, Jason, I don't let my guard down—no matter what the provocation." She grinned at him. "So what now? I could slice your throat, but that's such a messy business. Maybe I'll slice something else." She glanced suggestively lower then returned her eyes to his. "I may not be a bounty hunter, Jason, but I'm good. If you had been anyone else, you'd be dead by now. I have good instincts. Be grateful for my restraint and the fact I need you." She returned the knife to its place under her pillow. "Now, what else brings you here?"

Jason chuckled. "I'm impressed. You are good. I

actually came by to make sure you weren't hurt this afternoon."

Ali noted where his eyes strayed. She rolled off him and drew the sheet up. "I'm fine, no thanks to my uncle. He said you took care of the other two. Thanks again."

Jason shrugged. "No problem. But did you have to kill the third? We might have been able to get information out of him. The other two didn't know anything."

Ali stared at him. "Much as I might have wanted him dead, I left him alive. I coldcocked him, nothing more."

Jason tapped one finger against his lips. "I wonder…Sami, did you get any views of the area after we left?"

"Sorry, Boss. I kept my sensors on Ali."

Ali gasped and frowned. "Sami, do you mean to tell me you were watching me the whole time?"

"Yes Ali."

"Why you little voyeur. I ought to fry your circuits."

After a slight pause, Sami reacted. "I mean no, Ali. My sensors were all outside the dressing area. Honest."

"He's telling the truth, Ali." Jason chuckled. "I asked Sami to keep an eye on you, but circumspectly."

Ali sat up and crossed her legs, the sheet artfully draped across her shoulder. "In that case, I'll forgive him. Now, back to the original subject. What about the other two thugs?"

"Local hires, and probably the third as well. They were supposed to harass you, rough you up, and split. They'll be lucky to survive the week."

"What about you? Won't my uncle get suspicious if you're still here?"

"My departure is scheduled for an hour from now. If anyone does any checking, I'm on my ship. The bio-readings prove as much."

"Sami," Ali concluded.

"Yes," Jason confirmed.

The conversation died off. Ali noted the way Jason looked at her—the way his eyes showed his desire. A responding attraction filled her, and she leaned forward just the slightest in answer to his silent summons. The sheet slid off her shoulder. This time she didn't bother to retrieve the material.

The door chime sounded, and they jumped apart as if impelled by a giant spring. Jason pressed flat against the wall by the door as Ali struggled for her composure. She stood on the opposite side.

"Who is it?" she asked.

"Leksi, it's me, Dimitri. I can't get this damned door to open. I'll have to get maintenance to check the overrides. I found out you're leaving."

Just her luck. A close friend of her uncle's, although she wasn't sure why, Dimitri had powerful allies in politics and business. So unlike a minor official on a space station on the backside of nowhere. And Dimitri had been after her for years.

"Sami?" Alex mouthed to Jason, silently questioning the failed override.

He nodded.

Ali took a deep breath, trying to calm the rush of emotions roiling through her. "Dimitri, it's late. I want to get some sleep."

"You can't leave without talking. I heard about

Sean, and I wanted to tell you how sorry I am. I thought we could go for a nightcap. We have a lot to talk about. What about our history? We're good together."

Ali bit her lip in fury. She didn't need this right now, if ever. And history? Hah. She'd acted as his escort at official functions a few times but nothing more. Okay, he had charm, looks, and money—everything a woman could want. Just not her. Unfortunately, the more she said no, the more he chased her. Sometimes she thought he did so just because she said no.

"Dimitri, I'm too tired. Go home and we can talk tomorrow."

"Promise?"

"Yes, I promise. Now go away and let me get some sleep."

"All right. Good night, Leksi."

After Sami gave them the all clear, Ali breathed a sigh of relief. "I can't believe he's back already."

"Who is he?"

"Dimitri Kolanka. He's a friend of my uncle's."

"I've heard of him."

"Everyone's heard of him. He's on the president's council and has his fingers in just about everything important on Abboo."

"That's not exactly a recommendation."

"Yeah, well, that's Dimitri."

"Sami," Jason queried, "why didn't you warn us of company?"

"You didn't sound like you wanted to be disturbed, Boss."

Ali suppressed a chuckle as Jason muttered the same thing she had about frying circuits. "I think you'd better leave. I'll see you dirt side the day after tomorrow. Oh, and Sami? Thanks for the extra security."

"Not a problem, Ali. If you want, I can tweak the station AI to keep it after we leave."

"You can do that?"

"Yes, ma'am." He paused. "There, it's done. The program will respond to your voice code, no matter what room you're in."

The gift touched her. "Sami, if you were a human, I'd hug you."

"Awww shucks. Sleep well, Ali. Jason, the corridors are clear."

After Jason left, Ali climbed back into bed, but tossed and turned for a long time before sleep came, and then only to dream about a man with coal black hair and eyes the color of sapphires.

****

The day had not gone well from the start, and it didn't look like it would end any better. Ali had awakened from a sleep that had left her more tired than rested, and then spent the morning filling out reports on the previous day's attack. Fortunately, her uncle had been called away so she only dealt with his aide. The afternoon had been somewhat better since she'd been able to pack most of her things for storage and tie up loose ends, but then her uncle had called to invite her to dinner. She couldn't beg off without making him curious, so she'd agreed.

She sat in one of her uncle's overly soft chairs and tried in vain to find a comfortable position. Although everything looked neat, the room showed definite signs of neglect. The recycling area gave off an unappetizing aroma all the air fresheners in the quadrant couldn't eradicate, and the carpeting sported several large stains she didn't even want to think about. The disarray concerned her. Her uncle had always been so fastidious. One more sign of something wrong. But his health band glowed green—no drugs, no chemical imbalances. So what was wrong?

The bigger problem, though, pushed the mess in her uncle's apartment to a minor level. He'd also invited Dimitri—unfortunately. The last time Ali had dined with him, a waiter accidentally spilled the water glass on the table, splashing Dimitri. The entire table had stared as Dimitri screamed at the poor young man, and then had him fired. Afterward, he calmly regained his seat and went on with his dinner as if nothing had happened. She'd like to say his behavior seemed out of character, but she couldn't. As long as her uncle stayed with them, she supposed she could stand Dimitri for one night.

Fortunately, he hadn't shown up yet. She sighed and shifted again. The room closed in around her, and she fought the urge to leave. Her uncle had disappeared into the bedroom to take care of an important call, and Ali felt compelled to wait. She gave up on the chair and wandered around the room.

She saw a pile of papers on the sofa and glanced at the top one. The drawing looked like a sketch of a weapon, but not like anything she'd ever seen. She studied the schematics but didn't recognize the workings. Her uncle had probably drawn the sketch. Although he was a terrible shot, he enjoyed trying to improve the weapons they used. Oddly enough, some of his ideas were actually quite good.

This one looked like it would fit in the palm of her hand or a small ankle holster. Curious, she glanced through the other papers. They looked like rough sketches of the station and other structures. She hastily replaced them when she heard a noise from the bedroom and returned to her chair.

Her uncle had changed out of his normal station suit and wore a dark-red tunic and matching trousers accentuating the slight paunch around his waist. She bit her lip to keep from smiling. She knew her uncle to be a vain man, and anything less than her admiration would not be welcome.

"I'm sorry, Leksi, but I had to take that call. Dimitri has been delayed but will join us shortly. He said to go ahead and eat without him." He threw a semi-clean cloth over the table. The catering unit beeped, and he removed several dishes and placed them on the table along with three glasses of wine. "I hope you like what I selected. I think everything's ready."

Ali listened with a sense of mounting dread. She took the chair he held for her and sat down. He whisked the covers off the food. A huge slab of undercooked mystery meat took up almost three-quarters of her plate. A tiny mound of limp greens and what looked like fried tubers swimming in oil accompanied the meat. Ali barely controlled the nausea rising in her throat as she viewed the unappetizing mess.

She forced herself to eat the vegetables and sliced off some of the more fully cooked portions of the meat, which was tough and stringy and without any flavor. While she did eat meat, it never made up a large part of her diet, and her stomach roiled in protest. She made a show of cutting the slab into small pieces, and pushing them around her plate.

"Leksi, are you sure you want to go on this retreat?" her uncle asked.

Ali continued on with the story she'd concocted. "I think this is the best thing for me. The retreats are private and secluded and will give me time to think about things. What about you? There must be a lot of parties and events around the belt for you to attend, especially with Dimitri here. I know you don't spend all your time in your office."

He grinned, and then nodded. "I do attend public events when I can and go out to make sure people know I'm here and they are safe."

She smiled at him. "I'm sure there are a lot of women who'd love to be seen with you."

"A few." He gulped his wine and twirled the glass between his fingers. "My tour of duty is up in a few months, and I'm thinking of leaving the service. I'm getting tired of all the petty problems that go with being station commander. I'm thinking of getting a ship and making a tour of the inner planets. I'd like to have someone to go with me."

His unexpected announcement troubled her. He'd never mentioned leaving before this.

"Being the station commander can be a terrible job, but you've done well here. You've earned the respect of more than a few people, but there's nothing wrong in turning the station over to someone new. You deserve a rest."

She winced inwardly when he frowned. He appeared to have taken her to mean he couldn't handle things. She had to be more careful. Where had he gotten the credits for a personal ship? The question puzzled her even more. Commanders didn't make enough to outfit a ship for the extended time an inner tour took. She hoped he didn't plan to use her ship. Even before the pirates, the vessel would have needed a full refit before being ready for such an extensive journey. So much work would cost almost as much as a new ship.

"You only live once," he said as he put down his fork. "I'd like you to come with me, Lynette. We'll explore the inners together. We can spend the summer on Sherman's Planet and then go on to Abboo. Maybe we'll hop a cruiser and head for Ki's World. It would be wonderful. I'd take care of you. You'd want for nothing."

Ali gazed at him in horror. He hadn't confused her with her mother—he actually thought she *was* her mother. She had to get out of there, fast. And she had to get help for him. "Uncle Rod, I…" She faltered as his gaze locked on hers. *Stars, how did I get in this mess?* She had to stall him. "I'm sorry, but I can't give you an answer right now. Give me the time I need to sort things out. With some time and distance, I can decide where I'm going next. I promise I'll be back as soon as possible."

Ali thought she caught a look of anger on his face, but the image disappeared so quickly, she couldn't be sure what she'd seen.

"You're right, Lynette, but it'll be hard to wait. Meanwhile, the night is young. What do you say we send you off right?" He rose from the table, moved behind her and fingered her neckline. "I have something very special for you, Lynette."

She suppressed a shudder. How could she get out of this one? It took all her training not to jump up and run. He took his hands away, but her relief fizzled when he fastened a heavy necklace around her throat.

"I had this made especially for you, Lynette." He released the necklace and placed an open jewelry box on the table. "It has earrings to match."

Ali stared at the pair of earrings lying in the box. They were made of emeralds and topaz set in heavy gold. She fingered the necklace, sure if she looked in a mirror, she'd see the same design as the earrings. First the trip, now the jewelry. Too many things didn't add up.

"They are—they're beautiful, Uncle Rod." She stressed the *uncle* hoping hearing it would help him remember.

"Commander Matthews?" The computer's tinny voice interrupted them. "You have an emergency call."

With a muffled curse, Rod turned from Ali. "What now?"

"There's a priority one call coming in from a stranded freighter."

"Can't you deal with it?"

"They asked specifically for you."

Ali saw the opportunity to end the dreadful evening. "Go ahead and take the call. It's late, and I still have a lot to do before I leave in the morning." She stood and kissed him on the cheek. "I'll talk to you before I leave."

She grabbed the earrings and her bag and hurried out the door before he could stop her. As she escaped the apartment, she half wondered if Sami had rescued her with the fortuitous call, but then remembered Jason and Sami had already left . She'd gotten a few feet from the door when someone called her name. She turned around to find Dimitri smiling at her, his arm draped around a woman whose clothing left nothing to the imagination and who didn't have an escort guild badge.

"Going so soon, Leksi?" He held up a bottle of champagne and leered at her. "The party is just getting started. We could talk about our future."

She turned her back on him and hurried off to her own quarters.

\*\*\*\*

Ali tossed and turned on the bed, struggling in her dreams against the faceless man. In her nightmare, she fought against the hands pinching and prodding at her. Against the man who beat and bound and gagged her. She couldn't get free. "Let go of me," she screamed as the second man came closer, injection in hand. She felt the stinging pain as he hit the trigger. "No." Darkness descended.

Ali sat up in bed, trembling, her sheets wet with sweat. It took a few deep breaths before she could speak. "Lights."

The room brightened as she struggled to clear the nightmare from her thoughts. The dream seemed so real. She looked around the room—remembering in spite of her efforts to forget the events that had changed her life.

They'd come roaring at her and her roommate from between the housing units. Before she could react, she'd been struck down with a stunner, bound hand and foot, and tossed in the back of a dark vehicle. The days following were a haze of drug-induced images and pain. Her captors' faces were always covered, and their voices electronically distorted. There had been at least three, but she couldn't be sure there hadn't been more.

She did know the leader enjoyed pain—especially hers.

When the drugs he'd given her wore off enough for her to be aware of her surroundings, she found herself in a small, square, block room with one door, no windows, and no furnishings other than the cot she curled up on. She swam in and out of consciousness, never quite certain of the time, or even the day. After a while, thankfully, her mind shut down. When she woke up in the hospital, Sean had been there, and her roommate was dead.

Over the years, she'd hired various detectives to track down the men, but the leads were getting thinner. She wished she remembered more, but the drugs they'd given her had done their job well. She only remembered bits and pieces and couldn't tell the difference between a drug-induced nightmare and reality. But ever since, she'd hated Dimitri Kolanka.

She didn't have any proof, but she had a strong impression he'd been involved somehow. The experience had been the catalyst to changing her life. Fleet had been her saving grace. In the academy, she'd learned how to protect herself. That alone kept her sane each time the dreams came back. She had to believe if she'd had training before that night, the outcome would have been very different.

Ali thumped her pillow and snuggled back under the sheet. "I swear I'll get my revenge—first on the pirates for what they did to my family, and then on Dimitri Kolanka. I will survive."

Chapter Seven

The next morning, her uncle escorted Ali to the shuttle. "I'll miss you, Leksi."

Ali gave him a quick peck on the cheek. With some relief, she noted he'd used *her* name again. "I'll miss you too. I'll see you soon."

With a sigh, she climbed into the shuttle and took her seat. The trip to the spaceport at Delphi would only take three hours. She relaxed into the soft leather and watched the scene outside the portal while the ship drew away. The station sat at the halfway point between the asteroid belt and the planet, and heavy traffic moved back and forth—especially now as miners moved in for protection. She studied each passenger on the full shuttle. Other than a few station acquaintances, she didn't recognize anyone. Fortunately, the older woman who took the seat next to hers settled into reading, leaving Ali to catch up on some mail and other chores.

Before she'd gotten half-way through her mail, the shuttle jerked, sending equipment and people flying.

"What's happening?" Ali's seat partner asked, her voice quavering.

Ali had a horrible suspicion, but held back so as not to panic the group more than they already were. "Probably a minor glitch in the grav-systems. Relax and everything will be fine." She did some quick calculations in her head. They were about two and a half hours into the three-hour trip. A good personal ship could make the trip in two hours. The pirates—even faster.

"Gentlepersons, this is your captain speaking. We've had a minor malfunction of the propulsion systems. Our technicians are working on the problem. We apologize for the delay. Please relax and stay calm. We will be underway again as soon as possible."

Ali chewed her lip. The male voice coming over the speakers wasn't the captain. She knew Tom Kofsky, the captain, personally. He had a deep bass timbre, not this light tenor. She rose from her seat.

"Where are you going?" the older woman asked.

"I'm going to the restroom. Why don't you go back to your book? We may be here a while."

Ali headed for the bathrooms, but instead of stopping there, knocked on the steward's door.

A woman peeked through the security window, then opened the door. "Ali? I didn't know you were on board. Thank the stars." She pulled Ali into the steward's space and shut the door.

"Missy? What happened?" Ali knew the young woman in passing—one of Angelo Vito's nieces. Normally neat as a pin, her uniform showed deep creases, and an ominous red stain smeared the front.

"They...the captain. He's dead. They came out of nowhere. "

"Who?" Ali could guess without being told.

"I don't know. The cabin sealed off before I could hear more."

"Who made the announcement?"

"It's a generic tape we're supposed to use in emergencies. I used the one that seemed to fit best."

"You did fine, Missy. Do you have an emergency suit? I need to get into the cabin."

Missy opened a small cabinet and handed Ali an emergency suit. "I tried to get in again but couldn't."

"Did you try the secondary bridge?" She had to assume the rest of the bridge crew had met the same fate as the captain. She had a good idea who had hit them, but why had they gone away? Why hadn't they finished the ship off?

"I'm not cleared on the second. We haven't learned how to run it yet, but with so many people coming in, we're short staffed."

"Where's your senior steward?"

"I'm her." Missy's eyes welled with tears.

Ali sighed and then embraced the girl. "Okay, Missy. Relax. We'll get through this." She backed off to arm's length. "Now, first thing, I assume you have a clean shirt around here. Put one on and clean yourself up. Then put on a smile and go out there and see to the passengers. Show them what a Vito is made of. Can you do that?"

As soon as Ali invoked the Vito name, Missy's chin rose, her shoulders straightened, and a look of determination came over her face. "Yes, ma'am."

"Good. Get everyone into the emergency escape pods. If anyone asks, tell them it's precautionary to ensure the safety of everyone. See to your charges. I'll go down to the secondary bridge. Relax. I'll get us there."

A couple of minutes later, sealed inside the suit, Ali climbed down through a trap door to the lower level. It had been a while since she'd flown a shuttle, but the controls weren't much different from her own ship. She accessed the secondary bridge and checked the readouts. She didn't see anything majorly wrong, so she set course and got the vessel moving as fast as it could go, which was too darned slow for her comfort. Then she checked the external views.

The upper bridge looked more or less intact, but the solid film of ice covering the inside of the viewport told her there'd been a breach.

"Delphi Station, this is Shuttle One calling. Delphi Station, do you copy?"

"Shuttle One, this is Delphi Station. Who is this?"

"This is Captain A.K. Matthews, temporarily in control of the shuttle. There's been an accident. Assume captain and navigator are dead. Looks like the bridge has been breached."

"Ali? What the hell happened? Do you need help?"

"Audrey?" Ali thanked the stars she knew the woman on the com. "Yes. You got IMFs you can scramble? We took a bad hit, and I don't think they're done." Ali tapped her fingers as she waited for the station to come back.

"Scrambling. What's your ETA?"

"We were about an hour out I think." The proximity alarm went off. "Damn. They're coming around for another hit! Get those scramblers here or we might not be!"

The shuttle shook when the pirate ship opened fire, peppering one side of the passenger cabin and shaking the ship. Ali prayed Missy had been able to get the passengers to the escape pods in time. She did what she could to keep the boxy machine moving, but maneuverability wasn't one of the ship's strong points. Their attackers seemed to be targeting to stop, not destroy, the ship. Why? What were they after? Then she knew. Her. They were after her. But the attack made her think they wanted her alive. Why?

She saw the dark ship coming around to hit the second side and braced for the hit. When it didn't come, she checked her viewers and saw two IMF needles coming fast. One broke off and took off after the disappearing pirate. The other came alongside her.

"Heard you could use some help, Captain."

"That you, Rocko?" Ali relaxed and checked her nav-stats, correcting her course. As she watched, the ship veered again. The gyros weren't working. And her fuel was nearly gone. This kept getting better and better. Just great.

"Yeah, Ali. I've got your back. You're cleared through to Delphi—emergency status. Looks like they messed her up pretty good."

"I can't keep the gyros in line. You see anything out there that will keep me from going down? From what I know, they hit the bridge and starboard side."

"Your underbelly is pretty well gone. Can you go back to station? I'm not sure I'd want to land that baby."

"Negative on the station. I'm riding on fumes now. How bad is the damage?" She waited for Rocko to check the shuttle out.

"You sure you want to try this?" he asked a moment later. "I don't think there's any way you can land her in one piece. Can you launch the pods?"

Ali hit the controls to release the emergency pods. And nothing happened. "Seriously?" She slammed her hand on the console. "That's a negative on the pods. I don't have a whole lot of choice here."

"Okay, here's what you've got. Your starboard side and underbelly are a mess. If you can lay heavy on the port, you might make it, but it's going to be hell holding to course."

"Will she hold together on entry?"

"You might lose a few pieces, but she should. Hang on a sec."

Ali waited, knowing he was probably talking to his partner. He came back a minute later. "We lost the unfriendlies. No idea where they are."

"They fly ships made out of Myethean polymers."

"M-P's? We can't scan them."

"I know. Keep your eyes open. Okay, if we're going to do this, it has to be now."

"We'll flank you. Good luck, Ali. Glad it's not me flying that thing."

"Yeah, thanks. See you dirt-side." Ali flicked her microphone to announcement mode. "Gentlepersons, this is Captain Matthews. I am currently in command of this ship. There has been an accident, and the ship has sustained damage. You will be safe in your pods but the ride will be rather rough. Please strap in and prepare. Thank you. Captain out."

She mentally crossed her fingers. "Delphi Station, this is Shuttle One. We're starting our approach now. I'll be coming in on fumes and a prayer."

"We're ready for you, Captain. All other traffic is clear."

Ali tightened the straps on her seat and grasped the steering handles. "Rocko? You still there?"

"I'm with you, Ali. I'll spot you a drink at Tommy's when you're down."

"Make it a bottle. I don't think one drink will cover

this."

"You're on. Good luck."

Ali nudged the stick forward. The planet loomed in her port viewer. Starboard views were gone. Nothing like flying with one eye blind. "Setting coordinates for Delphi Station." She punched in the coordinates and waited three seconds for the auto-nav control to take over. When nothing happened, she let fly a string of invectives.

"Ali?"

"I've got no nav-com and no starboard control, Rocko. I'm afraid the air brakes are gone too. I'll have to do this manually." She heard Rocko's echoing language. Her job had gone beyond improbable to impossible. "There's no way I'm going to get out of this one," she muttered. "I'm sorry, Sean."

"Captain Matthews?"

To Ali's surprise, she heard Jason's voice in her ear at the same time Rocko's warning of a ship approaching.

"Wait, Rocko! He's a friendly."

She could sense the strain of the ship as it hit the atmosphere. The stick became a living thing in her hands, straining her muscles. "Hunter, I don't have time to talk right now."

"Where did you graduate on flying?"

"Third." She fought the stick, trying to keep the ship level. A tiny part of her brain wondered why he'd used her rank instead of her name.

She heard Rocko's laugh. "She graduated third only because she refused to take the basics class. Pissed off the instructor when she outflew him."

"Doesn't surprise me," Jason said. "Okay, Captain,

here's what we'll do. Can you see me on your port side?"

Ali glanced at the port viewer. "Yes."

"Okay, I'm going to get as close as I can. You stay on my six the whole way."

"I'll get caught in your wash."

"Not if you're dead on my six. And I do mean dead on. Screw this up, and there won't be anything to pick up."

"Got you." She had an idea what he had in mind. The tactic, if they lived, would go down as historically insane—but it might work. They had no other choice.

"Ali?"

"It's all right, Rocko. If this works, I'll need that bottle. If it doesn't… Enjoy one for me."

"Aye, Captain. Rocko out."

"Ready, Captain?" Jason asked.

"Go." The ship rocked as Jason took position directly in front of her, nearly against her nose. She could only see his port side—ridiculously small compared to the bigger shuttle.

She fought to keep his wing in exactly the same spot in her viewer. Sweat trickled down her brow, and she wished she could wipe it off. Her hands worked the handles while her feet worked the manual pedals. The air burned past them, blinding her further. She held onto the tiny picture of hope in her port viewer.

"Captain, I'm going to slow you down. It'll get bumpy."

"And it hasn't been? Go."

She braced for Jason's backwash as he hit his boosters. They would impel him forward and her backward. She flipped the switches for her own reverse engines, but nothing happened. Jason's ship appeared again in her port viewer as they emerged from the ionosphere into the upper atmosphere.

"How much time to station?" Ali asked.

"Ten minutes."

"I'm going to try cutting the engines and glide in."

"She's too boxy to glide. I'll give you another backwash."

"Can you do a five second burst?"

"Yeah. Why?"

"Trust me. In three-two-one. Now!"

Her straps bit into her chest and legs as the thrust hit her. "Four…three…two…one." The burst stopped. Ali cut all her engines. She could see the station in her viewer growing closer much too quickly. She counted to one hundred and blew out the emergency doors and ramps. The ship rocked but slowed down even more.

"What the hell?" Ali heard Jason's chuckle over her headset. "Nice trick, Captain."

She could see the landing pad but had no way to settle down. "I'm about out of tricks, though."

"Your friends and I might have one left. Sit back and hang on."

"Not much else I can do." Ali sat back in her seat. She'd done everything she could. The ship would either settle down to land, or not. They'd know in less than a minute. She gripped the arms of her seat as multiple thuds shuddered the ship, throwing her against her straps. In her viewer, the station grew closer—but at a slower pace.

And slower.

And slower.

Another buffeting, and the ship dropped. And

stopped.

Ali let her head fall forward, and she exhaled. They were on land.

"Delphi Station, this is Shuttle One, signing off."

"Shuttle One, this is Delphi. Captain, you and your escorts will go down as the best damn pilots we've ever seen. Welcome to Delphi Station. We'll get your passengers."

"Gentlepersons, welcome to Delphi Station. Please be patient while technicians open the pods and assist you in exiting safely. Captain Matthews out."

Ali hauled her helmet off and leaned her head back against the seat. "We made it, Sean."

"Yes, you did."

Ali didn't even open her eyes when she heard Jason enter. She recognized his scent as soon as he opened the door. That and the fresh air blowing in the open hatch told her she wasn't dreaming. She really had landed.

"Ali, I hate to say this, but you should get out of here as soon as possible. Even here, you're not safe."

"I know. And thanks." She glanced at him, and then blinked. The man standing in front of her did not look like Jason Cole.

Ali grabbed for her weapon, cursing when she remembered the suit covered everything.

"Who the hell—"

"Easy, Ali. It's me," the stranger responded softly.

To Ali's surprise, the blond-haired, blue-eyed man disappeared in a blink and Jason appeared. "Jason?"

"Yes." He held up a small controller. "This is a little tool we sometimes use. As myself, I can't be seen on station with you. As this persona, we're both safe.

Fortunately, you called me Hunter and not by my name since I use a different one with this face. I go by JC Draper here."

"But how?"

"Holograms. But they're not perfect. I'll use makeup and other artifices once we're on station. This will get me past a superficial look." He hit a button on the controller, and the blond once more appeared. "Now, shall we go, Captain?"

Chapter Eight

Ali had been to the spaceport many times but had never seen the rest of the planet. A religious group ran the private retreats at Delphi. They were renowned for their privacy and part medical, part mystical healing arts. Rich mineral deposits—especially the rare Ki crystals—found in the asteroids had led to a different sort of colony at New Nova, separated from the retreats by a harsh desert—a town less *civilized* many would say, catering to miners and the sort of people who came after them, out to make quick money any way they could. The mining had also led to the establishment of the space station and a security force.

She didn't have time to enjoy the views as a throng of officials descended on her and Jason. Her old friend and classmate, Rocko, pressed through them all and swung her into a huge bear hug.

"Damn, Ali. This is one that will make the books."

"For both of us. Thanks, Rocko." She turned to Jason. "This is the other flier."

Rocko stepped back and stared at Jason, then stuck out his hand. "Pleased to meet you, sir. You did some damned good flying."

"Not bad yourself—especially that last bit."

Ali cocked her head at the two men. Both were good looking, but even in his alternate persona, Jason had an air of power tightly leashed about him.

"Speaking of that last trick, what exactly did you guys do? I couldn't see a thing," Ali said.

"We let the shuttle settle on our ships' wings and flew you in." Rocko grinned at her.

"You what?"

They didn't get a chance to talk further as the media rushed in. "Captain Matthews. A statement. Captain, look here. Captain, how did it feel to fly a ship of the dead?"

Ali stared at the people. She knew they had jobs to do, but they were like so many vultures. To her relief, a phalanx of officials and security officers shoved through and surrounded her, Jason, and Rocko. They cordoned off the ship, helping the living to exit the vessel, and shielding the dead flight crew.

"Official statements are available from our communications officer. Please excuse us." The officials and security swept her, Jason, and Rocko through the crowd and away from the media. Finally, they reached the station offices and a semblance of quiet. Then they were separated and taken to different rooms for their statements.

"Tell us what happened," the security officer questioning Ali said. So she did, leaving nothing out.

"You're certain the pirates took out the bridge?"

"No. I did not see who or what attacked. All I know is what happened after the first problem. I'm sure you have the recordings of everything."

"What is your business here?"

Ali sighed. "I've already told you several times. I'm here for retreat. All I want to do is get some peace and quiet for a couple of weeks."

He looked up as a chime sounded in the room, then

nodded as if agreeing to something. Ali suspected he had a com button behind his ear. "You are free to go, Captain. If we have further questions, we'll contact you."

"If you have further questions, you'll have to ask the sisters. I'll be on retreat, and I do *not* want to be disturbed."

He shrugged and escorted her to an elevator. "This lift will avoid the media. Your room is 541. Your print is already on record. Enjoy your stay, Captain."

The doors closed before Ali could say anything. They opened a minute later on an empty corridor with her room near the middle. She laid her palm on the scanner and the door slid open. The inexpensive, generic room, blandly decorated in shades of tan and cream, held a bed, a single chair next to a small table, a tiny bureau, and an even tinier bathing area. She knew there were other, more comfortable and more lavish rooms available for tourists, but this area held the rooms reserved for those applying for retreat status.

Ali stepped in and found her small travel bag on the end of the bed. She took out a clean outfit and peeled off the bright yellow emergency jumpsuit she'd donned in the ship. Underneath, her sweat-soaked travel suit reeked. It joined the jumpsuit in the cleanser.

"Now me." She entered the bathroom and chuckled. The tiny bathroom on her ship seemed luxurious to this miniscule space. She stepped into the cleaning unit, sighing with pleasure as a water shower came up as one of the options. She turned the water to hot, lathered and rinsed quickly, then leaned against the wall and let the water run over her until it shut off. Three whole minutes of bliss. She toweled off and donned clean clothes. A quick glance at her watch told her as much as her stomach. She'd missed lunch and dinner. Before she met Rocko for drinks, she needed food.

"Time for some exploring." Plus, she wanted to find Jason. She headed for the main concourse.

There were so many things to see and do at the huge complex. In addition to the gates for those coming or going, there were theaters, shops carrying anything and everything a spacer would want, rooms for rent, and restaurants catering to every type of cuisine from multiple worlds. A small city in and of itself, the spaceport also held the main assayer office for the quadrant, a place she'd visited often.

An enticing smell tickled her nose, and her stomach rumbled in response. A short time later, she enjoyed a light meal at one of the smaller eateries along the third level concourse. From her table, she watched the transient population of the port as they went about their business. Ali searched the faces for one in particular, looking for black hair and a confident stroll, lingering as long as possible, but no luck. Nor did she see him in his blond persona.

A short time later, she strolled into a bar known for hosting IMF people. Sure enough, Rocko and his partner, Chino, were dead center in a group of people, some of whom she recognized, some she didn't. But they all had the look of being military.

"Hey Ali." Rocko motioned her over to the table where he perched. "Everyone, Ali's here."

A cheer went up around the room, and a pathway opened up between the door and the table. Ali made her way across, accepting the pats and congratulations for what they were—people who knew what they'd done. Unlike the media, these people understood what it had taken to bring the shuttle in.

Ali shared a couple of drinks, nursing hers. Although getting mind-numbingly drunk had a certain appeal, she knew it wouldn't help. She couldn't afford to let her guard down—even here. Her eyes scanned the crowd, looking for the one person she most wanted to see, but she didn't spot him anywhere.

Finally, late into the night, she begged off one more drink and headed for her room, relaxing when she made it there without incident.

"All the comforts of home." She prepared for bed, wondering what had happened to Jason. Had she trusted him too quickly? Where had he disappeared to? She fell asleep asking herself if she'd made a huge mistake.

****

A soft chime woke her the next morning at an ungodly hour, and she struggled awake, trying to get her bearings. Even though she'd only had a couple of drinks, her head felt as if she'd had several dozen.

A light breakfast sat in the catering unit, as well as a small package she opened. Inside rested a long-sleeved soft white robe and a note telling her all retreat participants wore the same clothing. She also needed to place her retreat preferences on file. Ali shrugged and did as directed. A few minutes later, a soft knock at her door interrupted her impatient pacing.

"Identify."

"Hi, Ali." Sami's voice greeted her as the door sprang open to admit Jason, once again in disguise.

"Hi, Sami. Come in, Jason." Ali stood aside for him to enter. Once the door closed securely, he reverted to his normal visage. Although the change startled her, one look at his handsome face made her heart thump a little harder. She turned away to hide her interest. What about the man challenged every sense she had? Even in the nondescript jumpsuit he had on, she'd never seen anyone better-looking. Maybe not handsome in the classic sense, like Dimitri, but more than good enough to get her heart pounding.

"What kept you so long?" Ali asked, her voice harsh as she tried to calm her racing libido.

"Getting worried, were you?" he teased. "I had some difficulty getting to you. Security is keeping a close eye on you. They're checking everyone coming and going in this section, and have spy-eyes all over the place, as do all the media outlets. Once you registered as a retreat participant, you were beyond their reach, so they settled in the outer rooms. They offered me several fortunes to bring you out. So much for you keeping a low profile."

"You think I planned this? Trust me, flying the transport shuttle under those conditions was no picnic."

"I believe you. But it's made our job a lot harder. We need to get out of here. This place is too accessible." He tossed her a gray standard-issue jumpsuit like his. "Put this on. We'll be going places where our regular clothes would be noticed."

"Why don't you give me one of those hologram things and we can walk out of here with no one the wiser?"

"First of all, they have to be specifically attuned to the holder. Secondly, they don't grow on trees. I'll use the one I have but you'll have to manage as you are."

Ali quickly changed into the suit, keeping her own

boots, banging her knees several times as she tried to maneuver in the tiny bathing room. She secured her knife in a special pocket in her right boot and stowed a small laser pistol in her left.

A knock sounded at the door when Ali emerged from the stall. She turned a puzzled frown to Jason.

"Sami?"

"It's her." The AI answered his boss.

Jason opened the door and admitted a tall, slender woman. She hugged him and turned to Ali. "Her?"

"Yeah. Can you do it?"

The woman circled Ali. "Say something."

"What? Who are you?"

"Sami has her on file. You can get the walk, talk, and other particulars from him."

"At least we're the same size. The rest should be no problem. I'll register as wanting seclusion," the woman said.

"She's already registered. Enjoy your vacation."

The stranger picked up Ali's discarded robe and smiled. "I will. Thanks." She handed Jason a bag. "She needs to change her looks, and a jumpsuit isn't enough. There may be eyes watching."

Jason grimaced as he took the bag. "Thanks. I didn't think of that."

The woman held her hand to her chest. "Oh, dear. The great Jason Cole forgetting something." She laughed and winked at Ali. "It's not much, but it should get you out of here."

Jason snorted as he handed the bag over to Ali. "You need a disguise. Put this on."

He turned his back as she took out a wig and cap. She also dabbed on some dark makeup the woman handed her. "I'm ready."

"Sami, are we clear?" Jason asked.

"Yes, Boss."

Jason opened the door and motioned Ali out. After the door shut, he turned to her. "I know you have questions. Please, hold them until we're out of here."

They strolled through the corridors reserved for employees, easing into the flow of traffic as if they belonged there. They kept conversation to a minimum as they rode down to the main concourse where they merged into the crowd. Ali matched Jason's pace, noting his speed and way of walking. With her nerves on edge as they were, she might move too fast, bringing undue attention. By the time he led her into a deserted corridor, Ali had no idea where they were. At the far end, a hatch opened onto a parking slot containing a small, covered air-sled.

The door eased shut after Ali, and she sighed with relief. "Phase one complete." She looked over the small craft. She'd used a lot of sleds, but this one didn't look like any she'd ever seen. Outwardly, it seemed almost the same as others—just slightly larger—but that's where the similarities ended. Compact like Jason's ship, a wide variety of electronics, most of which she'd only read about, packed the small space.

Jason pointed behind the seats. "Your stuff's in the back compartment. We don't have much room but I didn't have a lot of options on such short notice. The seats can double as beds, and the dome can be clear or dark, whatever we need. We'll go dark until we're safely gone."

Ali smiled. "If this is the best you can do on short notice, I'd love to see what you'd do with a little planning."

Jason tossed his gear in the back and leered suggestively at her. "Sometime I'll have to show you."

She snorted and frowned at him as she climbed into the passenger seat. Once they were on their way, she turned to Jason. "Okay, enough time. You want to tell me who that woman is and what she's doing in my room?"

"She's a friend of mine and is in need of some time off. I thought our cover would be better if someone actually went on the retreat. We get an added measure of safety, and she gets a much-needed break."

"She's a bounty hunter?"

Jason shrugged. "She's in the same business I'm in."

Ali stared at him. He hadn't answered her question. She had a strong intuition he wouldn't be forthcoming with any more information. Secrecy controlled his life. She let the subject drop—for now—but she resolved to discover more.

"Is Sami always around?"

"No. However, I needed to find you without alerting security. This system gave him a little trouble getting into it, but he managed. He'll withdraw as soon as we're gone."

"What's our first stop?"

"A place outside of town, within close proximity to New Nova. It's safe, so we can make plans from there."

As dusty kilometer followed dusty kilometer, Ali studied the man sitting next to her. He had charm as well as skills, but she sensed an underlying reserve. Oh, he was pleasant enough company, but he revealed very little about himself. One thing Ali did know, she didn't need to be afraid of him. If asked why, she couldn't say, but she knew the truth of her feelings.

Her eyes roamed over his muscular physique. He had a strong jaw line, softened by a day's growth of beard. When he smiled, it lit up his entire face, not at all in keeping with the image of a cold-blooded bounty hunter. She liked his intelligence and his concern for her safety and found the rare combination of traits permeating his being appealing. He should not be taken foolishly or lightly.

Shortly before dark, Jason set the ship down in the shade of a rocky outcropping. "I'm taking a circuitous route in case we're being tracked. Tomorrow I want you to run through the simulations on how to use this sled, and we'll figure out our plans from there. We'll reach New Nova by Saturday." He broke out two packets of field rations. "Vegetable stew with biscuits or stir-fried rice with vegetables?"

Ali grimaced as she reached for the stew. "I hope they've improved these things since I last had one." She popped the heat ring and waited for the meal to get warm.

Jason stirred his own meal, took a bite, and frowned. "I'm afraid not. Sometime I'm going to have to find the place manufacturing these things and put them out of our misery," he half-joked.

Ali grimly agreed as she downed her own meal. While field rations were complete with all the daily requirements to sustain life, they didn't do much to sustain the soul or the taste buds.

"What can you tell me about New Nova and the surrounding terrain?" she asked.

"It's pretty much like this. The sisters and brothers

at Delphi got the best of what there is on this piece of rock. There are two seasons at Nova—wet and dry—with no in between. We're coming into the wet season right now. We probably have a week or less before the weather gets really miserable. As for the town, like anywhere, parts can be pretty rough. It's about as opposite Delphi as you can get and is mostly there to support the miners. That's the reason the Delphis tolerate the town. Having this place keeps the less than stellar elements out of their area. A small deposit of Ki crystals nearby brought in the get-rich-quick hordes, along with the leeches who always follow behind."

"You make the town sound horrible."

Jason grimaced. "It can be for the unwary. Nevertheless, there are also some good things to recommend. We'll be getting there in time for the last of the High Season Festival—a time of parties and parades. If you stick to the main part of town, the festival can be safe and fun for families. It brings in a good many tourists from all over the quadrant. Kind of a last fling before the wet season descends."

After they finished, Jason set the security controls for the ship and leaned back in his seat and yawned. "Might as well get a good night's rest. We're going to have a long day tomorrow. Good night, Ali."

"Night, Jason," Ali responded as she settled into her own seat-bed. Sleep, however, eluded her while the man on the other bench consumed her thoughts. She could smell his cologne, hear his breathing. She even imagined she heard his heart beating, steady and strong—unlike hers which pounded faster than light.

What about him had her running hot and cold? He could be arrogant, demanding, dictatorial, and a loner—

definitely not her type. Now if she could only get her libido to agree with her logic.

Finally, Ali drifted off into a restless oblivion.

Chapter Nine

The journey continued, mostly in silence. Ali missed the easy bantering between her and her brother—his wry humor and teasing pranks always made time go much faster. Jason's reticence gave her ample opportunity to reflect on the past few months and her plans for the future. Ali refused to think beyond capturing the pirates. Her concentration had to be on them and not on any other possibilities—focused on succeeding where others had failed.

She ran through the simulations to familiarize herself with the workings of the air sled. The controls were more advanced than anything she had ever used, and yet were remarkably easy to work. As she looked over the schematics, one part of her mind wondered why Jason had such a powerful effect on her emotions. The difference between him and Sean, her uncle, or Dimitri could span a parsec. Ali silently scolded herself for even trying to compare them. Her uncle had intelligence, but no backbone. Dimitri had looks, charm, and money, but no honor, and Jason—he had looks and charm when he wanted, but also bravery and honor. Although, he lacked Sean's mischievous streak—the missing trait might not be a bad thing. She shook her head at the direction of her thoughts and went back to studying the ship's specifications.

"We'll reach our camp tonight. The pirates raided

the place early on. They won't be back, so we'll be safe. We can use the vacant camp as our base of operations," Jason said.

"How do you know they won't return?"

"It's been a year, and they haven't been back since. I set up alarms to alert me if anyone disturbed the area. Not many want to be as far from town as this place is."

Ali noted the tension in his voice and body and wondered what was bothering him. "That's fine," she said. She had a sense any questions would cause him to retreat further into his shell so kept her silence. Eventually, he would learn to trust her.

"How did your evening with your uncle go?"

Ali glanced at him, but he concentrated on his driving. It seemed odd to her he'd waited all this time to ask her about that night. So why bring it up now? "Fine. Why?"

"I'm wondering if you gave him any clues about what we're doing. Did he ask about me at all?"

"Only in most unflattering terms. You can relax, Jason. I was as tight-lipped as you seem to be."

Jason half-turned to her and grinned. "Touché. The commander claimed you were under his personal protection."

"He's terribly protective." Ali stared out the window. She refused to tell anyone about what had happened at dinner. When she succeeded with the task at hand, she'd need to check on things very carefully before notifying anyone of a possible problem with her uncle. If he planned to retire anyway, maybe she wouldn't have to do anything. She really didn't need one more worry to deal with, but this one lay high on her list.

"Another question. I know you attended Fleet Academy, but you had a full scholarship to the Science Academy. Since they only pick the best of the best, why the change?"

Ali's hands clenched on the simulation controls. "That's none of your business," she snapped. "And I don't appreciate you checking up on me."

"It's my business if you drag some kind of trouble into this mess. I want to know what's behind my back."

She stared at him, trying to get her warring emotions under control. "Do I look like the kind of person who gets into trouble?"

"Yep."

Ali forced a laugh and tried to appear relaxed. "After what happened to my folks, I decided I needed the extra training Fleet offered. I got all the combat skills along with an excellent education. Fat lot of good it did me."

From his expression, she knew he didn't believe her, but he did let the subject drop. "What about you? Why did you become a bounty hunter, especially an Orion Hunter?"

"For the adventure." His words said one thing, but his voice and look said another. What secrets did he hide? Ali bit her lip. Everyone had secrets—places not open to scrutiny by anyone. She turned to stare out the window, hiding her face and her emotions. She had to remain strong and in control.

"Ali, if you ever want to talk, I'm here."

He'd spoken the words so softly Ali couldn't be sure she heard them. "I'm okay. But thanks."

Chapter Ten

They traveled until dusk, stopping as the first of the three moons topped the distant hills. Jason parked the sled in a small grove of trees half-way up a steep mountain. "We'll set up camp here. There's fresh water and shelter," he spoke in a strained voice.

Ali wondered about his growing moodiness, especially here in this beautiful grove. She climbed down from the sled and stretched the kinks out of her back. "Are you sure this area is safe?"

"We're close enough to Nova, we can come and go as we want but far enough out we won't be disturbed. With the festival going on, we should be able to mingle without too much trouble." He leaned against one of the trees, staring at the setting sun. "I haven't been here in a long time. This grove belonged to a family I knew. They were killed in one of the first raids. They had a beautiful little house a short walk from here. They'd found a small pocket of Ki crystals. Not a lot, but enough for them to live on for a while. A year ago, the pirates hit. They killed the family, burned everything to the ground, and cleaned out the crystal."

Ali watched Jason as he talked. His bitterness and sadness were evident in the way he spoke and the way he stood. She eyed the peaceful site where a family once worked and played. Were they merely friends? Or more? "I'm sure your friends would appreciate your care of their land. A place like this is a treasure."

"What about you? Did you grow up in space?"

"Yes and no." She joined him at the edge of the grove. "We spent about six months of the year in space and the rest at various places around the system. Both my parents were in demand as crystal experts, and we traveled a lot."

"So you never had a home base?"

"Not really—" She paused, then continued. "—that sounds terrible. It wasn't, though. We had a place on Epsilon Eridani One we called home—Sean or I visited for the last time a couple of years before I left for the academy, but it never felt like *home* to us. Home happened to be wherever our parents were. No matter where we went, they made sure we were happy and safe. We never felt as if we were missing anything. I guess I'm a wanderer at heart."

"While nice at times, it can be a lonely existence."

"It didn't seem lonely back then. We had the entire universe as our playground and plenty of people around. There were even other kids at different times. I know it sounds bad, but we had fun and learned a lot in the process."

"Well, you're safe here. I promise. Why don't you take a look around while I fix us some dinner?"

"Oh, please. Not another field ration," she teased in mock horror.

Jason laughed. "No. How do grilled fish and a salad sound?"

"Heavenly. What'd you do, rob a grocer on the way? No, don't answer. I'd rather not know."

"If you're interested in cooling off, there's a creek and pools off to the west. You have twenty minutes."

Ali grabbed her pack and headed for the water. What she found stopped her in her tracks. The small creek poured from high in the mountain into a dazzling waterfall plunging to a series of five pools, the largest of which lay at the base of the small mountain and covered at least a couple of acres. A soft, mossy bank surrounded the clear water, and Ali saw where a series of steps had been cut into the rocky bank for easy access to the second pool. From there, she could see the short jump to the larger pond and steps cut into the bank for access to the upper pools.

"Bless you, Jason," she said as she stripped out of her traveling clothes. A few minutes later, she blessed him again as the shockingly cold water hit her bare skin. She dived beneath the calm surface, reveling in the invigorating chill. At one point, near the far side of the pool, she crossed a section much warmer than the rest of the water. She followed the stream to its source and found to her delight an area of the pool fed by an underground hot spring. Someone had walled the section off, partially enclosing the warmer water and having an underwater ledge for relaxing.

Ali swam back to her things, grabbed her bathing supplies and returned to the warm spring. She lost all sense of time as she relaxed. Finally, she swam to a ledge by the waterfall and climbed up to stand under the edge of the cascade, letting the stream flow over her. For the first time in more months than she cared to remember, she felt at peace.

\*\*\*\*

Jason glanced at his watch and smiled. Ali had been gone almost forty minutes. He knew the lure of the pools and bet she'd lost track of time. He covered their dinners and set off in the direction of the falls. What he saw when he got there made him stop in awe. There under the waterfall stood Ali in all her glory, and what a glorious sight she made. Her arms were raised to the waterfall as if in silent prayer. He watched her for a few minutes before a noise from behind him broke his reverie, and he reluctantly returned to the shelter. When he got there, he didn't know whether to laugh or throw a fit. A small gray-striped cat sat in the middle of his carefully prepared dinner neatly licking its whiskers. Of his dinner, not much remained. Only a few bones from the fish and the salad, upended in the dirt, had survived. He looked up as Ali joined him.

"I'm afraid dinner's ruined," Jason said, trying to keep the laughter from his voice. He retrieved a container of soup from their stores. "Looks like we'll have to make do."

"A cat." He watched as Ali approached the feline and allowed the animal to sniff her hand before she reached up to scratch it under the chin, earning her an instant rumbling purr.

"I'm impressed," Jason said. "Me-too doesn't let just anyone pet her."

"Me-too? What an unusual name. Is she yours?" She sat down and the cat leaped into her lap and kneaded Ali's legs before settling down.

"By default. She belonged to the family who lived here. I thought she'd died in the raid. I wonder how she's been surviving." He turned to the ship. "I'll see what else I can come up with for our dinner." A few minutes later, he set out soup, fresh biscuits, and fruit compote.

They ate their meal in companionable silence, Me-too providing the dinner music with her contented purring from Ali's lap. Afterward, Ali cleaned up while Jason checked the perimeter alarms he'd set out earlier. When she finished her chores, Ali crawled into her bunk, the cat curled up at her side.

Jason returned to find the campsite organized and Ali sound asleep, a slight smile on her beautiful face. The cat opened one eye to see who had entered then settled back down. Jason sighed and stared out at the starkly beautiful landscape. The three moons lit the barren plain at the foot of the low hills. Off in the distance, the city lights brightened the horizon. He picked out individual constellations. He loved this place and knew his brother had also. Though harsh, the land held a beauty all its own.

"Well, Zack, I finally brought a girl around for you to meet. Only problem is, you're not here to see her, and it's my fault. I should have been here for you and Corinna and the kids." He turned back to the shelter to stare at Ali. "Damn it. Why did you have to come into my life? I can't afford to care about you, and it's too dangerous for you to have any affection for me. I can't rest until those pirates are dead, and even then, I'll be gone again on some other mission. You need someone stable—someone who can give you a home."

No matter how much he tried, he couldn't picture himself with anyone but Ali or think of her with anyone else. But he knew it would never work. His job didn't allow for commitments. He crawled into his bunk vastly aware of the woman a few short steps away as sleep eluded him.

****

The next morning, Ali woke early, a sense of

rightness and calmness soothing her. She listened to birds chirping in the trees surrounding the shelter as she stretched the kinks out of her back. The sun hadn't yet made its appearance, but she had enough light to see Jason had gone from his bunk, nor did she see the cat anywhere. A quick search didn't find him at the campsite or the pools, so she made a quick round of the alarms. At the second one, she spied him a short distance away kneeling at the base of the largest of four grave markers. She watched him for a few minutes while he brushed debris away from the site.

She returned to the shelter, made breakfast, and straightened up. Not that the area needed it, but she needed something to occupy her hands. A short time later, Jason joined her.

"I suppose you're curious about them," he said as he accepted a cup of coffee.

His awareness of her didn't surprise Ali. "Only if you want to tell me."

Jason wrapped his hands around the steaming mug and stared into the dark brew as if the answers he sought were there. "It's where I buried my brother, his wife, and their two kids a year ago."

He threw a rock across the clearing and grimaced as it bounced off the trunk of a tree. "They killed the entire family for some surface crystal Zack had uncovered."

Ali laid her hand on his arm. She knew his mood exactly. "I'm sorry."

"I should have been here!" His words echoed through the trees.

"Then you'd be dead too. I know. They have no scruples, Jason. Be thankful you weren't here. I saw what they did to Sean. At least you were spared that." Too late, Ali realized what she'd said. She saw the expression on his face change when he figured out she'd been lying. She hadn't just heard their voices but knew their faces.

"What do you mean you *saw* what they did?" Jason demanded.

"I meant I had to clean up the ship after they left," Ali hedged.

"Try again," Jason demanded, his tone flat and cold. "You were drifting, barely alive. When I found you, you weren't capable of cleaning up yourself let alone a ship."

Ali stared at him. "You found me? You were the one who took me in? Why didn't you tell me? Why didn't Uncle Rod? Why'd you disappear?"

"I had an appointment I couldn't miss. As for your uncle, he made it clear having an Orion Hunter find you didn't sit well with him. Now, back to your statement. What do you mean, you saw them?"

She dropped her shoulders in defeat. "Sean installed a special surveillance camera a week before the raid. I downloaded the data before the repair crews found it. The camera caught everything. I saw it all."

"The data wafer—do you have it with you?"

"No," she lied. She knew if Jason had the data, he'd leave her behind and she refused to be left out. Jason stared at her, but she gazed right back at him without flinching.

"I'm beginning to wonder how many other things you haven't told me."

She gestured around the campsite. "I'd say we both have some secrets." She softened her voice, trying to ease the tension. "What about Me-too? Was she a pet?"

As if on cue, the cat strolled out of the woods, twining around Jason's legs.

"She belonged to Toni, Zack's daughter. Toby, my nephew had a pet lizard, and anything Toby had, Toni wanted. Her favorite phrase was *me too,* thus…"

"Me-too." Ali finished. She laughed and then sobered. "Jason, I do know how you're feeling. In a way, I'm glad I know. You're not in this for the money so you'll see it through to the end. This makes us equals."

"We always were, Ali." Jason's eyes met hers.

Ali caught his look. She needed to change the subject before it got too personal. She pointed to her simple denim pants and plain white shirt. "Is my outfit all right? I didn't know what the locals might wear so I settled for simple."

"Simple works fine. The locals are mostly grubbers or those who make money from the grubbers." Jason looked her up and down. "Actually, you look too good. If we're not careful, some pimp may want you for his crib."

"Me? Not a chance. If anyone tries, they may find themselves speaking soprano, if they can still talk."

"Ouch. Remind me never to get on your wrong side. Is there anything else I should know about, besides your bloodthirsty attitude?"

"Many things. However, I think I'll make you figure my flaws out. A girl has to have some secrets."

"I'd say you have more than your share."

Ali bit her lip and looked away. "That reminds me. Shouldn't we be getting to work?"

Jason walked over to where she sat, and looked

down at her. "Afraid of me, Miss Matthews? Or of yourself?"

Ali stared up at him and countered, "Neither. Right now, we can't afford to be distracted. Talk to me after we've taken care of the pirates."

He ran his fingers across her cheek, tracing her jaw line. "I'll hold you to that."

"I expect you to," she tossed back.

****

Jason berated himself for doing what he'd wanted to avoid. He couldn't afford to get involved with anyone right now. Chances were one or both of them wouldn't survive this mission, but he had to finish this. He shouldn't tempt her—or himself—with something that would lead nowhere.

"You're right, Ali. We need to keep our heads. Since I don't want my boss lady cutting off my source of income, or anything else, I'll behave."

Ali grinned mischievously. "Yeah. Right. Now, as to business, what do you know about the pirates and why they haven't been caught?"

Jason set up a portable data reader and initialized the machine. "As you know, the raids are widespread and seemingly random, but with your information, we've been able to establish a pattern. We assume they'll hit Jones next, so they'll be ready for them. My boss has already given Jones a heads up, but the pirate group is large. In space, they use anywhere from three to five high-speed ships. They used a land transport here, but we have no clue where they came from. We can't find any base." He pointed out different pages of data on the reader, allowing Ali time to read and assimilate it all.

Vicky Burkholder

"This isn't the only planet in the quadrant they've hit, but it is the one they've hit the most often. They have to have a fairly large base, one able to hold all the ships, personnel, and even a refining and manufacturing area. I don't think they're going to farm out their raw materials when they've gone to all the trouble to steal them."

Ali took over the reader, scanning through the data quickly as he talked.

"Other than it's a large area to search, there's no reason not to find them. They could be here on the planet or on one of the larger asteroids or one of the moons. It's possible they even have some security people in their pockets. That wouldn't surprise me. You said they talked about New Nova. What exactly did they say?"

"Basically, they couldn't wait until they got back to Tillie's."

Jason pursed his lips. "Tillie's is a brothel we've had under investigation several times. It's been reported she uses non-guild members and caters to depraved tastes."

He didn't tell Ali that every time they raided the place, they found nothing, and every undercover agent ever sent in either came back empty-handed or didn't come back at all. Of the two, the latter happened more frequently.

"Okay, today we'll check you out on the sled and some other special equipment. We'll figure out our next moves afterward. I know you can handle a pistol, but how handy are you with the knife you have in your boot?"

Ali grinned and slipped the knife out. "Give me a

---

target."

Jason picked out a knot on the trunk of one of the trees.

"Standing still or running?" She flipped the knife and buried the blade in the center of the knot.

He nodded as she retrieved the blade. "How about a moving target?" He tossed one of their dinner plates as hard as he could. A second later, she impaled the plate, dead center, on one of the trees. Jason didn't bother to conceal his astonishment. "I think I'm very glad you recognized me that night in your room. Okay. What about hand-to-hand combat? Should we try, or you just want to tell me your ranking?"

Ali grinned. "Could be fun finding out, but I'll tell you I placed second in my class."

"Only second?"

"I missed one match due to a bout with the Altarian flu."

Jason blew out a low whistle. "You missed an entire match and still ranked second? Plus, you managed to finish first in your overall class ranking." Her skill impressed him more than a little. "I think I need to get you to teach me a few things. Is there anything you don't know?"

"I'm not good dealing with people, especially strangers. In addition, I don't know how to fly your sled. I've seen a lot of air sleds, but that one is different from anything I've ever used."

Jason led the way to the small craft. "It's a special design." He spent the rest of the morning showing her the controls and testing her on different maneuvers. He had to admit she learned fast. By the time they broke for lunch, she knew as much about the sled as he did. In a few hours she'd learned what took most people the better part of a week to pick up.

"Why don't you go enjoy a swim, and I'll take care of lunch. We'll take the afternoon off and get back to work after dark. Accuracy in bright daylight is one thing. In the dark is something entirely different."

Ali wiped a trickle of sweat from her face. "Agreed. Why don't you join me? We both need the break, and I'll help you with lunch later."

Jason hesitated only a second and nodded. "Sure. I'll be there in a minute." He waited until she'd left and followed slowly. When he got to the pools, he found her standing beneath the falls again. This time she wore a brief swimming suit. He skinned down to his own suit, dived in, and swam over to the ledge.

"So, what do you think of our little area?" he asked.

"This is beautiful." She jumped back into the water, came up under Jason, and yanked him off balance so he fell backward into the water.

He came up sputtering and chased her across the pool. "You will pay for that, woman." He grabbed for Ali, but she slipped from his grasp and swam toward the edge where the water dropped down to the lake.

Before she made it halfway across Jason caught her and dunked her, making it her turn to come up sputtering. He splashed her from behind and submerged before she retaliated. He surfaced near the bathing pool. "Guess water sports aren't your strong point," he called, but to an empty pool.

Where had she gone? He trod water, looking for telltale signs of her swimming underwater, but he didn't see any. Suddenly, she surfaced, straight up, only centimeters away from him, showering him with water.

Ali climbed up on the rock wall and laughed at Jason. "You forget. I grew up with an older—and bigger—brother. My mom came from a water planet. Every time we were anywhere near a pool or water source, we went swimming or boating. I'll admit I'm not the world's strongest swimmer, but I do know how to hold my breath."

Jason climbed up beside her and chuckled. "That skill could come in handy in a lot of places."

"How deep are these ponds?" Ali asked. The geologist in her looked at the surrounding area. Something about the place intrigued her—something more than the waterfalls and pools. She looked at the way a sharp, if low ridge surrounded the lake. It might be a natural lake, but for one thing, she didn't see an outlet and yet the water didn't appear stagnant. There had to be an underwater outlet.

Jason pointed up the cliff. "The first one is the smallest. It's actually nothing more than a big watering hole, and the water runs through there quite fast. The second one is slightly larger in size, but no deeper. If you could keep your balance in the flow, you'd probably be able to walk across without getting your knees wet. Except for the lake, this one is the largest and deepest."

"I see your brother put some work into the them."

"Zack and I spent an entire month working on this. His wife found the warm spring and insisted we block it up for the bathing area. The whole section is partly natural, partly what we did."

"You did a good job. It's beautiful."

"Thanks. The lake is completely natural and

extremely deep—deep enough to hide my ship, which I've done on occasion. We never found an outlet, but there must be one underwater somewhere because the water's always fresh. There are even a few fish if you're of a mind for sport."

Ali leaned back and let the sun dry her off. The light bounced off the waterfall, treating them to a constant rainbow adding to the beauty of the glen. The warmth and sound of the waterfall made her drowsy, and she lay back against the rocks and drifted off to sleep.

She'd been in the middle of a delicious dream when the shock of cold water dropping on her bare stomach woke her with a start. "What? Jason! You…"

He dived in and swam across to the far side of the pool before she could retaliate.

"Come on, partner. I don't know about you, but I'm hungry, and we have work to do." He laughed at her, climbed out of the pool, and headed toward camp.

Ali looked around. The sun hung low in the sky. She'd slept almost the entire afternoon away. Her stomach rumbled, reminding her she'd never had lunch. She grinned and jumped back into the water.

Back at the shelter, she changed into a black thermal suit for the night trials they were going to do. Jason had dressed in a similar outfit.

"Pasta salad okay with you?" he asked.

"Sounds great." Ali got out the plates and utensils while Jason got out a food packet. When they'd set up camp, it had amazed Ali how much he had stowed in the little sled. He'd had the tent, cots, food, and water stores for at least a week, and more. He certainly knew how to pack. "Garlic bread?" she asked and reached for another pack.

"Of course. Oh, and get out some more of the fish stores for Me-too."

"Okay."

The cat purred her appreciation as they sat down to eat in companionable silence. Jason looked at the table and snapped his fingers. "You forgot something."

Ali looked around and then noticed the small smile on Jason's face. "Okay, I'll bite. What did I forget?"

Jason went to the sled and retrieved a small, reinforced box. He brought it back to the table and set it down. "You forgot this."

Ali watched him open the box. He pulled a large, well-wrapped, fist-sized round object from the box. She laughed when he unwrapped the prize and handed it to her with a flourish. "Rainbow fruit? You managed to get a rainbow fruit and bring it here?"

"Of course. Just because we're roughing it doesn't mean we can't enjoy ourselves." He got out a knife and split the bright globe into halves.

Ali ran a finger across the split. The large fruit had been aptly named as it ran from bright orange at the outer edge through multiple colors to end up at the dark purple center. Tiny edible black seeds dotted the different layers. She licked the sweetly tart juice from her finger. "Ummm. I much prefer eating one to wearing one."

"Oh, I don't know. You looked rather delicious drenched in rainbow juice."

Ali laughed and dug into her dinner. Their easy bantering continued throughout the meal.

A short time later, after they'd cleaned up, Ali tugged up the hood on her outfit while Jason looked on in approval. He did the same and handed her a lightweight helmet. "We'll start at the pools and practice without infra-reds first—night scopes only. I'll take lead. You follow in ten minutes. When you get to the sled, hit the lights to signal your arrival."

They got to the pools, and Jason melted into the darkness, disappearing quickly into the dark woods surrounding them.

Ali checked to make sure her weapons were set on practice mode. She waited the allotted time and followed Jason into the trees. She followed the trail to the sled. Twice he tried to ambush her, and twice she eluded him, but barely. The third time, he managed to sting her in the leg before she hit him with what would have been a lethal shot. She made the sled and reached for the lights when her instincts stopped her. The exercise had been too easy. She switched off her night scope and carefully touched the side of the sled, fingers sliding delicately up the side to the switch. Sure enough, she found a wire—a booby trap. She grinned as she followed the wire to the source and disarmed the trap in the dark. A minute later she hit the switch, bathing the area in light and herself in white foam.

"Ka-boom. You're dead." Jason said from the canopy of the sled.

Ali sputtered as she wiped foam from her face. "A second trap? You set a second trap?"

"You can't be too careful, partner. Always have a backup plan. Always. You did get away from me and disarm the first trap. Not many people could do that."

Ali grinned and swatted some foam at him. "Yeah, I did manage to kill you, what, three times before you got me?"

"Don't let that get around or my reputation would be ruined." He frowned in mock horror as he climbed down and handed her a towel. "Ali, I want you to make me a promise. If something happens to me, I don't want you to take any unreasonable chances to save me."

Ali studied Jason. "I'll promise only if you'll agree to the same thing." Ali knew she'd never leave him behind, and she was pretty sure he'd feel the same way, but she'd agree. You never left a man behind, no matter what. But who knew what the future might bring?

"Agreed. Looks like we're stuck with each other, so let's make the best of our time. Okay, your turn to be the hunted."

Ali took off in a different direction. Earlier in the evening, she'd spied a possible hiding spot high in a tree on the edge of the camp. She'd almost made it when Jason ambushed her from the front. "That's not fair," she complained. "You have the advantage of knowing this terrain better than I do."

"When we find the pirates, we'll be in their territory," Jason pointed out.

Ali nodded. She'd made a mistake a first-year cadet wouldn't make, and under other circumstances, it could have gotten her killed. "You're right. I got sloppy. It won't happen again."

"We'll see. Okay, let's try again."

They practiced a few more times before Jason called a halt. He handed her an energy bar and a bottle of water and led her to a rocky outcropping. They sat overlooking the dark desert, feet dangling over the edge, with nothing but air beneath them for a thousand feet. A sudden flash in the north got both their attentions.

"Jason, did you see that?"

"Yes. Looks like it came from north of New Nova."

"Any ideas as to what it is?"

"One, but that doesn't make sense. The flash looked like a ship's trail but shorter, and there aren't any bases out there."

"None that we know of. What if it's one of the pirates?" In her excitement, Ali jumped up and started pacing across the narrow outcropping. "This could be the break we've been waiting for."

"And it could be tourists taking a night flight." Jason knew better. The trail didn't match one for a shuttle or land sled. Whatever had taken off had been big—and powerful. "Ali, I want you to wait back at the camp. I'm going to go into town and find out what I can. I'll be back before daybreak."

Ali stopped pacing and stared at him. "You want me to what? Not on your life. This is as much my fight as it is yours."

"I'm asking you to trust me on this. I'm going someplace you can't. Not yet. I'll bring back some costumes so you can move around freely after this. Promise me you'll stay here."

Reluctantly Ali nodded—but only because she had an idea of her own. "Be careful and watch your six, Jason." She watched him leave, feeling very alone. After he left, she looked around the neat campsite in frustration.

She grabbed a flashlight and some tools and packed them along with a couple of energy bars in a backpack and headed for the pools. A short time later she grinned in triumph. She would definitely have something to show Jason when he got back. She slipped off her backpack and got to work.

## Chapter Eleven

Jason parked the sled in a dark alley next to a five-story inn and restaurant and climbed out. Halfway between the sled and the entrance to the alley, he paused and rapped at a dark door set flush in the solid wall. A small opening appeared in the door, and he stuck in his right hand. A couple of seconds later, he heard a faint click and went through the door into a closed vestibule.

"Please remain still for ID verification," a sultry female voice instructed him. He held still while a beam of light played from his head to toes. A minute later the inner door swung silently open, and Jason strolled into a well-lit room jammed with all sorts of electronic equipment. A portly man, black as the midnight sky, completely devoid of hair and wearing a bright lavender robe, sat at a console in the middle of the room. His fingers nimbly danced over a variety of controls.

"Hi, Jase. Make yourself comfortable. I'll be with you in a sec."

Jason looked around for a chair and finally found one under a pile of wires and connections. He gently extracted the seat, rolled up to the console, and waited quietly until the man finished his task. Jason marveled at the chaos in the room. No matter how many times he came here, the amount of equipment crammed into the tiny space always amazed him, and Marty constantly added more. When it came to electronics, nobody could match Marty's genius. Marty also had the reputation of being one of the best innkeepers in several star systems.

Finally, he turned and grinned at Jason. "I knew I'd be seeing you soon. What brings you to New Nova? Somehow I don't think you're here for the festival."

"I'm not. I need your help."

"That's what I'm here for. Ulric sent me a packet of information for you via Sami, so I figured you'd be in sooner or later." He reached into a voluminous sleeve and extracted a data wafer. "Do you want privacy?"

"As if you don't already know what's on this," Jason chuckled. "Give me the gist."

"I'm hurt you think so little of me, Jason. You're right, of course, but I'm still hurt." The older man grinned. "Okay. Some of this you already know, but I'll recap. Aleksia Matthews. Graduated first in her class from the academy. Highest scores ever, with one exception." He looked meaningfully at Jason, who had never been beaten.

"She's an over-achiever, especially in combat techniques. Specialized in hand-to-hand. At the same time, received her PhD in geology. Only daughter of Lynette and Andrew Matthews. Both multiple PhDs. They focused on Ki crystals and were the ones who discovered its energy potential, including the unique qualities of red crystals and the possibility of using it as a replacement in ship propulsion. Has one brother, Sean, who is missing and presumed dead. He holds degrees in business, electronics, and geology. Family has multiple holdings in several areas. I won't bother with the portfolio download unless you're looking for her credit rating." He paused until Jason shook his head. "Suffice it to say, after probate, Miss Matthews will never hurt for credits. She served two years with the Fleet then went reserve and left to join her brother. Word has it there's a contract out on her. Funny thing is, there's a counter contract. If anyone hurts her, the second buyer will pay double for her killer."

"Next subject—Commander Rod Matthews. Assigned here as a junior officer straight from the academy fifteen years ago. He lost his right arm when the cruiser he'd been on chased down what they took to be a pirate ship. Turned out to be a low-level smuggler. Interesting thing is, only the cargo bay sustained damage. Our good commander's battle station lay elsewhere, but it put him on the fast track as he managed to plug up a major breach in the hold."

He snorted as Jason grinned. Neither one of them had any use for officers who received their rank without earning it the hard way.

Marty continued, "Other than that, the commander's had an undistinguished career. If not for the smuggler, he probably would have played out his career as a lieutenant, but not much more. Likes the good life but stays within his bounds. Basically, a dull character with nothing going on anywhere with the exception of some very powerful friends—one in particular is Dimitri Kolanka."

"I knew he traveled in high circles. What I don't know is why."

"Final subject—Dimitri Kolanka. Extensive holdings, although nobody knows exactly where his wealth comes from. As it is, he has a more-than-comfortable income, but is rapidly going through his funds with his, um, somewhat extravagant lifestyle.

While nothing has been solidly proven, he has a lot of allegations following him around concerning his exotic tastes in physical pleasure. Has contacts at all levels of business and industry, but especially high ones in government. It's rumored his connections are all compliments of extensive blackmailing, but there's no proof, and any time charges are brought up against him, the witness either recants or disappears. Again, without proof of his involvement. He's very careful to be in a public place with lots of publicity when an *accident* happens."

"In other words, he's got the scruples of a Denebian slime devil."

"Fewer. Be careful with him. We're digging deeper but haven't gotten anything solid yet. And his association with Matthews doesn't fit his profile. He's slumming here, and we don't know why. I do find it interesting that, considering his tendency to avoid anything appearing nasty, the commander, not the local gendarmes, looked into the recent incident at Delphi."

Jason started. "What incident?"

"Where have you been? No, don't answer. I don't want to know. Seems that two days ago, the retreat wing of Delphi station suffered an explosion. Whoever did it used a very special type of device even I've never heard of. The lab is already working on the breakdown. Speculation is, the device was based on Ki crystals. Three rooms destroyed—no bodies found—but the authorities assume the occupants were still in the rooms as none of them has shown up for the retreats. In an unprecedented spirit of cooperation, the brothers and sisters gave the authorities the names of the missing. Two men and one woman. Do you want their names?"

Jason chewed the inside of his lip as he thought. He could guess who the woman was. The incident could work to their advantage if she remained dead for the time being. "Just the woman's."

Marty raised an eyebrow. "One Aleksia Matthews."

That confirmed Jason's guess. "Did Kate get out all right?"

"For the most part. Minor injuries. A couple of days at the med unit on Orion, and she'll be fine. But she says you owe her." He swung around to the monitor. "I assume the latest gossip is not what you're here for. Now, what else can I give you?"

Jason digested the information as he tucked the data wafer in his pocket. "Approximately an hour ago we saw a flash north of the city. It looked like an abbreviated ship's tail."

Marty touched a few keys. "Funny you mentioned that. Look at this. I picked it up from the satellite about the time you saw the flash." He touched a few controls and a large, dark, blurry image appeared on the view screen. As Jason watched, the fuzzy image grew larger and then suddenly disappeared.

"Can you clear up the picture?" Jason asked.

"This is cleaned up. Even I couldn't read the original."

His admission surprised Jason, but he nodded. If Marty couldn't read it, it couldn't be read. "Damn. They did it. I wonder how many they have."

"Would you like to enlighten me as to what the hell you're talking about?" Marty asked.

"The pirates. One of their hits netted a substantial amount of Myethean polymers—enough to build an entire fleet—or a small space station."

"An undetectable station? That would be an interesting problem."

"Interesting isn't exactly what I would say. Any theories as to where their base might be?"

"I followed the trail of the ship back as far as I could, but didn't see anything at all that looked like a base. It has to be large enough to house ships, personnel, land vehicles, and from what you say, manufacturing. There simply isn't anything in that direction large enough. The same for a five-hundred-kilometer radius. Nothing. Do you want me to expand the search?"

Jason glared at the blurry image on the screen as if he could will it to divulge its secrets. "No. I have some other leads to follow up on. Thanks anyway." He hesitated. "Do you know if any geologic maps were ever made of the surrounding area?"

"Probably. I'll check the archives. Are you looking for anything specific?"

"I'm not sure yet. Send it to Sami if you find anything. One more thing. Has there been any unusual activity at Tillie's lately?

"No. In fact, it's been abnormally quiet. I heard a rumor she pulled up stakes and moved out to one of the asteroids. Do you want me to check?"

"Yes. Send a flash to Sami. Thanks, again."

"Not a problem. Jason, watch yourself out there. These are nasty buggers, and you've been on their tails long enough to be a target. I don't want to see you gamble away your life for nothing."

"This time I've got an ace up my sleeve. Marty, do you have any empty rooms? I need to rent two, one with extra security."

Marty cocked his head, thinking. "It's a little tight right now with the festival, but I'll have something by evening. How much security are you looking for?"

"The max, but I'll take what you can give me."

"I'll see what I can do."

"Thanks. Oh, before I forget, do you have any beignets around?"

"But of course. Zeus?"

"Done, sir. They'll be up in a minute," the AI said.

Marty turned back to Jason. "Is there anything else?"

Jason shook his head. "Not yet. We'll see you at sundown." A few minutes later, he headed back to the campsite.

The pale light of dawn shone over the site when Jason returned. Ali had coffee steaming in two mugs when he strolled into the clearing.

"Hi, partner," he said as he dropped a package on the table. "That coffee smells good. I figured you'd be up, so I brought us some breakfast." He opened the package to reveal a dozen beignets, still warm from the oven.

Ali inhaled the aroma and smiled appreciatively. "You are definitely a handy man to have around, Jason Cole. What did you find out in town?"

He took a bite of one of the donuts before answering. "That you have good instincts. It looks like they have a base somewhere north of town, but it doesn't show up anywhere. It also looks like they might have already built a ship from the polymers. The flash we saw means they were probably testing the ship."

"That means they're getting ready for another raid.

We have to stop them before they get a chance to kill any more innocent people. We need to move our base to town. The only way I can identify any of them is if I'm there."

"Much as I hate to admit it, you're right. I've secured a place for us at an inn. The place belongs to a friend of mine, so I know we'll be safe there."

After breakfast, Ali and Jason packed up the camp and prepared to move into town.

"Do I have time for a quick swim?" Ali asked as she wiped a trickle of sweat from her face. The high humidity and heat made the process slow and tiring. Even eating lunch seemed too much trouble.

Jason glanced at the storm clouds gathering in the distance. "Yes, but make it a quick one. That storm will be here soon. You go ahead. I'll follow in a few." He watched as Ali took off down the trail before he turned to the sled.

"Sami, you on?" Before they'd left Delphi Station, Jason had instructed Sami to keep the ship in readiness. He knew in an emergency the little ship could get to them in thirty minutes.

"Yes, Boss. I was beginning to wonder about you."

"I've been busy. Has Marty sent you anything lately?"

"Bunches of geological data. How do you want it analyzed?"

"Look for anything large in the area around New Nova, perhaps a hidden canyon or something similar. Concentrate on the northeast area but give me anything in a hundred-kilometer radius. We're moving our base of operations to Marty's Inn. We'll be there by tonight. You have anything else for me?"

"Some local news you might find interesting. An explosion in town this morning destroyed the establishment known as *Tillie's*. Fortunately, there were no major injuries."

"Damn. That's a little too close for comfort. Sami, after local sundown, I want you to move the ship to this location. The grove is closer than where you are now. We may need to get out of here fast, and I want you nearby. Go to stealth mode and use the lake like before. I'll talk to you later."

"Right, Boss."

Jason strolled to the pools, wondering how to break the news to Ali.

"It's about time you got here," she teased as she floated in the warm water, then she changed positions and frowned at him. "What's wrong?"

Jason blinked. He'd thought he'd controlled his face enough so she wouldn't suspect anything. He'd have to remember and be more careful. Quickly and unemotionally, he told her about the bombing of the retreat hotel and Tillie's brothel.

"Did anyone get hurt?"

"In Tillie's, no. At Delphi, it's assumed two men and one woman were victims." Jason debated telling her she was one of the *assumed*.

"Assumed? Why not definite?"

"The bomber used a special type of incendiary. There's nothing left to identify."

She cocked her head. He could almost see the thoughts going through her mind. "Am I one of the *assumed* dead?" She paled when Jason nodded. "Stars, I have to tell my uncle I'm okay. And what about your friend?"

"My friend is fine. She got out in time. As for your uncle, think about this—if you're dead, we'll have a little breathing space. Alive you're still a target. Dead, you're a problem solved."

"I'm not sure I like being a problem solved, but I see your point. So, what do we do now?"

"We stick to our plan. We'll move into town and work from there."

"Before we do, I have something to show you. Change into your swimming duds and come in."

Jason looked at the looming clouds. "We don't have a lot of time before the storm hits."

Ali grinned. "This won't take more than a few minutes. Meet me at the waterfall."

By the time he dived in, Ali had climbed out to stand under the waterfall. "What are you looking at so intently?" he asked as he trod water.

"Come up here and see." She reached down a hand to help him out. "But watch your head." She stepped through the waterfall.

With a shrug, Jason followed her. The solid rock wall in front of him stopped him in his tracks, and Ali had disappeared. "Ali?" he called. "Where are you?"

Ali poked her head out from behind a large rock to his left. "I'm here. Look what I've found. Watch your footing—it's slippery and low." She handed him a glow stick and held up her own as she led him around the rock. "When I first saw this place, I thought this looked like a good area for caves. So, while you were gone, I did some exploring." She ducked through a narrow slot behind the rock followed closely by Jason. They sidestepped a short distance through the narrow slot before the cave opened up into a large cavern.

Jason stared in awe at the view. The vastness of the room swallowed his small light. Huge columns of rock reached from floor to ceiling, some streaked with thick bands of Ki crystals, their colors sparkling. Smaller stalactites and stalagmites studded the area like giant teeth, their crystalline compositions reflecting his light.

"Isn't this incredible, Jason?" Ali called from further into the cavern, her voice echoing off the rocky walls. "Look at this place."

"Incredible doesn't begin to describe this place. Are those bands of crystal?" He ran his hand over one of the thick columns of shining rock, gulping as his light reflected red.

"Yes. Without my equipment, I can't tell how pure the vein is, but I believe it's high grade, maybe even red. Hard to tell in this light. It's probably one of the largest deposits ever found outside Abboo."

Jason shook his head. "All the scrabbling Zack did on the surface and this was here the whole time." He shivered and rubbed his arms. "It's cold in here."

Ali laughed. "Most caves are. The ambient temperature is usually around thirteen degrees Celsius year-round." She handed him the jacket she'd brought in during the night and slipped into her own.

He gratefully tugged the warm coat on. "You look like you're enjoying this."

"This is my first love. When I'm not crawling over asteroids or planets, I'm crawling through them. There's nothing quite as exciting as struggling through a tight passage only to emerge in an underground fairyland of crystal."

"Ali, we simply don't have time for this right now," he reasoned as she studied the rocky columns.

"Oh, I know. I just wish we did. I'd love to see where it goes." She turned to him with an impish smile. "Do you think the owner would mind if I came back sometime and explored more fully?"

"I'm sure he wouldn't mind at all," Jason said, his voice as excited as hers. "In fact, given the right incentive, he could probably be convinced to join you."

Ali backtracked to the entrance. "I can't wait."

"We'd better get moving," Jason said above the rising wind, "or we're going to get caught in the storm. I don't want to be out here in one. They can get pretty violent around here."

Ali quickly dried off and donned a pair of shorts over her bathing suit. "I'm ready now. Oh. I almost forgot. What about Me-too? We can't just abandon her."

He decided to tease her a little. "She'll survive. She has before."

"Jason, even you can't be so cold-hearted. We are not going to leave her here."

Jason grinned at her. "Relax. I'm teasing. I won't abandon her. We can take her with us. But you have to hold her while I drive."

"Done. Thank you."

"No worries. She's all the family I have left. I'd never let anything happen to her."

Ali nodded as she headed for the sled. They found the cat sitting there, almost as if she knew they were going away. Ali scooped her up and settled her in the back of the sled. The bright afternoon sunshine turned dark as the threatening storm raced in. A few minutes later they were on their way to town, barely ahead of the rain.

They stopped in a small alley empty of any other vehicles.

"Don't take more than you need," Jason directed. "We may have to move fast when the time comes. Oh, and put this on." He handed her a garishly painted mask and pulled one on over his own head. He picked up Me-too and led the way to the front of the inn.

Ali giggled as she followed Jason.

He stopped, puzzled by her humor. "What?"

"I'm sorry, but come on. Where else would you find a big man wearing a pair of bathing shorts, boots, a warm jacket, and a red and yellow rooster's head? And carrying a cat!"

He snorted, but grinned. "Yeah, well, you should see yourself. I'd say we make a good pair."

"Reservations for Cole," Jason spoke to the automated receptionist. The door buzzed, and they went through.

The lobby had been tastefully decorated in shades of navy blue, tan, and maroon. Though not large, soft chairs and potted plants made the area inviting. There were no windows, but ambient lighting more than made up for their lack. Several people milled around the room, talking quietly or relaxing in the chairs. Ali noted some of them wore garish clothing and masks even more bizarre than hers and Jason's.

"Marty sends his apologies, but he has only one room available," a young man dressed as a Harlequin greeted them. "Your room is on the fourth floor, front, and is keyed to your prints. Enjoy your stay." A lighted arrow appeared in the wall directing them to their lodgings.

"I'm, ah, sorry," Jason apologized to Ali as she

registered her palm print on the door. "I asked for two separate rooms."

"Jason, would you stop worrying? This isn't a problem. After all, we've been sharing accommodations for a couple of days already." Ali shouldered her bag and followed the arrow to their room. When Jason opened the door, they saw a large, well-appointed room luridly decorated in deep shades of red with a huge round bed situated in the middle.

"I am going to strangle Marty," Jason muttered.

"Now that is a bed," Ali said as she lost the battle with laughter.

Chapter Twelve

"I'll sleep on the floor," Jason said as he tossed his bag on the single chair near the window. "If I can find a spot." He yanked off his mask and tossed it on the tiny table next to the chair.

Ali removed her mask and looked straight at him. "Jason, don't be silly. This bed is large enough to hold the entire fleet with room left over."

He looked at the bed and grinned. "I guess you're right. I'll take the door side. You've got the window."

A flash of lightning briefly lit the room followed closely by a deafening clap of thunder. Ali glanced out the window at the downpour. "I'd suggest dinner, but not if we have to go out in that."

"Afraid of a little rain?" Jason teased. "This is just the beginning. But not to worry. They have an excellent restaurant downstairs. We can eat there." He buzzed for reservations. A minute later, he turned back to her, a disappointed look on his face. "Looks like we'll have to make do with the catering unit. The storm sent everyone inside, and they're booked solid."

The room monitor beeped at them. "Message for Jason Cole."

Jason opened the file and broke into a big grin. "Forget the catering unit. We've been invited to dinner."

"What? Where? And what do you mean *we*? Who

knows I'm here?"

Jason dug in his pack. "The man who owns this place is an old friend of mine and can be trusted implicitly. He's invited us to join him in his private booth. There's a back entrance so we don't have to go through the dining area or the rain. We can relax and eat, and nobody will be the wiser. You're in for a real treat. Marty is from a place on Old Earth called New Orleans, and in addition to his other talents is an incredible cook. He's famous for his jambalaya."

"Whatever jambalaya is. So when's dinner?" Ali asked. She mentally went over the clothes she had in her small bag. They were mostly practical, traveling clothes, nothing to wear on an evening out. Then she remembered the microfiber dress she had tucked in one pocket of her bag. It would do nicely.

"In an hour. Oh, and do you have anything other than travel gear? If not, I can get you something from the shop downstairs."

"An hour is fine if I get the shower first. As for the clothes, I'll see what I can whip up." She grabbed her bag and headed for the bathroom. "See if you can find something for Me-too. She's probably hungry. Oh, and you'd better figure out something for a litter box." Ali shut the door on Jason's amused face and snapped the lock with an audible click. Then she got her first good look at the bathroom. She immediately broke into loud laughter.

"Ali? Are you all right?"

Jason's innocent question sent her into another paroxysm of laughter. Tears streamed down her face as she opened the door. "You have to see this." She stepped to one side, allowing room for him to enter.

When he did, she watched his face, giggling again when his mouth dropped open.

"I can't believe someone would actually do this on purpose."

Jason joined her in laughter as he surveyed the space nearly equal the bedroom in size. Gold-veined mirrors covered the ceiling and two walls. Filmy pink and red material held up by cherubim aligned along the edge of the ceiling and draped the other two walls. On the floor lay a thick white carpet patterned with gold, red, and pink roses.

In addition to an expansive shower cubicle, a sunken bath—large enough for several people—sat center-stage. Vibrant paintings in the tub itself left absolutely no doubt as to the activities of the participants. She found the toilet in one corner of the room hidden by a moveable screen covered with more of the suggestive paintings.

"Let me guess," Ali said when she could breathe again, "the honeymoon suite." She broke into laughter again as Jason muttered something about Marty and space and no space suits. Ali shoved at him. "If I'm not out in twenty minutes, send in a diving team." Ali took her dress out of the pocket of her bag and hung it over the screen. The humidity from her bath would help to straighten out any wrinkles in the soft material.

Twenty minutes later she donned a light robe she found hanging on the back of the door and wrapped a fluffy towel around her head. She grabbed the dress and emerged from the room.

"Your turn, partner," she said to Jason. She noted small food and water dishes sat in one corner of the room along with other feline necessities. Me-too had curled up in the middle of the bed, contentedly purring. Jason disappeared into the bathroom, and Ali went to work. She'd brought very few cosmetics, but some quick work with tinted powder sufficed. She fluffed out her short curls as they dried. Finally, she slipped into the dress.

A wide strap across one shoulder held up the soft material. From there, the skirt dropped in a long flowing line to her feet. The melding of color gave the simple cut an incredible look. The artful blending of shades of gold changed hue as the light changed. Ali wished she had some kind of jewelry to go with the gown and then remembered the necklace and earrings her uncle had given her the night before she'd left. She dug through the bag. She'd planned to drop them off at the security bureau but had been sidetracked. She took the box out. She rarely wore jewelry, but the set went perfectly with the dress, if in an overly ornate way. She opted to wear the necklace and placed the earrings back in her bag. Finally, she felt as ready as possible. Then Jason emerged from the bathroom.

She stared at him in admiration. A creamy white silk shirt open at the neck hugged his body. The full sleeves tapered down to French cuffs in which he had placed round black studs. He wore black pants and his high black boots. Ali could picture him in one of her historical novels standing on the bow of an ancient sailing ship. He was every centimeter a desirable, incredible man.

"You've been holding out on me," she teased. "Or do you always carry clothes like that in your travel bag?"

"It pays to have friends in high places. Besides, I

could ask you the same question. Surely gowns like that aren't standard pirate tracking fare. Lady, when you whip something up, it reaches new heights. Aleksia Matthews, you are truly beautiful."

Ali dropped into a brief curtsy. "I thank you, kind sir. Are you ready?"

He held out his arm for her to take. After checking the corridor, he escorted Ali to an elevator around the corner from their room. "This is a private car accessible by handprint. The public ones are at the other end." He placed his palm on the panel, and a minute later the doors opened.

The short ride down felt so smooth, Ali didn't know when they started or stopped. When the doors opened, she half expected to see the same corridor. She stepped into a lighted alcove containing three doors. Jason laid his palm against the one in front of them. The silent door sprang open to reveal a small room furnished with a table and several chairs. Muted lighting kept most of the small room in shadow, but Ali saw that, unlike their room, this one had been tastefully decorated in dark blue, cream, and gold. She also noticed someone already seated at the table. Their host?

Jason stepped in the room and brought Ali in with him. "Marty, may I present Miss Aleksia Matthews. Ali, this is Marty Jameson."

Marty rose from his seat, and kept rising, towering over her by at least a head and a half. Easily the largest man she had ever seen, he also had more bulk than most people and didn't have a speck of hair on either his face or head. He stared at her, and she had the strangest sensation he was assessing her worth. Relief flowed through her when he gave her a slight nod.

"My dear, you look absolutely ravishing. In fact, I'm beginning to wonder why Jason isn't doing that right now."

"Marty." Jason glared at the big man.

Ali giggled.

"Ali, you'll have to forgive him. I think somebody spaced his brains and forgot to take his body."

"As if anyone could overlook this body," Marty said as he sat back down. He indicated a seat for Ali and Jason on either side of him. "It is good to finally meet you. Sami has told me a lot about you."

"Then you have me at a disadvantage," Ali said. "Because I know absolutely nothing about you."

For some unfathomable reason she liked the big man. He was certainly not like anyone she'd ever met, and she couldn't even begin to guess his age. But he had kind eyes and a happy manner that spoke volumes. He also had a soft, drawling accent she'd never heard before.

"What you see is what you get," he said.

"I see an awful lot," Ali quipped.

Jason laughed. "Marty, you've met your match. Now, how about some dinner? Or are you going to let us starve to death?"

"Patience, Jason. The food will be here momentarily." He swiveled in his chair. "What do you say we see what's happening on the floor while we wait?" Two panels on the wall opposite them slid apart, revealing the packed dining room below. Ali shrank back into her chair. The last thing they needed now was for her to be recognized.

Jason reached for her hand. "Relax. The window is one way. We can see them, but they can't see us. Do you see anyone you recognize?"

Ali leaned forward and looked over the crowded room. More than half the revelers were in some kind of costume, most with masks. "It's impossible to tell with the costumes."

Jason nodded. "Agreed. Marty can give us access on the room monitor so we can keep a watch on things from there, but I doubt if you'll see anyone. This isn't the sort of place their type would patronize."

Marty grinned and leaned toward Jason, his whisper carrying across the table to Ali. "Speaking of rooms, how do you like yours? The credit goes to Sami."

Ali gasped. "I'm going to fry his circuits."

Marty laughed, a deep, happy sound triggering her own giggles. Soon all three of them were laughing over the atrocious room.

"You'd be surprised how many requests we get for that room," Marty said. "I'm losing a lot of revenue by giving it to you."

Jason raised an eyebrow at Marty. "Uh-huh. And I'll bet you'll bill Ulric double since there are two of us."

Marty placed his hands over his chest. "Oh, I'm mortally wounded. You're right, but I'm wounded."

"Yeah, right. So what's for dinner? Or did you invite us here to be subjected to your rapier wit?"

"Jason, would I ever keep food from the hungry? That is a sacrilege I will not tolerate. But, since you asked, we're having grilled shrimp with peppers, mushrooms, and pearl onions dusted with my special Cajun spices, and served over saffron rice. And for dessert, something special for the two of you. Another suggestion of Sami's."

"Uh-oh," Ali said. "I think we're in trouble."

"Not at all, my lady. It's a delicate sorbet made of rainbow fruit."

Ali looked at Jason and started laughing again. "I…I think…maybe Sami needs some reprogramming."

"I'd have to agree," Jason said. "You'd better believe I'm going to have a long talk with him."

The ambiance progressed through a dinner Ali declared to be the best she'd ever had, to lighthearted bantering between the three. After dinner, they watched an entertainment troupe performing for the diners below. Finally, the evening wound down, and Jason led a very tired Ali back to their room.

On the elevator, Ali realized she still knew almost nothing about Marty, but he had learned an awful lot about her during their time together. She half wondered if Jason had put him up to the interrogation.

"Why don't you get some rest?" Jason opened the door to their room. "I have some things I want to check on. I'll be back in a few minutes."

Ali yawned, too tired to care about anything other than sleep. "No problem. See you in the morning, partner."

He nodded and left. A minute later, he returned to the dining alcove with Marty. "So, what do you think?"

"That she is undoubtedly one of the best-looking women I've ever seen." He grinned when Jason glared at him. He tapped the arm of his chair, and a hidden door opened in the back wall, revealing his lab. "By the way, you've got the entire floor to yourselves. To keep things looking right, I put some of our people up there." He led the way into the lab and waited for the door to close. "Okay, here's what we've got. According to the DNA test from dinner, she is exactly who she says she is. Over the years, she's had a few flings, but no serious romances—no skeletons in the closet waiting to jump out at you. Except for her family, she's pretty much a loner. According to the head office, she's been cleared almost up to your level. We're authorized to take her on officially if she so desires. So, do you want to recruit her or just bed her?"

Jason's gave him a raised eyebrow in answer. For some reason, her lack of partners made him unaccountably happy. "For right now, I want to keep her alive. She can visually ID the pirates, or at least some of them. I know she's got the information on a wafer, but I haven't been able to find it yet."

"You're losing your touch, my boy. I'd say this girl has gotten under your skin, but you don't have any under that armor you wear. Okay, we'll let the recruitment go for now. Have you told her who you are yet?"

"No. She thinks I'm nothing more than a regular bounty hunter, and that's the way I want to keep things for now. Finding these pirates is our focus for now, both as Ulric's agent and as a hunter. So I'm on the hunt. I'll worry about recruiting her later."

Marty shook his head. "You need to tell her. She's not stupid, and eventually she'll figure something out. When she does, she'll be unhappy you weren't honest with her."

"I'd say that's a two-way street. She's not exactly been forthcoming with me, either," Jason shot back and then paused as an alarm went off on Marty's console.

Marty swung around to the monitor. "Get up to

your room now. Someone's trying to break in. I'll alert Ali."

Before Marty had finished the sentence, Jason headed to the room. He paced as the elevator lifted him to the floor. "Is the hall clear?" he asked while he yanked his laser pistol from his pocket.

"Up to the corner," Marty's voice came over the speaker. "I activated the sticky field, but they must have a nullifier. There are three of them. No response from my guys."

As the door opened, Jason heard a loud *pop* coming from the direction of their room. He stood flat against the wall and peered around the corner. Two men were watching the corridor while a third aimed a strange weapon at the door. Two other men lay sprawled on the floor. He could tell from the positions of their bodies they were dead. So much for Marty's men.

Jason took aim and shot the first man as another explosion reverberated through the corridor and one of the men ran into the room. The second man fired at Jason, eradicating a section of the wall above his head. Fortunately for Jason, the man had nothing to hide behind. A quick shot took that one out. Jason sprinted down the hall, pausing when the third man came flying back out of the room and landed in a heap at the base of the opposite wall.

"Ali?" Jason called. "Are you all right?"

Ali stuck her head out the door. "Yes."

She stepped out and checked the man she'd taken down while Jason examined the other two. "This one's out cold, but alive. How 'bout yours?"

"Dead." Jason tried to keep his eyes from the short

robe gaping open at the waist. He could tell she had nothing on underneath. He heard a noise from the direction of the elevators and swerved around, his gun at the ready.

"Jason?"

Jason relaxed as Marty's voice echoed through the hall. "Come on out, Marty. It's safe."

Marty strode into view, followed closely by a floating platform. He looked down at his men and sighed. "Damn. I didn't expect an attack this soon. Put all of them on this and come with me." He turned around and saw the wall. "Jeeze, Jason, couldn't you have stopped him before he destroyed the wall?"

"I was a little preoccupied." He took a pair of binders from the platform and used them on the unconscious man.

"I need to change and check on Me-too," Ali said. "I'll be right back."

Jason could tell from the tremor in her voice the entire episode had shaken her, and he was pretty sure she recognized one of the men—the one who had burst into her room. She needed to learn to mask her face. Her expressions gave everything away. Thank goodness Marty had alerted her before they'd gotten in so she'd been ready for them.

While she changed, Jason dumped the two thugs' bodies on the pallet and laid the other two bodies gently on top of them. Finally, he placed the third thug on top. He turned around and picked up the odd weapon. "Ever seen anything like this, Marty?"

Marty took the piece to examine. "No. Let's get this down to the lab and see what comes up." He looked up as Ali joined them, all business. "Let's go."

Between Marty and the pallet, the elevator's space shrank, and Jason found himself pressed face to face with Ali. He suspected Marty had planned this on purpose. It would have been easy for him to send up a crew to take care of the bodies.

Ali's heart beat against his chest from under the thin shirt she'd donned. He inhaled her scent, a mixture of the citrus soap she favored overlaid by the sharp tang of sweat—the after-effect of the preceding moments. Her head came to just below his chin and felt so right resting there, her hair as silky as he'd imagined. Over the top of her head, he noticed the smug smile on Marty's face and vowed to get even with the man. The trip down took far too long for his comfort.

****

As soon as Marty took the pallet out of the elevator, Ali climbed down and stood staring at her surroundings. Instead of the basement she'd been expecting, she saw a huge, dimly lit room full of tables covered with a wide variety of equipment. Glass walls partitioned off several offices, all of them currently empty. Two men came through a door at the far end of the room and walked toward them.

"Lights, full power," Marty ordered as he maneuvered the pallet away from the elevator. He waved at the men. "Mike, Rick, put the prisoner in Room One and take the unknown bodies to Joey. Full ID spectrum. Have Sandy see to the other two and make appropriate arrangements. Then see what you can make of this." He handed the one he'd called Mike the weapon used on Ali's door. "Oh, and send someone upstairs to make repairs."

"Already done, Marty," Mike said. He took the

weapon while the other man took the bodies away. They both disappeared through the same door they'd entered.

Ali took in everything around her then turned to Jason and Marty. Jason had the sense to look embarrassed while Marty grinned at her. "Okay, which one of you wants to tell me what's going on? Unless I'm very much mistaken, this doesn't look much like a typical hotel basement, and I don't think you're just an innkeeper."

"I told you she'd figure something out sooner or later, Jase." Marty laughed.

"If I didn't know you better, I'd swear you set this whole thing up," Jason growled at Marty.

Ali looked from one to the other in frustration. "If you two are done squabbling, I'd appreciate knowing what the hell is going on."

Marty looked at his watch. "Oops, I'm being paged. I'll be right back." He took off as quickly as a man his size could move, which proved to be surprisingly fast.

"Coward." Jason called after him. He turned to Ali. "Let's go into an office where we can at least sit down." He led her into the nearest cubicle and took the chair behind the desk while she sat in another.

She knew Jason was stalling. If the events of the evening weren't so serious, she'd laugh.

"So, which branch of the government do you work for? I'd say some kind of special services." Although Jason masked it quickly, the telltale look on his face told her she'd hit pretty close to home.

"Before I answer your question, let me ask one of my own. How seriously do you take your oath of loyalty to Fleet?"

Ali cocked her head to one side as she thought about his question. Like all graduates of the Academy, she'd been required to take an oath of loyalty to Interplanetary Military Forces, a formality the students recited by rote. There were a lot of problems with the government and even within the IMF, but the basic tenets were good. So did she agree with the tenets and laws she had promised to uphold? Yes, she decided, with no reservations. She took a deep breath and exhaled. "Very seriously."

Jason nodded. "Okay. I'm going to hold you to your oath. What you're seeing here is so far beyond top secret only a select few know. You're here because my bosses have already cleared you. There is a lot I won't tell you, so don't ask. What I can tell you is that being a bounty hunter is my cover, as I'm sure you've already guessed, but the hunt I'm on is serious. As you know, I have personal reasons for going after the pirates. I also have professional ones. I've been tracking them for better than a year, and this is as close as we've ever gotten. I gather you recognized the man who got into your room?"

"He was one of the pirates who breached my ship." She looked up as Marty entered the room.

"Is it safe?" Marty asked.

Ali laughed. "Only if you'll promise to make me a batch of those wonderful beignets for breakfast."

"Done." He took the larger chair behind the desk as Jason joined Ali with another chair.

"So, what's the news?" Jason asked.

## Chapter Thirteen

"Not good. The third man's dead. Your weapon took care of the first two, but even if you hadn't, they'd be just as dead. All three had a microchip implanted in their necks. We don't know what triggered them, yet, but the lab is working on them. We had slightly better luck with the weapon, but it's too soon to say more than it's made of Myethean polymer and is crystal based."

Ali blanched. She remembered the sketches in her uncle's apartment. She debated telling Jason and Marty. It would be disloyal to her uncle, but she couldn't be sure of his innocence any more. "Um, Jason? I don't know if this means anything, but I think I saw a drawing of such a weapon recently."

Jason raised an eyebrow at her. "How recently and where?"

"The day before I left, in my uncle's apartment. I thought they were some sketches he'd made. He liked drawing things like weapons and equipment."

"Marty?" Jason looked at Marty who nodded. "Okay, Ali. Thanks. We'll have someone look into your uncle and his sketches. What I'd like to know is how they found us so quickly. Ali has been reported missing, presumed dead at Delphi. We went from there straight to Zack's place, and this is the first we've been here. How'd they know she was here?"

Marty ran his hand over his chin. "I wonder.

Zeus?"

"Yes, sir." A very dignified voice answered him. Ali cocked her head in puzzlement.

"Your AI, I assume?"

"Oh, excuse me." Marty smiled at her. "Ali, meet Zeus, our AI. Zeus, this is Aleksia Matthews."

"Pleased to meet you, my lady. And I am not his AI. He is my human."

"My apologies, Zeus." She bit back a chuckle.

"Business, please, Zeus. I need a sensor scan of the inn. Concentrate on the fourth floor."

"Yes sir. Visual display or hard copy?"

"Visual."

"Very good, sir." A diagram of the fourth floor of the inn showed up on the screen. In one corner, a tiny red light blinked at them.

"That's our room," Ali said. "What is it?"

Marty shrugged. "Zeus, can you ascertain the source of the alert?"

"Negative, sir. It is some kind of tracking device, but the signature is unusual."

Marty tapped his finger on his lips. "Ali, I noticed you were wearing some jewelry tonight. Not to be unkind, but you don't strike me as the type to wear such an ornate piece."

"I usually don't, but the piece went so well with my gown I thought I would this time. Why? What's wrong?"

Jason turned a puzzled frown on her. "So, in a bag where you're carrying the bare necessities, you just happened to have a necklace like that?"

"Uncle Rod gave it to me right before we left. I didn't have time to put it in security." She looked from one man to the other. "Is something wrong?"

Jason nodded one time at Marty and rose. "I'll be right back."

Ali looked at Marty. "You think my uncle bugged my necklace?"

"How well do you know your uncle?" Marty asked.

"He's my uncle. What do you want? I mean, I've known him my entire life. But I don't know much about him, I guess."

"Zeus, talk to Sami. I want you two to find out what you can."

"Yes, sir. Am I to understand you want it in minute detail, sir?"

"Down to the genome."

"Yes, sir."

Ali looked up at the monitor. The red light moved with a steady pace. "Marty? Look at the light."

"Zeus, give me a split visual."

"Yes, sir." A picture of Jason swinging Ali's carryall showed up on one half of the screen while the other half showed the original diagram. They watched Jason as he traversed the corridor to the elevator and rode it down, the telltale light moving as he moved.

"I think that pretty much settles our question," Marty said when Jason joined them. "You were on the grid the entire way."

"Where is the necklace, Ali?" Jason asked. He handed her the bag.

Ali removed the jewelry box from the pocket. "There are earrings too." She opened the box. There lying on white silk were the necklace and earrings.

Marty let out a low whistle. "This is what an uncle gives his niece these days? These are some works of art." He picked up the necklace and held it up to the light. "Commanders must be making a heck of a lot more these days. These are Terran. You can't even find gems like this in this quadrant." He retrieved a small scanner from the desk and skimmed it over the necklace. He paused, frowned, tapped the scanner and ran it over the necklace again.

"It's not the necklace, is it?" Ali said. She blew out a breath she didn't know she'd been holding. If her uncle was responsible, it meant one thing—he was somehow involved with the pirates, and she didn't want to think about that scenario.

"No." Marty put the necklace back and ran the scanner over the earrings. A high-pitched beep sounded from the instrument. He removed the earrings and placed them on the desktop and ran the scanner over them again. It beeped at them again. "It appears to be just the earrings. Ali, if you don't mind, I'd like to keep these. We need to know what they're using to track you."

Tears threatened. Her own uncle. How could he? "Keep them. Keep the whole set. I don't ever want to see them again." She clenched her hands until her nails dug into the palms. The pain helped her focus. "Do you need me anymore?"

Jason shook his head. "Right now, we all need some sleep." He led Ali back to the elevator. "I'll be up shortly."

She nodded and leaned against the wall as the doors closed. The adrenaline rush faded, and exhaustion set in. When she got off, the slightly more awake part of her brain saw the wall the pirate had shot out had been fixed, as well as her door, and none of it looked repaired. The new parts blended in as if they had always been there. If she didn't know better, she'd swear nothing had happened here.

Once in the room, Ali washed up and finally crawled into the bed. After the past few days of sleeping on the narrow camp bunks, the large, soft bed felt as if she were sinking onto a cloud, and she sighed in sheer pleasure. But pain tempered the pleasure—pain that her uncle could do this to her—to her family.

"Uncle Rod, how could you?" A deep sadness and anger replaced the concern over his mental state.

A few minutes later, the door opened. Ali reached for the knife under her pillow.

"Ali?" Jason's whisper pierced the silence.

"I'm awake." She released the knife and rolled onto her back. "I assume the floor is secure?"

"The whole building has been secured. Marty has sentinels on every floor, the roof, and positioned around the street."

"He has so many people here?"

"Not that I know of. Some of the surveillance is mechanical. But we're as safe as possible."

"Thanks." The other side of the mattress sagged with Jason's weight. The silence grew once more as she became more aware of him lying only a short distance away. Her breathing quickened from the close proximity. For an eon, neither spoke.

Jason and her reaction to him so unnerved her, she forced herself to think of her uncle. Could he be one of the pirates? If not, why the tracking device? But how could he be one of the people who'd killed her parents and Sean? "Do you think my uncle has anything to do with this mess?"

"I don't know. He's the commander of the largest station in the sector, giving him the power, but I don't think he's the leader. No offense meant, but he isn't the leader type."

"He isn't. But he wouldn't try to kill me. Not my uncle."

"You'd be surprised what a man is capable of when given enough incentive. However, I think you're right. He wouldn't try to kill you. But what about his friend, Dimitri? You haven't even mentioned him."

Ali froze—her breathing stopped. She jumped from the bed as if the sheets had grown thistles. Most times, she could forget the attack, like a bad dream. She didn't know for sure, but something tickled the back of her brain. Something told her Dimitri had been involved.

"Ali? Are you all right?"

She heard the concern in Jason's voice, but she refused to respond. After a moment, she forced her voice to remain calm, unlike her body that shivered even in the warmth of the room. "I'm fine." She yawned expansively. "Why don't you get some sleep? I think I'll sit here by the window a while." She settled in the chair, tears streaming down her face, while she struggled to control the emotions threatening to overwhelm her. *Perhaps you are the lucky one, Jason Cole. Sometimes emotions can get the better of you.*

Long after Jason's even breathing told her he slept, Ali reclaimed her side of the bed, but a relaxing rest evaded her. Nightmarish images plagued her dreams as she helplessly watched her family ambushed while Dimitri laughed at her. He wore a garish mask that throbbed and pulsed in wild, hypnotic colors. Like before, bindings held her helpless, unable to do more than watch in frustration, screaming out her hatred.

\*\*\*\*

Ali's thrashing around and cries woke Jason. He rolled over to her and gathered her in his arms. "Ali? Ali, come on, wake up." He grasped her arms as she swung her fists at him, still caught in the throes of some nightmare. "Ali!" He finally succeeded in calming her, but she still trembled violently.

Suddenly, Ali attacked Jason. "Get off me you filthy bastard. If you touch me again, I'll kill you. I swear. Get off me!"

Jason realized the nightmare still held her in its clutches and backed off, even though it was the last thing his body wanted to do. Ali became a fierce wildcat, striking out at him with a skill few matched. While trying to restrain her, a part of his brain wondered what had made her react so violently. Yes, he knew about the attack on her and her roommate, but how bad had it been? A simple kidnapping wouldn't lead to this kind of reaction. He knew from her files she'd had extensive rehab after the kidnapping, but the file didn't say what kind or what had happened to her. A lot of it had been redacted, which led to the questions by whom and why? He'd have to get the higher ups to look a little deeper.

It took him time and all his skills to subdue her without hurting her, but eventually he did. "Ali! Wake up! It's only a dream."

\*\*\*\*

Jason's words finally got through to her mind. The nightmare loosened its grip, and she regained her senses. She looked up to see him staring down at her, a bright red mark staining one cheek. She met his probing

164

stare directly. "You can let me up now. I'm all right. I'm sorry, Jason. I haven't had a nightmare like that in a long time." She gently touched his face. "I, um, suggest if I have any more, you run for cover."

She retrieved a med-kit out of her carryall and took out a small tube she held up to his face. "Use this on your face and any other bruises. It'll help."

"It might help if you talked," Jason suggested.

"No, it won't. We both have secrets, Jason, so let's keep out of each other's lives. Unless you want to tell me about your past, leave mine alone." She returned to the bed, curling up in a small ball in one corner, refusing to get near him. With the nightmare still fresh in her mind, she couldn't allow him, or any man, to touch her.

Ali arose the next morning before Jason stirred. She knew the moment he awoke. She could feel his eyes boring into her as she programmed the catering unit. He had every right to be angry with her. She had been nasty to him when he'd just been trying to be kind. Ali sighed as she went into the bathroom and ran the water in the tub. They had been getting along so well, and now she'd probably ruined everything. Ranting like a madwoman and beating him up was no way to endear herself to a man.

She fretted over what Jason thought about her after last night as she stepped into the water. She had drawn him in and then shoved him away. He'd responded to her, but why? Because he wanted her, Ali Matthews, or because of her availability? Could she let him in, and then let him go out of her life? She sighed and sank back, letting the hot water soothe her.

When the water cooled, she dried off, donned a

robe, and went back to the outer room. Jason had tea and a light breakfast of beignets and fruit ready. She waited for him to say something to gauge his mood.

"Ah, so you didn't drown, as I feared," Jason teased as she re-entered the room. "I'll get my bath while you dress, if you left me any hot water." He tossed her a brightly colored pair of shorts, a top that would reveal more than it hid, and a long veil to hide her hair and face. "You might want to try these. We'll look like the other tourists—although what you have on isn't bad at all."

Ali glanced down when Jason chuckled and she glared at him.

"Sorry, Ali, but you look damn good in that robe. I think I'd better make mine a cold shower."

Ali watched him go. After last night, she hadn't known if he'd even speak to her again, and here he was, teasing her about her lack of dress. A man of many moods, and she liked each one of them. She also appreciated his strong sense of self-control.

She quickly donned the outfit he'd provided, trying futilely to stretch the skimpy fabric. A short time later, he emerged from the bath wearing a pair of black, form-fitting shorts with studded suspenders crisscrossing his chest, leather sandals strapped up to his knees, and nothing else. Drops of water still clung to the tiny hairs on his chest. Deep blue eyes stared at her across the tiny table, and she shivered in spite of herself. With Jason, she experienced emotions she'd never had before. Mostly, he made her feel alive.

"What about the earrings?"

Jason grinned. "We attached it to a drone and sent it on a trip. Right now, my dear, you're rafting down the nearby gorge."

Ali laughed. "I hope I'm having a good time."

After Jason looked her over and handed her a demi-mask, they went out for a look around. He smiled at her wide-eyed astonishment as she surveyed the town. There were three main boulevards criss-crossed by several smaller streets. Off each street were alleys, some connected, some not.

The streets were dark red and smoothly paved, but the buildings drew the eye. None stood higher than five stories with most being only two or three but taking up entire quads or even blocks. They were painted every color of the rainbow and then some. A bright purple restaurant sat next to a lime green shop that co-existed next to a vivid red bar. One building even had a rotating color scheme on a holographic front.

"You didn't tell me the town was this colorful. It's like a maze inside a kaleidoscope."

Jason laughed. "I didn't want to spoil the surprise. The buildings only look this way during festival. By next week, this will all be back to muddy red and tan. The town fathers wanted New Nova to be different so people would come back. As for the maze, it actually is one. If viewed from above, you can see the pattern. Anytime someone wants to erect a building in town, they are assigned a specific lot in keeping with the pattern. Other than that, there are no rules."

"Well, it certainly is remarkable."

The rain had ended during the night, but the air remained heavy with humidity made worse by the high heat. Ali silently thanked Jason for the skimpy outfit as anything more would have been instantly soaked with sweat. He'd chosen their outfits well. They blended in with the tourists roaming the streets. To the casual observer, they looked like any other revelers, but their seemingly random wanderings took them steadily toward the north. Once they were out of the main thoroughfares, they made a more direct route, but stopped short when they heard a woman's scream come from one of the myriad side streets. Ali determined the direction almost as fast as Jason.

"Watch your six, Ali."

"That goes for you too."

They took off at a quick run and came up on a small band of thieves in the process of robbing a tourist group. Before the six thieves knew they were there, Jason knocked one of them unconscious, and Ali took out a second one. The remaining four rounded on Jason and Ali. They took up back-to-back positions and waited for the attack to come. All thought left as instinct, honed by rigorous training, kicked in. The thugs were inept and uncoordinated, relying more on brute mass than finesse. Of the four, only one offered more than a token resistance, but Jason easily outmatched him. The fight ended almost before it began. In a few minutes, the four joined their compatriots on the ground. Jason removed the straps from his sandals and securely bound the unconscious thugs together.

"Do you have a security contract?" Jason asked the leader of the tour group as Ali checked each of the thugs. A brief shake of her head told him she didn't recognize them.

"Yes," one man said. "I called them when we were first attacked, but they never showed up."

"Then I suggest you call the locals, and I'd also file

a complaint against whomever you were using. You shouldn't be this far from the festival." He looked at a little girl cowering in a corner of the alley, tears flowing from big frightened eyes. He knelt down in front of her and smiled. "It's all over, little one. You're safe now." He gently wiped her tears away. He looked up and saw a young couple standing protectively nearby. The man thanked Jason as the woman picked up the little girl.

"Thank you for your help," the leader of the group said. "I've never seen anything like you two. You wouldn't be looking for work, would you?"

Jason turned toward him. "No, thanks. You'll be fine now. But I suggest you head back to the main district and stay out of the back areas."

The local police arrived, and after a few brief words with Jason and Ali, they were free to leave.

"I wonder what those people would have thought if they'd known you were an Orion Hunter," Ali said. "You were amazing with that little girl. Does every female you meet fall under your spell so easily?"

"Actually, it's a ploy to win you over to my side," he responded.

"Then you're wasting your time. I've been on your side ever since you ruined my best jumpsuit with your rainbow fruit back on the station."

Jason chuckled. "Ditto for me. You're good. I'd trust you at my back any time."

"I wish I could say the same."

"What do you mean?" Jason asked, confusion in his voice. She kept her eyes on the ground, unable to look at him.

"We both know you'd like nothing better than to drop me off as soon as you don't need me anymore."

Jason grasped her arms in a strong grip, his gaze intense, never wavering as he quickly kissed her. "Then make sure I need you."

As quickly as he'd grabbed her, he released her and strode away.

Ali struggled to regain her shaky composure. She studied him. How could he kiss her like he had and then walk away? She shook her head, doubting she would ever understand him.

Late in the afternoon they returned to the inn for a much-needed break. Ali massaged her aching feet while Jason lounged in the chair. She sensed his gaze on her. "Do you ever get tired of it, Jason?"

"Of what?"

"Of the traveling, the fighting, the looks when people think you're a bounty hunter?"

Jason turned away from her and stared out the window. "I don't always enjoy what I do, but it's a job needing to be done, and I'm good at what I do. I like to think because of me, someone somewhere will feel a little safer—a little more secure—like that little girl in the alley. I don't intend to spend the rest of my life doing this, but for now, this is what I am." He looked back at her.

Ali noticed the wistfulness in his voice and manner. "So, what happens to make someone like you quit?"

Jason shrugged. "I don't know. I've never known an agent to quit. Most times, they go into an administrative role or end up dead."

"Doesn't that bother you? Is the excitement worth the danger?"

"Let me ask you this. A little bit ago in the alley,

weren't you excited? Didn't the danger give you a rush?"

Ali thought a minute before she answered. "Danger, yes, but not terror or death."

"But they're the same thing. You live with danger every day, especially when you're off planet. The smallest slip out there, and you're history. Death surrounds us. It's unavoidable. That's why I live like I do. Live for the moment. For the now."

"Aren't you ever afraid?"

"Of course, I am. Only a fool doesn't get afraid, but I can't afford to show it—not even to myself. You learn to use the fear. The edge keeps you alert. However, you can't let emotions control you—you have to control them. Otherwise fear becomes terror and you're helpless. In this job you can't afford to let terror take over. You can't ever let your guard down. It's an exciting life, don't you agree?"

"No. To always be afraid, never to know peace? That's not something I'd call exciting. The people you go after must feel that way. They're always running, always looking over their shoulder. And even you. There's a very thin line between them and you."

"Like I said, Ali, I live for the here and now. This is who I am right now. Who knows where I'll be tomorrow or next year? I take my risks, the same as you. And like you, I have problems that need solving. Right now, this is one way of solving them."

Ali didn't know what to say to him. She couldn't very well ask him what he meant, not after telling him to stay out of her private affairs. "Have you ever backed away from something?"

"No. I guess I've believed even dying was better

than being helpless."

"Have you ever considered you believe what you do because you don't think much about your own future? After all, you have no one else to consider."

"That's why I stay alone. As soon as I allow someone else into my life, I put them in danger, and I won't do that. It's bad enough my brother and his family are dead. I can protect myself, but I'm not very good at protecting others. If I'd been there…"

"I think you're wrong, Jason."

He shrugged. "That's your opinion. Tell me, who would you rather have with you? A bounty hunter? Or the agent?"

"Aren't they all the same?"

"Not necessarily. There are multiple sides to everyone."

"Then in that case, I choose Jason Cole."

He looked surprised. "Why?"

"Because Jason will live longer than the hunter or the agent, and I'd like to have him around for a very long time."

"I wish I could be Jason Cole, but I'm not even sure who he is any more. It's been too long."

"I think he's closer than you know, and I think his family would be proud of him."

Jason snorted. "Now that's where you're wrong."

"You're the one who's mistaken, Jason. If you'd been there, you'd be dead too. Don't let what happened cloud your thinking. I know those emotions. If you dwell on them, they'll destroy you."

Jason raised one eyebrow. "What about you? Are you listening to your own words?"

Ali sighed. "I'm not perfect. There are things in my

past that affect me. The bruise on your cheek is stark evidence, but I've learned to go beyond it—most of the time."

Uncomfortable with the conversation, she rose from the bed and called up the catering menu. "By the way, in case you didn't get my signal, none of those thugs in the alley were from the group of pirates who hit my ship."

"It doesn't mean they couldn't be part of the gang."

"True, but I don't think they are. The pirates are too professional, too sure of themselves, and too well trained. These guys were inept, and they weren't out to kill those tourists. Plus, if what Marty said about the microchip is true, they'd be dead by now, and I think we'd have heard."

Jason nodded. "Good thinking. I'm going to see Marty. I'll be back shortly. Don't open this door to anyone."

She tossed him a neat salute. "Aye, aye, Captain."

Chapter Fourteen

A few minutes later, Jason strolled into Marty's domain. "What have you found out?"

"Hello to you too." Marty used his foot to shove a chair Jason's way. "Not much more than we knew earlier. The tracking device was crystal based. It's been ground up and mixed with the platinum in the setting. Quite ingenious. As for our uninvited guests, we do know the chip is encoded with a timer and a micro-receiver. Best guess is, check in regularly with the boss or checkout. That's one way to keep them from talking. Oh, and the device seems to be susceptible to a crystal pulse. Joey's trying to cobble something together for you. A direct hit anywhere on the body should deactivate the receiver."

"Should?"

"What can I say? We don't exactly have someone to try one on." Marty shrugged. "I understand you had some excitement in town."

Jason didn't even bother to wonder how Marty knew already. He assumed the man had contacts everywhere. "Nothing we couldn't handle. Just some local thugs trying to roll the tourists."

"I know. They're third timers. Rehab didn't work so it's reconditioning time for them. You might be interested to know those types of incidents are increasing in that area. Petty thugs who've never done

174

much are stepping up to the big leagues, and there are a lot of non-locals moving in. When they're caught, they don't know more than what they've been conditioned to."

"Sounds like someone is trying to empty out the nice people from that end of town."

"So, what are you going to do?"

Jason grinned. "Go back, of course. Nobody ever accused me of being nice. Oh, can you take care of Me-too if Ali and I get tied up?"

"I hoped you'd ask. I'd be happy to."

Something in his tone warned Jason. "Marty, just take care of her. No funny business."

Marty held his hands out in a show of innocence. "*Moi*? Never. Though… if you wanted to breed her, I could give you good odds."

"Marty!"

"Okay, okay. Just saying. Cats are worth a lot of money. But I'll see she's well taken care of. I promise."

"Fine." Jason rose. "Now, if you'll excuse me, dinner calls."

"Your lady made some good selections. I had the kitchens beef up the selections for you. None of this bourgeois swill for our best."

"Thanks, Marty."

By the time he returned to the room, the catering unit had delivered their meals. He sniffed appreciatively at the dishes covering the tiny table. "Mmmm. That smells good."

"What did you find out?" Ali picked up her plate and sat cross-legged on the bed.

"You were right about the thugs," Jason said as he took the chair. "They were locals who have records of similar attacks on tourists. The northern section of the city has had a marked increase in minor problems like this. The town cops can't keep up with them. For every group they catch, three more get away, and not all of them are residents. Someone's importing them from outside. Unfortunately, nobody can get any information from them. They've been reconditioned."

"Reconditioned?"

Jason heard the astonishment in her voice. Reconditioning, although not unusual, cost a lot of money, and the person or persons in charge were doing it with a lot of people. "Not getting bored, are you?"

"Not a chance. But that means someone with a lot of power or money or both is heading this. So no help there. I guess we keep looking. 'Fraid you're stuck with me."

"Sweetness, I'd stick with you anywhere," Jason teased.

Ali's smile faded. "Jason, please don't say that."

Jason looked at her and nodded. "Somewhere, someone hurt you, and I'm sorry nobody protected you. When you're ready to talk, I'll be ready to listen."

He saw the tears glistening in her eyes. Thanks to her files, he knew almost everything, but she couldn't know that. He had to let her come to him. He hoped it didn't take too long. She needed to get rid of the monkey on her back before the problem became so deeply embedded the damage couldn't be fixed.

She nodded. "This is something I have to deal with when we've finished with the pirates. Rest assured, it has nothing to do with them." She set her plate aside. "If you'll excuse me, I need a shower."

Jason watched her go. He programmed the catering

unit for a stiff drink. When it arrived, he downed the fiery liquid in one gulp and ordered another. It was going to be a long night.

****

When Ali emerged from the bathing room some time later, she found Jason softly snoring in the chair, an empty glass on the table. One whiff told her all she needed to know. Between the sleepless nights over the past week and the stress, he'd earned some indulgence.

Ali figured she bothered Jason as much as he did her, a new experience for both of them. Although she'd had plenty of offers over the years, she'd never given herself to any man. She'd never wanted to, until now. As she sat in the middle of the big bed petting the cat, she studied Jason. His face, relaxed in sleep, gave him an almost boyish look. He might profess to being a loner, but she'd bet her entire fortune he was also lonely. He didn't have an easy life. Somehow, she had to show him he could trust her and they could be friends. She covered him with a light blanket and lay down to sleep.

****

"Jason? Ali? Are you two decent yet?" Marty's voice interrupted their breakfast the next morning.

Ali flicked on the monitor, and Marty's sober face appeared. "What's up?"

"The pirates hit again last night."

"Where?" Jason asked.

Marty hesitated and then answered, pain lacing his voice. "End of the Universe camp. All ten families are gone. There's a general exodus from the belt to all points elsewhere. Universe was one of the more heavily armed camps."

The glass Jason had been holding shattered in his hand, and he looked surprised as blood welled from several small cuts. Ali retrieved the medical supplies and knelt on the floor in front of him so she could tend to his hand while he talked to Marty.

"Did you get any downloads?"

"Sami managed to get a partial, but nothing useful. No one and nothing saw them coming."

Ali looked at Jason as the news sank in. "They did it," she whispered.

"We were going out to the grove this morning then hitting the bars tonight. In light of this news, though, I think we'll take a quick trip around the belt to see what we can find. We'll be back in a day or two."

"Agreed. I'll send some data to Sami for you to look at. Be careful, you two."

Jason sat back in the chair and studied his hand. "They've built undetectable ships. What the hell do we do now?"

Ali shrugged. "We keep doing what we've been doing. This is a new glitch but doesn't change anything. Jones Base has added extra security and cut down production. Most of the outer miners are grouping together or moving inward. All we can do is keep looking."

"Then I guess we'd better get going."

Ali nodded and cleaned up the breakfast mess. She'd give him the time he needed to come to terms with the new deaths. From his reaction, she figured he'd known the people. She'd heard of End of the Universe camp. She and Sean had been scheduled to meet with them in a week. That wouldn't happen now...for several reasons, none of them good.

When they walked out to the ground car, the heat hit Ali with an almost physical force. In the short minute it took them to get to the vehicle, perspiration broke out, wetting her thin clothes. "Is it always so hot in the city?"

Jason nodded and opened the doors. "Yes. Unfortunately." They climbed into the air sled, and he set the environmental controls. By the time they took off, the interior felt considerably cooler.

"This isn't unusual for this time of year. Believe me, when the rains come, you'll wish for some of this heat. The storms we've been having each evening signal the beginning, and they're nothing. It can get nasty here during the wet season. I told you there's a wet season and a dry one. Well, the dry one is hot. Brutally, unremittingly, miserably hot. The wet one isn't. There's no in-between. Haven't you ever been here before?"

"No. The only times we came on planet, we stayed at Delphi or Jones Base. We never needed to go anywhere else." Ali watched the terrain pass by. When they'd first arrived on planet, the area had been mostly dry, barren expanse. Now she saw patches of green and even a few flowers.

"Then you've missed a lot. Being on the coast, Delphi has a moderate climate that stays pretty much the same year-round. This far inland, the weather tends to be fiercely disparate. It can be dangerous, but also exciting."

"It figures you'd love this," she teased. "Why don't they enclose the city under a dome? Then they could control the heat and rain."

"That's why. Most of the people who live here are

independent in the extreme. They don't want to be controlled and don't want their surroundings controlled either. Several years ago, the town council tried to get a dome approved, but the residents raised such an outcry, it's never been proposed since then. Plus, the proponents were all voted out of office during the next election."

A short time later they arrived at the same grove they'd left the day before. When Ali hopped out, instead of the oppressive heat she'd expected, the breeze felt cool and refreshing.

"Why isn't the temp as hot here?" she asked.

"The ridge behind us shades the worst of the sun, and the trees and waterfalls do the rest. The grove is usually about ten degrees cooler here than in the city, but don't let the coolness fool you. You can still get a nasty burn out here. The thin air doesn't offer much protection."

Ali wrinkled her nose. "If I got burnt, wouldn't you take pity on me and take care of me?"

Jason laughed, mischief crinkling the corner of his eyes. "Miss Matthews, if you don't know by now that these hands are itching to take care of your body, then you're blinder than an asteroid rat."

"Then I guess I'd better be careful." She smiled. She made a show of smoothing on a layer of cream to soothe her skin. She could tell from his sudden intake of breath her motions were having an effect on him and decided to tease him a little. "I can't have both you and Marty after me. Which should I choose? So many decisions."

"Me? In competition with Marty? I'm hurt."

"More like your ego is hurt. Might do you some

good to come down off that ivory tower of yours. At least I know you're a man of your word, even if your ego does get in the way."

"I'm shocked. How could you think such a thing of me?" Jason held his hands up to his chest in mock humility.

Ali raked her gaze over him. "Very easily. Don't you ever think of settling down, Jason?"

"I've never been tied to one place, Ali. At this point, I don't know if I could settle down."

"Then don't," she countered. "Build a place here to use as your home base, and then hire someone to manage it for you. That way, you can come and go as you please, but you'll always have a home—someplace to come back to. And I don't know how much land your brother staked, but you should make sure it includes a good portion of this mountain, especially the mining and mineral rights. With all that crystal we found, you'd never have to work again."

Jason looked out over the desert spreading to the horizon. "I've worked in space and on so many different planets, I've lost count, but any time I think of home, I think of this place. Your idea might be something to consider."

"Of course, it is." She grinned at him.

"Oh, so because the idea came from you, it's automatically brilliant?"

"But of course."

Jason had to laugh. "Yeah. How about some exercises and then a swim before we get to work on the data? I don't know about you, but I'm in need of some physical activity."

"That sounds fine. What do we have to do to get to

Sami?"

"Nothing. He's here. The lake is deeper than it looks. The ship can't be seen from above and is accessible only through the airlocks. We'll work out then join him for lunch."

"That's wonderful. I thought we'd have to go back to Delphi or something."

"You're not the only one with brilliant ideas."

"Touché. So, what do you want to do?"

Jason raised his eyebrow at her and then laughed when she blushed. "I'll go down to the bathing pool. When I'm ready, you try to sneak up on me. I'll let you know as soon as I hear you. The exercise will be harder in daylight because I'll see you coming."

"Sounds like fun."

"Fun has nothing to do with this. These rehearsals might save our necks. Give me five minutes." He strolled to the pool, whistling a light tune. Once there, he removed his boots, belt and shirt. "Anytime you're ready," he called.

Ali suddenly appeared next to him. "Was that quiet enough for you?" she teased.

Jason shook his finger at her. "You cheated. I wasn't ready."

"Hopefully the pirates won't be ready either."

"Right. Ready to try again?"

Ali grinned. "See you later." She returned to the sled and got out her bag. She'd give Jason a few minutes to enjoy himself and then surprise him again. She changed into her regular boots, loading them with the weapons she normally carried. A noise behind her startled her. She grabbed her knife and whirled to see what had caused the sound.

Jason stood up from his vantage point at the edge of the clearing. "You're fast, but not fast enough. I could have killed you."

Ali nodded. "You're right. I thought only of getting to you, not you getting to me. You caught me this time, but it won't happen again."

She replaced the knife in her boot. When she rose, Jason stood next to her. She held her breath but didn't move as he reached out to touch her hair. She sensed his desire and his hesitation. His touch was so gentle, so unlike the man who had attacked her. She could give herself to this man—someone who could chase the ghosts away, but still, she hesitated. No matter how much she cared for him—and she had to admit she did—the fear remained.

"Ali? I'm not those other men, but if you don't want this, all you have to do is say so."

Ali barely registered his whispered words, but she heard the sentiment. He knew she had issues from her nightmares, but...how had he known there'd been more than one man? Then she realized. Marty. He'd probably given Jason a file on her. But...

"How much do you know?"

"Not a lot. Just about the kidnapping and your stint in rehab."

"I don't remember a lot of it."

"This is up to you, Ali. I won't deny I want you, but the choice is yours."

She could refuse. But did she want to? She looked at the man she'd come to care for deeply, and more than that, trusted. She took a deep breath and let go of her old fears. Her parents and Sean were gone, but she was still alive. She needed to start living her life in the present instead of some fuzzy past. She sank to the soft moss blanketing the area and tugged Jason down with her.

Jason's arms encircled her as his lips found her mouth, searing her with a kiss that demanded an answer. His breathing hitched as his mouth trailed from hers to her jaw and down her neckline. As her hands kneaded the muscles of his back, their mouths met again, swiftly, and hungrily.

Jason broke away from her with a shudder. "I'm a man without a home, Ali. I can't promise you a future when I don't know if I have one. We have right now. That's all I can offer."

She put a finger against his lips. "Shhh. Here and now are enough, Jason. I want you. No promises from either of us. Just two people sharing what they can when they can."

"Stars, woman, where did you come from?" he whispered as his mouth once again found hers. Eager hands found and discarded clothing.

A maelstrom of emotions spinning out of control caught Ali. Her senses came alive with his touch, taste, and smell. A burning desire built from her center, spiraling upward until she thought she'd burst with need. As if with a will of their own, her hands stroked the muscles of his back, reveling in the strength there. She climbed until she exploded in a haze of passion.

Ali didn't know if she was dead or alive.

Alive, she thought. Wonderfully, totally, completely alive.

Jason rolled over onto his back, carrying her with him. Her heart slowed down as her breathing returned to normal. Never in her entire life had she felt like this.

She drifted off to sleep, the sound of Jason's heart beating in her ear.

\*\*\*\*

Jason listened as Ali's breathing slowed, telling him she was asleep. Gently, he shifted her to a more comfortable position and covered them both with a light blanket. He was not inexperienced with women, but what had happened between them was like nothing he'd ever known. She had given herself to him completely, responding to his every move with an instinct that defied her past. Just thinking about their activities made him want her all over again. He had thought that, like the other women he'd been with, having her would ease her from his mind. Instead she was entwined even more deeply. How could he take her into danger where she might be hurt or worse? If they were going to survive this mission, he had to forget this had ever happened. An impossibility if he ever heard one because like it or not, he was in love with her.

He wrapped his arms protectively around her. "Stars know how this is going to turn out, Ali, but for now, I'm all yours."

\*\*\*\*

Ali awoke and stared into eyes the color of sapphires. She smiled as Jason kneaded her back muscles, working his way from her neck down. She wrapped her arms around him, nibbling at his shoulders as his hands continued to work their magic. Her ragged breathing matched his. They made love slowly, but the experience was even more satisfying than the last time.

Much later, Jason playfully slapped Ali on her bare rump. "We're never going to get anything done this way. Time to get to work." He dressed and headed for the pools as Ali complained about demanding men.

Their lovemaking showed Ali Jason had a gentle, loving side. He needed to be reminded it existed. However, the timing could have been better. If his affection toward her changed, he'd be more determined than ever to leave her behind, and she refused to let that happen. She joined him in the pool, relishing the cool water.

A short time later, refreshed from their swim, they enjoyed a light lunch in the ship's galley. Entering the ship hidden underwater had been relatively easy. They packed their gear into waterproof bags, dived into the lake, and swam to the airlock. Sami pumped the water out, and they entered the ship. Since they couldn't move the sled in, they camouflaged it as thoroughly as possible in the grove of trees. Only someone doing a very determined search would find the vehicle.

Sami had turned on the monitors so they could see the surrounding terrain. Ali could understand why the locals loved this harsh land. The stark barrenness had its own kind of beauty. Tall monoliths of native rock towered over bare sand that shifted and changed with the wind. The boundary between dry desert lowland and green foothills looked as if some giant hand had drawn a border with the desert on one side and the hills on the other. No matter where she looked, she had a sense of vastness that would never be tamed. This was a wild land that called to the souls of those who dared settle there. Though they'd been here for several days, she hadn't really looked at the area before. Not like this. It pulled to her, as if she'd become a part of the land.

"Sami, have you had a chance to analyze the data Marty sent?" Jason asked.

"Yes."

Suddenly, a loud sonic boom reverberated through the ship. "Sami, location of that sonic." Jason scrambled from the galley to the bridge. Ali threw their leftovers into storage and joined him. She belted into her seat and snapped on her display.

"North of the city. Cause unknown, but appears to be outgoing," Sami said.

"Power up and get moving. I want to be on their tails ASAP."

"Jason." Marty's voice piped over the system. "I had a blip on my monitors."

"We're on it, Marty. I'll get back to you. Go, Sami. Don't be nice," Jason instructed.

The gravitation pressure forced Ali against the back of her seat as the small ship took off in an almost straight up pattern. The seat cocooned around her, buffering her against the worst of the G's. As they left the atmosphere, the pressure eased, and she could breathe easier. "Sami, are you tracking them?"

"There's nothing to track. However, I've extrapolated a possible heading from the atmospheric trail they left."

"Where's the trail heading?" Jason asked.

"Antares Station. You want me to follow?"

Jason turned to Ali, a thoughtful look on his face. "No. Set course for End of the Universe camp. I want to see what's left. Can you extrapolate where they originated?"

"On the screen now."

The monitor lit up with a view of the desert north of town. "X marks the spot, but there's nothing there."

Ali and Jason scanned the surface, looking for

anything that might mean a base, but there was nothing to see.

"What about caverns?" Ali asked. "Is there anything underground?"

"Nothing shows on my scans. Sorry, Ali," Sami said.

"Ali, why don't you get settled in while I talk to Marty? I'll give you a yell when we're clear," Jason said.

"Aye, aye, Captain." Ali tossed him a mock salute and walked back to her cabin. She had enough training to know Jason wanted to discuss some things with Marty she didn't have clearance to hear. While curious, she wouldn't jeopardize his trust by eavesdropping. She stowed her things in the small cabin. Like the rest of the ship, this area appeared neat and practical, but somewhat plain, as if rarely used. Here there were none of the murals that decorated the other sections. "Sami?"

"Yes, Ali?"

"Can I see a schematic of the ship and whatever systems I'm allowed access to?" She figured she might as well put the time to good use and get to know the ship.

"Boss says you can see what you want within reason. Yell if you have any questions."

"Thanks, Sami." The physical schematics appeared on the wall monitor next to her bunk. She spent the next hour studying everything she could about the ship. A few times she ran up against blocks and assumed those were systems Jason wanted kept secure. At one point, she saw details she thought would come in handy in the future—override codes—a glaring error she could use. Smiling, she memorized them. She blanked the screen as Jason knocked on the open door.

"Ready for your tour?"

"Let's see what I can do," she countered as she led the way. She turned right and ducked through the hatch. "Storage hold—seven thousand two hundred cubic meters. Can also be used as a small landing bay. Controls are on the port side, two meters from the main hatchway." She glanced at Jason's astounded face and laughed as she ducked back through the hatch. "Next are two cabins, one on each side of the central passage. In front of that, starboard side is the galley—fully stocked. Port side is the access to the engine room below the ship and one of the smallest—but well stocked—sick bays I've ever seen. She runs on white Ki crystals and is deceptively powerful. Final section is the bridge."

Jason shook his head as they entered the bridge. "You learned all that in an hour? I know your skills as a pilot, but how are you as a navigator?"

"Horrible—both planet-side and out here in space."

"What? Something you're not perfect at? I'm shocked." He offered her the second seat as he took the pilot's place.

Ali laughed. "Sean used to tease me I could get lost on my own ship without a map." Her laughter died as she thought about her brother. Jason offered her a hand, but she shook him off. "I'm good."

"Yeah. Okay, let me show you some of the things you couldn't get from the schematics." He showed her some of the systems and took her through some simulated situations to familiarize Ali with the ship.

A short time later, they landed at End of the Universe camp. The miners had been surprised at a meal, their weapons unused, and the useful portions of the asteroid stripped by the pirates' more advanced technology. Jason and Ali made their silent way through the destroyed camp. Tears ran down Ali's cheeks as she studied a picture of a young woman with short blonde hair and the pale skin of someone who spent most of her time in space. It matched one of the bodies they'd gathered. Another life cut short. Ali and Jason finished their grim task, piling the bodies near the airlocks for a recovery team to take care of, and re-boarded the ship in silence.

They checked on several nearby sites, but the results were the same everywhere. The pirates had cleaned them all out, leaving no survivors behind. Ali mapped the camps on a chart, adding them to the data they already had. As the day went on, Ali grew steadily more depressed. Finally, Jason called a halt for the day and ordered Sami to hold course for their next destination.

Ali leaned her head on her arms on the table. She wanted nothing more than to cry but refused to give in to her emotions. She knew if she let go, she wouldn't be able to stop. Her awareness of Jason a short distance away didn't help Ali's emotional turmoil. Right now, she wanted his hands on her body, anything to replace the death surrounding her, yet she didn't know where she fit in his world. Nothing made sense anymore.

## Chapter Fifteen

"Ali?" Jason laid his hand on her shoulder, and she looked up at him. The hunter drew her up into his embrace, crushing her lips with his. He picked her up and carried her into his cabin. "I've never met anyone like you, Aleksia Matthews. You take away all my control."

"Of course." She tugged her top off, deliberately provocative. She needed to forget, and losing herself in his embrace, even if only for a short time, sounded better than any other alternatives. Her clothes—one slow piece at a time—joined his on the floor. "After all, you're costing me plenty, so you'd better earn your keep."

Jason ran his hand down her side, making her shiver with delight. "And how much is this worth?"

"Ummmm, about fifty credits."

"Only fifty? Then how about this?" His mouth closed over one breast, teasing the sensitive peak as his hand kneaded the other.

Ali moaned with pleasure as waves of heat spread from the center of her being outward. "About a hundred."

"And this?" His hand moved lower. He stroked her, and she arched against his hand.

"Everything I own," she whispered. Ali's fingers dug into his shoulders as her body arched and pulsed, heat filling her. Her orgasm, when it came, left her weak and panting.

"I don't know about you, but I'm ravenous," Ali said when she could speak again.

"Your wish is my command." Jason rose from the bed. "Would you like anything in particular?"

Ali breathed out a satisfied sigh. "I think I just had it."

She admired the way his muscles moved as he wrapped a towel around his waist. He really was the most incredible man she had ever met. She wrapped the bed-sheet toga style around her body and followed him into the galley.

He laid out a light meal, and they ate in companionable silence until the first pangs of hunger were appeased.

"So did I earn my keep?" Jason asked as he wiped a drip of fruit juice from Ali's lips.

Ali caught his hand and held his fingers against her lips, licking at the tips. "I'd say you more than adequately earned your keep. But remember, I'm a very demanding boss, and I demand you earn your keep thoroughly and often."

He drew the sheet away and lifted her onto his lap. "Is this often enough for you?"

****

After a late start the next day, they scouted several other asteroid sites but found nothing of any value. All had been abandoned, but very few looked like the pirates had hit them.

"We'll be stopping at AS-257 for a break," Jason relayed late in the day.

"Joey's Place?"

"You've been there?"

"No. I know the place by reputation. My parents stayed there at various times, but I stayed on the ship with Sean. I've heard some strange stories about Joey's, most of which I can't believe."

Jason laughed. "Oh, you can believe them. Joey runs two establishments on opposite sides of the 'roid, connected by a security and administration tunnel where they handle the running of both. One side is clean and neat and caters to families. The other caters to those with different tastes."

"And which side will we be staying in?"

"You, my lusty wench, will be staying on the ship while I scout out the lower forms."

"That's not fair. We're supposed to be partners. I need to be with you."

Jason shook his head. "Not a chance. One look at your gorgeous body and the pimps will be fighting over first rights. You'd set off a bloodbath."

"What good will keeping me locked up do? How am I supposed to identify anyone if I can't see them?"

"Through Sami. You can see any of the public areas on the monitor."

Ali did some quick thinking. She could tell from his narrowed gaze he expected her to raise a fuss, but actually she'd been hoping for this break. Being alone would give her a chance to view the data wafer without Jason knowing. But would Sami? She had to know that first.

"I assume Joey belongs to your network." She paused, but he remained tight-lipped. "Okay, no more questions. That works for me." She yawned widely. "I'm a little tired anyway. Maybe I'll take a shower and a nap." She looked up at one of Sami's monitors. "Um, Jason, not to be nosy or anything, but does Sami watch my quarters? Um, he didn't see us…"

"No. He doesn't monitor the cabins unless one of us tells him to. You can shower and sleep in peace."

Ali gave him a quick peck on the cheek. "Thank you. Good luck, partner. And watch your six." She strolled back to her cabin, feeling Jason's stare.

****

"She's planning something, Sami."

"I agree with you, Boss. Her heart rate and respiration both increased when she questioned you about me. What do you want me to do?"

"Under no circumstances is she to leave this ship. Park at the high security slip and engage a double lockdown. That'll keep her here and keep out any curiosity seekers. Let me know if there are any problems."

"Done. Docking now."

****

Jason entered the corridor leading to the alternate hotel. Lurid murals decorated the short hall. About halfway through, he checked to make certain he was alone and placed his right hand against one of the pictures—directly on top of a woman's breast. A few seconds later, the wall softened, and he made his way through to a small cubicle.

"Please remain still for ID verification," a disembodied voice instructed him. Again, he waited until he heard a click, and the inner door swung silently open.

"Hi, Joey." Jason grabbed a tiny, gray-haired woman in a crushing bear hug. Josephine, aka Joey, was one of the Fleet agents' greatest assets. He'd trust his life with her—and had on more than one occasion.

"Jason, you naughty boy, put me down," she scolded as she patted her short hair back into place. "I thought I recognized your slug, but the family side? Since when?"

"Since I'm not alone." He shook his head at her questioning look. "I'm here on business. I'm tracking down pirates and have the only eyewitness to one of the raids with me. She's on the ship. You have anyone due at the security lock?"

"Ah, the mysterious Aleksia Matthews. Marty clued me in. Fortunately for you, nobody's due in right now so you can have the slip. I'll let Sami scan in. Now, I assume you didn't come here to see an old woman, so what can I do for you?"

"Oh, Joey, you know I love you. However, I do have a reason. The pirates are stepping up their raids. They're getting bolder and hitting larger stations. Sami has some data for you to look at. With the information Ali had, he's mapped the pirate hits out by place, time, and material taken. Can you compare the results to whatever files you have? Pipe the final to Sami. Have you gotten anything more on the weapon or implant?"

"No more than what Marty gave you. The weapon is a unique design. We think we can duplicate one, but haven't gotten very far yet. As for the implant, that one's giving us even more trouble. We removed them from the bodies. Two of the three self-destructed before we could figure out anything. We're being extra careful with the third. You'll know as soon as I do. Now, what's this I hear about you giving Marty a cat?"

"You mean Me-too? He's just taking care of her until this mess is over. Why?"

"Something came up so she's with me. Mind if I keep her a while?"

Jason knew that sly look on Joey's face. She may be old, but she could still out-deal and out-bluff almost anyone he knew. "She comes back to me when this is over."

"Agreed. Mind if I breed her?"

Jason hid a grin. Now he knew what she had in mind. Cats were rare but welcome commodities in space. Joey would reap a small fortune for true-bred kittens, and he knew Me-too would be safe with Joey. "Only if you split part of the proceeds with me."

"Eighty-twenty."

"Hah. She's my cat. Thirty-seventy."

"Yeah, but I have to do all the work. Sixty-forty."

Jason played a hunch he didn't really have. "Marty offered me better odds. Fifty-fifty."

"Done." She shook Jason's hand. "That old fart Marty would have bred her to every tom in the quadrant and cut us both out. You let me take care of this, and we'll all come out to the good, including Me-too."

Jason laughed. "Thanks, Joey."

"Oh, before you go, a bit of news. Your witness has been officially been declared dead. Her uncle has already started probate proceedings."

"Damn. Thanks, Joey." He planted a kiss on her mouth and left the room. In addition to being a licensed physician, Joey had one of the best analytical minds he knew. If the raids had a pattern, she'd find one. Between the information they'd been gathering, the geological data from Marty, and Ali's information, maybe they could finally put these pirates out of business. He checked his watch. He had a little bit of time before he needed to meet Ali. He left the family side and headed for the less-savory area.

As he entered the bar, the bartender—who worked undercover for Fleet—greeted him with a nod and a bottle of Jason's favorite ale. "Thanks, Leo." He took a long draught and made small talk as he surveyed the room. The place looked pretty much the way he remembered—dark, noisy, and rough, but a good place to gather information. After about a half hour, he saw the woman he'd been looking for, but she had a customer.

Patrons packed both the bar and the casino in the next room, so he stayed at the bar. He had a good vantage point as he could see everyone who came or left and what they did. Most of the patrons were prospectors drinking and gambling away their profits as their kind had been doing for centuries. A few were off-duty military or security enjoying some R and R. The rest were a mixed group of spacers, traders, and others enjoying the ambiance of Joey's. There were other bars around the belt, but none like hers. When you stopped here, you knew the games were honest, the drinks pure, and the physical pleasures taint-free. For those reasons, the place did a rousing business.

It was also one of the best-run undercover operations in the system. Jason had finished half his ale when he overheard a grubby miner boasting about his Ki crystals strike. He gave a special signal to Leo. The bartender refilled the miner's drink, along with a slap on the back for good luck. Hopefully, the tattletale Leo left there would let security track the man for a while. He also noted which patrons seemed inordinately interested in the miner's luck. Jason finished his drink and nodded at Leo. A few minutes later he left. He'd promised Ali he'd be back at least an hour ago. On the way, he stopped by private catering and ordered a meal to be delivered to the ship. With the secure berth, they could remain docked on the asteroid, but he'd keep Sami on alert anyway.

****

After Jason left the ship, Ali sat on the bed, but not to sleep. She tugged off her top and tossed it aside, leaving her bra on. She used the tip of one fingernail to split open a special seam in the side of the bra and pried out a tiny data wafer. Next, she picked up her travel bag and opened a hidden pocket in the bottom. A minute later she slipped the data wafer into a portable viewer. Tears streamed down her face as she watched the scene unfold. Sean never had a chance. She took a deep breath and exhaled slowly, then watched the wafer again—this time making mental notes of each of the pirates' faces. There would be no mistaking who they were when she found them—and she would find them.

She glanced at her watch, appalled at the time that had passed. She stored the viewer and resealed the wafer into her underwear. A quick sonic shower refreshed her, and she donned a pair of crisp black slacks and a silky black shirt, finishing as Jason announced his return.

"Hey, Ali, I'm back. Did you have a good nap?"

Ali smiled at Jason. Her outfit had the desired effect. She stretched, straining already tight material taut over her breasts. "I got exactly what I needed." She experienced a pang of guilt about the deception, but then reasoned she hadn't lied, just misdirected. She tamped the guilt firmly down.

"If this is what a short nap does for you, I'm going to give you more breaks. You look incredible."

"Thank you, sir. Now, put your tongue back in your mouth and wipe up that drool. It's a good thing nobody else is here. They'd think you lost your wits."

"Only over you."

The arrival of the serving cart interrupted them. "I hope you don't mind," Jason said. "I took the liberty of ordering for both of us."

"Since we appear to have the same taste in food, no problem. Thanks." She lifted the lid off her plate and sniffed appreciatively at the casserole. It appeared to be some kind of seafood in a creamy sauce served with delicate noodles and sweet, tender snow peas. Ali didn't even want to begin to guess the cost. "I can't believe they import snow peas and seafood. Their food overhead must be incredible."

"Actually, lower than you think. Like your friend Vito, the restaurant owns another asteroid a short hop away. They've converted the interior to hydroponic gardens and fish farms. They also grow other proteins for those who are averse to seafood. They even offer tours."

Ali laughed as she speared some peas. "Well, wherever this comes from, the taste is excellent. Could you imagine what a place we'd have if we joined Angelo, Joey, and Marty in one place?"

"The three of them would corner the restaurant business for several systems."

Ali took another bite of the casserole. "I think they already do. We've got to introduce them all sometime."

While they relaxed, Jason ran his fingers up Ali's arm. "You have the most incredible eyes."

"Only my eyes?" Ali teased as his hands sent ripples of pleasure through her.

"Ali Matthews, you have a wicked mind."

"Where you're concerned, Jason Cole."

Their clothes made a trail from the galley to Jason's cabin. She let Jason do what he wanted with her and responded in kind as he drove her to heights she hadn't known existed. Her senses spun out of control as he tantalized every centimeter of her body.

"You are so beautiful, Ali. Your body is so sweet." Ali's slender frame suddenly stiffened. "What is it? What's wrong?" He rolled off and drew her to her side to look at him. "Ali, talk to me. Is it about your kidnapping?"

Ali closed her eyes and took a deep shuddering breath. "What I'm about to tell you, nobody knows. I hope you still think the same about me when you hear what I have to say." Slowly and quietly, she told Jason about the attack. "I'm partly to blame, Jason. I should have been able to do something. If I had, maybe Jeanie would still be alive. The detectives I've hired have given me quite a few leads, but no proof. I think…I mean…" She sighed heavily. "I have my suspicions the first man might have been Dimitri, but no proof."

Jason kissed her. "Don't blame yourself, Ali. Men like that aren't normal."

"I know what you say is true, but Jeanie's still dead."

"Ali, do you remember what you told me earlier?"

Ali frowned. "When?"

"When you told me I couldn't afford to let the past affect me. You've kept this bottled up for so long, the emotions are eating you alive."

"Actually, according to the therapists, I've adjusted amazingly well."

"Yeah? And exactly how many of them went through what you did? You may have adjusted, but it doesn't mean you're over what happened. This had a huge impact on your life and your psyche. Because of this, you changed your entire focus. Instead of being a straight scientist, you went for something that included extreme physical training." He fingered her face. "And you can't tell me the incident doesn't still affect you. The effects are there, in your thoughts, in your dreams. You can't get away."

"What bothers me more is I can't remember."

"You will when you need to. Even with the drugs, the memory is still there, just inaccessible. It means a lot to me you felt safe enough with me to tell me the truth. When we're done with this mission, I'll help you deal with him. We'll take care of him together." He paused. "We might have another problem, though."

"What?"

"Remember the retreat hotel?" Ali nodded, and he continued. "You've been officially listed as dead. That means your uncle inherits everything."

Ali frowned. "What if I send a notice from retreat? Under emergency situations, they allow that."

Jason's visage mimicked hers. "I think I can arrange that. You'd have to word your note very carefully so as not to give away our position. The notice will carry an official ID code. We'll have to figure some things out. I can't have you going broke on me."

Ali laughed. "Oh, so that's all I'm worth to you? A paycheck?"

"Woman, if you don't know better than that by

now, you never will," he retorted. "Of course, you are the one paying the bills for this mission."

"I'll pay your way, Jason. Just be sure you don't get into trouble because of me. Watch your back."

"Right now, it's my front I'm more interested in," he said huskily as he drew her on top of him.

**\*\*\*\***

Ali awoke to an empty bed and ship. "Sami? Where's Jason?"

"I'm not sure, Ali, but he left a message for you. He told me to tell you to stay here, and he would contact you later."

Ali picked up her things and straightened the galley and cabins—assuming Jason was doing whatever he did with the agency. After a shower and a change, she sat down to a tasty, if lonely meal. Finally, with nothing left to do, she paced from one end of the ship to the other.

"Ali?" Sami's voice interrupted her in mid-stride.

"What's up, Sami?"

"I thought maybe you'd like to see the hotel. I can show you the facilities on my main screen."

Ali shrugged. "Anything is better than waiting around." She made her way to the bridge and settled into her seat. Sami soon had her laughing as he gave her a guided tour with a commentary proving he did indeed have a sense of humor. They were passing through the main lobby when something caught her eye.

"Sami, back up. I thought I saw something."

Sami obliged and scanned back over the lobby. "There. Stop." Ali sat up in her chair, her mouth suddenly dry, as she watched a strange man stalking Jason. Ali ran for the lock. "Sami, open the lock. Now."

"I'm sorry, Ali, but Jason gave me strict orders to keep you here."

"Sami, that man is one of the pirates. He's going to kill Jason. Let me out of here." She pounded her fist against the lock.

"Ali, he'll be all right. Relax."

"Relax. You binary dimwit." Ali thought quickly and then smiled. "Computer. Manual override, Lock A-1, Command Alpha Two Three One Nine Zero Heinlein times three."

The lock slid open. Ali heard Sami cursing as she hurried through. That would teach them to leave her alone so much. The command only worked on non-essential systems, but it had succeeded. She quickly made her way through the corridors to the main lobby, remembering the directions from Sami's tour. Fortunately, there were very few people about, so she made good time.

She slowed as she heard two men arguing. The sound came from a corridor on her right. She followed the noise, moving as quietly as possible. When she got there, she stopped out of sight. Carefully, she peeked around the corner. Jason's back was to her. In front of him stood the pirate holding a small laser pistol. They were so intent on each other, neither noticed her. She jerked her head back, not wanting to distract Jason or draw the man's fire.

Her fear-numbed body felt sluggish. Had they seen her? She risked a second peek and watched Jason closely, noting the way he stood, the confident way he moved.

Ali risked another look at the man who'd challenged Jason. Tall and definitely overweight, he looked like he hadn't seen the inside of a shower in weeks. Young in age though—his beard had barely grown beyond the fuzz stage. By the way he swayed on his feet, he was probably drunk or drugged, and she knew the battle could have only one outcome.

"It doesn't have to be like this, Davis," Jason said in a steady voice. "Put the pistol down and we'll talk."

Ali caught her breath as another man stepped into the corridor and joined the young one. She recognized him as well. As quietly as possible, she reached down to her boot and withdrew her knife.

"Come on, Hunter. You can take both of us, can't you? After all, you're an Orion Hunter."

Ali stepped out and threw her knife as the second man fired his laser. Seconds later the fight ended, and the two killers lay dead on the corridor floor. Jason yanked Ali's knife from the first man, wiping the blade on the dead man's shirt. A security officer entered the corridor followed by two med-techs.

"Hunter Cole?" the security officer acknowledged Jason. "We'll review the tape, but the guard on duty has already witnessed you were the accosted party." He looked at Ali. "Ma'am, you'll have to come with me. Even though you were of help, you aren't registered to carry a weapon here."

Jason stepped in. "It's all right. She's with me. If there are any questions, ask Joey."

The man released Ali and nodded. "If there's a warrant on either of these, where do you want the credits posted?"

"Joey has all the particulars." He turned to Ali as the men left, his jaw clenched. "What the hell are you doing here?"

"Are you all right?" Her voice rose barely above a whisper.

"Yes. You didn't answer my question."

"Did you know those two men?"

"I knew the one from wanted vids. The boy babbled something about his father. Security will let me know their identities later." He looked at her, his head cocked to one side. "Why?"

"They were on the ship with Sean. Those are two of the pirates."

"What? Are you sure?"

"I'm sure. You can look at the file yourself." Too late, Ali realized what she'd said.

Chapter Sixteen

"I thought you said you didn't have the data," Jason responded slowly. The stunned look on his face told her everything.

"Do you know how dangerous it is for you here? There could be pirates anywhere. We have to get you back to the ship. Now." He hustled her through the lobby.

Ali trotted to keep up with him. "Don't tell me you didn't suspect. I couldn't tell you I had the wafer, because I didn't want to be left behind—and you know you would have."

"You're right, I would have. But now, it looks like the safest place for you is with me. Sami had better have a damn good reason for letting you out."

Ali gulped. "Um, don't blame him. I used the manual overrides."

Jason spun around and stared at her. "You did what? How the hell did you get those commands? Wait. Don't answer that yet." He grabbed her hand and dragged Ali behind him, ignoring the startled looks of the few patrons lingering around. One look at Jason's face and they hastily got out of the way.

Jason hauled Ali into the ship. "Sami, cycle this lock shut and make sure it stays shut this time. Better yet, take us out to a parking orbit." He rounded on Ali. "You have some explaining to do. First, the codes. How did you get them?"

Ali rubbed her arm, more to stall for time than anything. She hadn't expected Jason to be so furious, but when she looked at the situation from his point of view, she guessed he had the right.

"When I first came on board, you let me look at the schematics."

"Certain ones. The codes aren't in those."

"Not exactly. Some of the schematics include parts of Sami's code—something that shouldn't be there, by the way. Anyway, I found the code buried in a secondary subsystem."

"How many codes do you know?"

"The one for the docking ports." She paused, reluctant to reveal the rest, but knew she had to. "And the air locks and main engine control."

\*\*\*\*

"What?" Against his will Jason started to chuckle. Whatever her faults, he had to admire her. In the year since Sami and his kind had been on line, nobody had ever found those codes. At least nobody who'd ever reported they did. He'd have to pass the information along. He took two cups out of the cabinet and filled them with coffee. "Okay, now about the data wafer."

Ali sighed, but then nodded. She reached under her shirt and retrieved the wafer under Jason's very interested look.

"You've had this on you the whole time?"

"Well, not the entire time."

"You know what I mean." Jason took the wafer and slid it into a data slot. A minute later he watched in horror as the scene unfolded. He drew Ali into his embrace. Not only had she survived the brutality of her kidnapping, but this as well. Most people would have ended up in a rehab center, but not her. He watched the tape in silence. There were no words, no comfort he could give her. Thank the stars he hadn't had to see this happening to Zack. He didn't know if he'd have had the strength to endure what she did.

After the data ended, they sat there in silence. When what seemed like hours later, Ali shifted position to talk. "There's something else, Jason. Something I've been thinking about for a long time. We've been over all the sites, both out here and on the planet. What's the one thing they all have in common?"

Jason frowned, then shrugged. "You tell me."

"With the lone exception of my ship, all the other sites were destroyed. On the planet, they burned everything of value. Out here, the camps were breached and scuttled. Of them all, only my ship remained intact and able to be repaired. I find it strange they'd leave mine alone. My ship is an older model and not worth much on the open market."

"Why leave your ship intact? I've already put the question on our list of things that don't make sense. Unfortunately, the list is getting rather long."

"So what do we do now?"

"We eat some dinner. I'm hungry."

Ali smiled and laid out table settings while Jason heated their dinners.

"When do we go back to the hotel?" Ali asked.

"We? *We* aren't going anywhere. You're staying here while I go back."

"Jason, my going makes perfect sense," Ali argued. "We need to find out if there are any other pirates at the hotel."

"You are not going back in there, and especially not to the lower side. We'll get you a look another way. Let me see what Joey can do."

Ali slammed the rest of the delicious dinner into the recycler. "I need to see the people. I can't do that from here."

"You are not to leave this ship!" Jason roared. "Sami, as soon as I leave, I want you to seal this hatch and absolutely no one but me gets in or out. Especially Ali! Park this thing elsewhere."

"Aye, Boss."

"I love you too, Jason," Ali whispered as Jason stormed off.

****

Jason returned a short time later. "We're all set. Now you can get a look at everyone without them knowing you're here. Sami, bring the station monitor up in the galley. Code J-0113. Show split screen with current time."

Ali looked at Jason. "I probably don't want to know about this, do I?"

"Even if you did, I couldn't tell you yet, but if you join us after this is all over, I'll let you in on a few secrets. Now, since everyone passes through the lobby both coming and going, I got the downloads for the past hundred hours. That'll be enough to start with. The right half is current time, the left is the tape."

Ali sat down to her task. It didn't take her long to call him back. "Jason? I think I found something, but from this angle, I'm not sure."

"Sami, enhance this image, and give us another angle. Oh, and give us full screen. We'll go back to split screen later."

"No problem, Boss." A few seconds later, the image on the monitor changed to give Ali a better look at three men sitting at a table in the lobby.

"See those three sitting there?" Ali said as she pointed at them.

"Yes."

"They're pirates."

"You sound pretty certain."

"I am," she said quietly. "I've seen the wafer more times than you can imagine. I watched two of them beat up Sean. Do you see the ring the redhead's wearing?" Jason nodded, and she continued. "It belonged to our dad. Mom gave it to him on their last anniversary. The design is one-of-a-kind, and the last I saw it, Sean had it on his right hand." A single tear traced its way down her cheek.

"Stay here. I'll be back. Sami, compare the images on Ali's wafer to these. Pipe me when you've confirmed them."

"Jason—"

"Ali, please don't argue with me on this. I can do things officially that you can't. I know how much you want to be there, but let's keep this legal. The best thing you can do is study the rest of those records. You are my best lead and my only witness. I need you here, safe."

"You don't play fair."

"You're just finding that out now?"

While he was gone, Ali studied the rest of the records but didn't see anyone else she recognized. To keep busy, she puttered around the ship, but she couldn't find much to do on the neat little ship. Well into the wee hours of the morning, Jason returned, looking tired and grim.

"They didn't give up anything," he said, rubbing his hands over his face. Dark circles shadowed his eyes, and his shoulders drooped.

"What will happen to them?"

"They've already been taken care of," he said. "Less than thirty minutes after we captured them and confirmed their identities, they went catatonic and died. They all had chips."

She knew his frustration, and he'd been on the case longer than she had. "Are you all right?"

"Yeah, but we need to leave here. Once the news gets out about the three at Marty's and now these, someone's bound to get curious. And too many people saw us together in the corridor."

"Where will we go?"

Jason sighed and ran his hand over his head. "I'm not sure yet. Probably Marty's. Even with the attack there, he's beefed up security so it's safer than anywhere else—except here." He took her hand and dropped something onto her palm. "I think this belongs to you."

She opened her hand and couldn't stop the tears as she looked at her father's ring. "Thank you."

"I knew it had to be his or Sean's because of the initials inside the band."

She blew out a long, shuddering sigh, then shook off past memories. "Jason, I'm glad we caught them. That's eight people we don't have to worry about. They were dangerous men who put no value on human life. They're part of the group who killed both our families along with dozens of others. Even if they were reconditioned, that can only do so much. The tendency to kill had to be inside them. I'd be willing to wager they had warrants out on them from before the raids."

"They did. Quite long ones." He drew her against him and wrapped his arms around her waist.

"If they're being reconditioned and implanted, then someone powerful is controlling the puppet strings. That's not something you do on the fly," Ali said.

"Not to mention the base we still haven't found. The leader has to be someone with money—a lot of money. Somebody important is running this, and he has security in his back pocket. This case is taking far too long to solve."

"Marty's is the closest we've gotten to the base. It has to be there somewhere. Why don't we get some sleep and figure things out in the morning?"

"Sleep isn't what I need right now," Jason said as he ran his hands down her back. "You are."

"I hoped you'd say that." Ali led the way to his cabin. No thoughts of pirates or danger or doubts crept in as the two lovers moved together. The universe shrank down to a narrow bunk in a serviceable cabin on a small ship.

****

"I need to go back to the station," Jason announced at breakfast the next morning.

"What? Why? I thought we were going back to the planet."

"Your uncle is the closest Fleet officer of sufficient rank to handle yesterday's mess. Joey sent him a data flash, and he is requesting my presence to clear up some details." He didn't tell her that Marty, Joey, and he had decided going back to the station would be the best solution to keeping everything legal. Too many

212

people had seen Jason at the hotel with the pirates. They had to keep the operation clean and above board. He also had growing concerns about rumors of Ali being with him getting back to the station. Maybe he should have let her send a message after the bomb at Delphi, but at the time, it hadn't seemed wise.

"When do we leave? Maybe I can get in some shopping on the station while you're busy. Your stores could use some re-stocking."

"Right now, if you're ready. However, you won't be getting off the ship. I want you to stay on board. Sami can put in the orders for restocking, and I'll pick them up."

"The security scans will show my earlier involvement."

"No, they won't. It's not a request, Ali. This is too dangerous." To him, that ended the matter. He could tell from the narrow-eyed frown she gave him, she did not like being left behind, but what she wanted didn't concern him. Only that she be kept safe did.

****

Jason leaned against the wall in Rod's office as he waited for the commander to sign the releases for the five dead men. Dimitri sat on a chair in the corner. It took all Jason's self-control to keep his hands off the slime ball's throat. He studied the man and didn't see much of any worth. The oaf sat there flicking a small knife open and shut. With difficulty, Jason wrenched his attention back to the commander. He seemed nervous, as if something bothered him more than just Jason being there.

"I suppose you believe you're vindicated in taking those men out of circulation," Rod said as he shoved a credit voucher at Jason for his ID. "There's a reward listed for three of them."

Jason put his print on the voucher. "Thanks."

"I heard you were seen at Joey's with a woman with unusual eyes," Dimitri said. The knife flicked open.

Jason did some quick thinking. He'd been afraid someone had seen Ali. "Oh, you must mean Tommi. She has one green eye and one brown one, and the cutest little dimple on her right hip. She's one Magdalene you don't want to miss. Next time you're there, tell her I sent you. Maybe she'll give you a break on her fee. Even if she doesn't, she's worth every credit." Jason sighed as if thinking about the call girl.

Flick. The knife closed. "I understand you met Leksi when you were here the last time. Did you know she's disappeared and is presumed dead?"

Flick. Open.

"I'd heard something like that." Jason pretended to ignore the knife and watched the man's eyes. It was like looking into the face of a snake, something he'd done once or twice—and he preferred the snakes.

Flick.

"Are you interested in earning some credits by helping me find her?"

Flick.

"What's your offer?" Jason caught the surprised look from Rod and the disdain in Dimitri's face. He knew exactly who held the power here, and it wasn't the commander.

Flick. "Five thousand credits."

"That's a healthy reward for someone who might be dead. Trouble is, I have a higher offer from someone else. Besides, the commander here warned me to stay away from her."

Flick.

Rage colored Dimitri's cheeks. "The task would take someone like you to find her and bring her back."

"Thanks for the compliment. However, I'm afraid I'll have to decline. I've already accepted the other job, and I won't go back on my word."

The knife struck hard into the antique desk. "One day someone's going to kill you, Cole, and I hope I'm there to cheer him on."

There it was—the challenge he'd been waiting for. He'd been threatened by men a lot better than this lump of lard. "I don't die easily. Now, if we're done here, I have other places to be." Jason turned his back on the commander and his friend and left the office, aware of the glare boring into his back.

****

Rod called one of his aides into the office. "Follow that man and check out his ship. Don't lose him. I don't trust him." He turned to Dimitri. "You shouldn't have baited him. I'm beginning to think you're losing sight of what's important."

"Not at all, Rod," Dimitri sneered as he stabbed his knife once more into the desk. "In fact, I'm quite sure I know now what is important more than ever. It's a shame your ability to think has come too late to do either of us any good. But remember this—do things my way and we'll have her back for us both to enjoy again." He left the office, his knife still sticking in the desk.

****

Jason sensed the aide following him as he visited

several of the shops on the station, arranging for supplies and goods Sami had ordered to be delivered to the ship. His com-link buzzed. He strolled into a noisy bar and made his way to an empty booth at the back and ordered ale. He smiled when his shadow perched uncomfortably on a stool at the end of the bar nearest the door.

Pretending boredom, Jason leaned his head on his hand in order to hear better. "Sami?" he whispered.

"We've been scanned, Boss, but everything's taken care of."

"Okay." Jason sipped at his drink. So, the commander suspected him of something. The measures he'd put in place were working, and the scan would show the ship to be empty. He lingered over his drink, enjoying the discomfiture of the officer. Tired of the game, he finished his drink and headed for the airlock. The supplies were there as well as a delivery person. Jason smiled as he recognized another one of the commander's aides, conspicuous in the ill-fitting loader's uniform.

"Sorry, Hunter, but I couldn't load them. If you'll give me the code, I'll load 'em for you."

Jason handed the man a two-credit slip—an insulting tip. "That's fine. I'll take them from here. Thanks." He whistled as he stepped into the ship and began unloading the supplies. The man watched a few minutes, trying to peer into the ship, but finally had to leave. Jason finished and cycled the hatch shut. "Sami? We're leaving. Where's Ali?"

"Right here." She stepped out from behind the airlock. "What'd you find out?"

"Later. Right now, we need to get away from here

before the commander comes up with some reason to board me." He made his way to the bridge. "Sami, set course for Zack's. Call me only if there's an emergency. Got that?"

"Yes, Boss. Enjoy yourself."

Ali giggled as Jason muttered about smart aleck AI's. A minute later, he and Ali were lost in their own world.

****

A few hours later they landed at the clearing. "I'm going to run into town to check out some things. You stay here on the ship."

"Aren't we going to camp?"

Jason shook his head. "We're into the wet season. We're better off in the ship. With the weather, Sami will be hard to spot so he can stay in the clearing. I need you to work on the scan Sami took when we left and see if you can spot anything." He removed the camouflage and retrieved the sled from its hiding place.

Ali nodded. "Tell Marty I said hi."

Chapter Seventeen

When Jason returned to the ship, he didn't see Ali anywhere.

"Sami," he called in desperation, "Where is she?"

"Outside. Over the top of the ridge to the northwest. There are three other life signs below her."

His heart hammering, Jason grabbed a set of rain gear and his pack and took off up the trail. The mud made for slow going, but at least the rain had stopped for the moment. Once he got to the top, he got down flat on his stomach and used a scope to find Ali. He almost missed her but caught the slight glint coming off her laser rifle. She lay about fifty meters away, hidden by a large outcropping of rocks and wearing a gray and brown slicker that blended with the surrounding scenery. Jason scanned farther and saw the three men below her. They were working on what looked like a grounded sled. Creeping through the brush, he made his way to Ali.

She glanced at him and motioned for him to get close enough for her to whisper in his ear. "Those are three of the pirates. They landed near the clearing, but they didn't see the ship or me. They were there long enough for me to identify them with Sami's help, then they headed in this direction. They seemed to be having sled trouble, so I followed them."

He shot her a look of exasperation.

"Don't worry. I was careful."

Jason peered around the rock at the three men. One indeed worked on the sled while the other two lounged in the dubious protection of the rocks. An open design, the sled would make for an uncomfortable ride in the wet weather. They weren't out for a joy ride in this. Their work gave him an idea. He dug around in his pack and came up with an empty bag he rubbed in the dirt. He whispered, "I'm going to go down there to see if I can talk to them. I'll pretend I'm lost. Around here, that's a weekly occurrence."

As Ali started to protest, he stopped her. "Keep your gun trained on the one working on the sled. If anything happens, you take him out and I'll handle the other two. Ready?"

She nodded. "Be careful."

Jason kissed her lightly and headed back up the ridge. A short time later, he scrambled down the slope about a hundred meters from Ali's position. He had a bulging sack he'd filled with leaves and other debris to make the pack look heavy. He'd also made judicious use of the wet mud to dirty his clothes and face.

"Hey," he called as he neared the three men. "Can you help me?"

The three men instantly stood and faced toward the slope, staring at Jason.

Jason scrambled down the slope. "Can you point me toward the nearest dry spot? A town? A hut? Anything? I lost my way a while back and can't get my bearings in this damned wet weather. I can pay a little, but not much until I make a bigger strike." Jason made sure to move slowly. "Heard this range would be easy pickings for a miner, but there's barely more than a few rocks and rain." He stopped a few feet from the men, making sure he didn't block Ali's line of sight.

"You picked the wrong place for mining, mister," the middle one said. "Most miners are out in the Belt."

The men continued to face him, their hands on their weapons. "Not too many miners left out there what with all these raids going on." Jason knew the men were studying him as much as he studied them.

"This isn't a good place for miners," the second man agreed. "You'd be better off heading back to New Nova or Delphi."

"Can you at least point me in the right direction?" he asked, keeping up his ruse. "What I did mine is weighing rather heavy. Took me nearly six months to scrabble this much."

The tension ratcheted up a notch as Jason watched the three men look at each other.

"Thought you said you didn't have much money." The second man leveled his gun at Jason.

"I don't."

"But you've got a sack full of crystal. That's worth more than a few credits."

Jason grasped his bag tighter, like a frightened miner might, his fingers on the handle of the pistol hidden inside. "I can pay you after I get my find valued."

"Maybe we'll take what you have now and skip the middle man. I think you'd better hand your bag over to us, and we might let you live." He tugged out a weapon and aimed the barrel at Jason.

"This is all I have. You can't take it," Jason whined.

The next events happened quickly. The talker fired

his weapon. As he did, a large hole appeared in his chest, and he went down. His shot went high, barely missing Jason. Jason scrambled for the rocks, taking out the other two on his way. Once the firing stopped, he climbed out. After checking to make sure they were dead, he motioned for Ali to join him.

When she got to him, he grinned. "Looks like you saved my skin. Thanks, partner."

"You took an awful risk, Jason. What if I'd missed?"

"You? Miss? Not likely." He told her what the men had said, which didn't amount to much. "You check the sled while I check them. But be quick."

Jason came up empty, as did Ali. "We've got to get out of here. Someone will be looking for them, and we've got to be away before they do."

"Shouldn't we hide them?"

He nodded and looked around. "There's a hollow in between those two big rocks over there. We'll put them in there and cover the hole over." With some effort, he picked up the first man and carried him to the rocks.

"What's the hurry?" Ali asked as she dragged another body to the cleft.

"Your uncle had me followed on the station. I wouldn't be surprised if he landed someone here on the planet to tail me." He hauled the third body and dumped it in with the other two then motioned Ali to back away. A well-placed shot from his weapon brought down a shower of stones, neatly covering the dead men. "They probably put a tracer on us, which means they've followed us as far as the planet. Even Sami can't evade everyone."

"Jason, I have an idea about where we can stay," Ali said as they returned to the ship. "What do you think about the cave?"

"That it's cold."

"You mean to tell me the great Hunter Cole is afraid of a little chill?" she teased. "Look at it this way—we can work from there, and Sami can head back to Delphi or somewhere else."

"That's an excellent idea. You'll have to figure out a way to keep me warm." He gathered their things. "Nobody knows the cave is there, and it's safer than having you in town." He turned to her. "Ali, this business is getting nasty. Are you sure you want to go on?"

"More than ever. We've taken out almost a dozen of them. That's eleven fewer madmen left to prey on other families. I said I planned to stay in this to the end, and I will." She picked up her carryall.

"In that case, I want you to promise me something. If anything ever happens and we're separated, you will go to Marty or Joey. They'll protect you."

Ali grimaced. "We'll worry about that if it happens. Now, shall we move into our new quarters?"

With some maneuvering, they moved everything they'd need into the cave behind the waterfall and even managed to keep most of their stuff dry by bundling it into waterproof containers. Jason ordered Sami to move to Delphi.

"What do you say we head to town to do some scouting?" Jason asked when they'd finished.

"Ready when you are."

"No, you're not." He handed her an over-sized miner's hat. "We can cover your hair, but we need something to cover your eyes."

Ali looked at the hat and nodded. "I can go you one better. Give me ten minutes." She urged him toward the entrance to the cave. "Get the sled ready. I'll be right out."

A minute later Ali emerged, dripping, from the water and disappeared behind some shrubs alongside the path as a puzzled Jason waited. A short time later, a slightly overweight, stooped miner's mate emerged. She had a slight limp and the pale skin of someone who'd spent her life in space. Short ebony curls streaked with gray escaped from under her cap, not quite covering the wicked looking scar running from her right eye to her temple. Watery blue eyes peered around the site as if looking for someone.

"Excuse me, sir." The deep-voiced woman attempted to smile up at Jason, but her expression turned into more of a grimace. "Can you give me a ride to town?"

Jason grinned as he looked over a transformed Ali. "Where did you get this disguise? It's perfect."

Ali stood up straight and smiled. "While we were on the station, I had Sami add some things to your supply list. Don't worry—the records were taken care of. Nobody looks at a miner's mate twice, so she can pretty much go where she wants. I've got a couple of other disguises too, but I thought this one would be the best."

Jason walked around Ali, studying the disguise from every angle. "Even knowing it's you, I don't see anything of you beyond the disguise. You wouldn't by any chance have something for me in your bag of tricks, would you?"

"What about the hologram controller you used before?"

"I've always found reality beats technology every time. It is possible to get past the controller. A physical disguise is harder to get past."

Ali tossed a bag at him that he caught easily. "Good thing I came prepared. Change into these, and I'll do your make-up." A short time later, nobody noticed an older mining couple disembarking from their muddy sled in front of Marty's Inn.

They spent the evening moving from bar to bar in the small town, picking up whatever news they could. In each, they took seats at the bar rather than a booth in the back and made careful small talk with the bartender but learned very little. In the wee hours of the morning, Jason stopped their hunt, and they returned to the cave.

In a brief break in the storms, the three moons shone down on the pools, and Ali knew she had never seen a more beautiful spot. She loved it more each time she came here. She shed her clothes, bundled them into a waterproof package, and climbed behind the falls. Jason secured the sled and followed. By the time he got in, Ali had a thermal heater set up and had a light meal warming for them both. She wore a robe and nothing else.

"Woman, you are incredible," Jason said as he joined her. He nuzzled the back of her neck sending shivers through her.

"It's late. Aren't you hungry?" she asked as she turned in his arms.

"Not for that kind of food," he answered as he opened her belt.

"You, my handsome hunter, are a man after my

own heart."

****

Ali wandered around the lovely dining room in Marty's hotel, where Jason had asked her to wait while he went to get the others. She'd expected to be taken back to the same dining alcove as before, but Jason had led her through a different set of doors. The table appeared to be made of some kind of dark wood polished to a high sheen and lit with real candles, something she rarely saw. A snow-white lace runner extended the length of the table. On either side were two place settings in crystal and thin china. In a time when most utensils and platters were endlessly recycled, this room paid tribute to an older, more elegant age. Ali thanked the stars she'd taken extra time to look her best.

The door opened and in walked Jason, resplendent in black slacks and a creamy white silk shirt. He escorted an older, gray-haired woman who had an impish grin and sparkling blue eyes. They were followed closely by Marty.

"Ali, I'd like you to meet Josephine Burns, also known as Joey of Joey's Place." He presented the woman to Ali.

Joey took one look at Ali and turned to Jason. "Stars, man, this is the partner you told me about? You'd better marry this girl before Marty does."

Marty enveloped Ali in a huge bear hug. "Hi, Ali. Welcome back. If this rogue hasn't married you yet, I'd love for you to have my children."

Ali cocked her head at Marty. "It depends on the terms you're offering."

Joey guffawed and slapped Marty on his arm.

"Looks like she's got your number, you old reprobate. Ali, it's good to finally meet you."

They chatted amiably while the serving cart quietly delivered their meals. Ali sniffed appreciatively at the covered platters as Joey served. The meal started with a light delicately seasoned broth and crusty rolls along with a crisp salad. Then came a spicy rice dish. Next followed a grilled white fish with a variety of roasted vegetables. A creamy citrus sorbet perfectly cooled their palates. A variety of wines accompanied each course.

"So, Ali, what do you think of my room?" Marty asked as they finished their dinners.

"I think it's incredibly beautiful. This is even better than the dining room we were in the first time. Some of these pieces must be museum quality."

Marty grinned. "If you can't bring the man to the beauty, you bring the beauty to the man. It's a good thing Ali identified those pirates you got. Have you shown her any records she might be able to recognize others from?" Marty asked Jason.

"No. I never thought of that, but it might be a good idea." He looked at Ali, who frowned at him.

"Okay. Let's get down to work," Marty said as Jason and Joey cleared the table, stacking the dishes on a nearby cart. "Zeus, work mode, please."

Ali jumped as the beautiful wood table changed to a white, laminated worktable. The muted lighting of the candles switched to utility lighting, and the cream and blue walls disappeared only to be replaced with banks of monitors and other electronics. Even the carpeting beneath her feet gave way to smooth tiles in a random pattern of whites and tans. "Holograms? You did this all with holograms?" she asked, amazed at the transformation.

Marty grinned from ear to ear. "Well, a little more than that. What do you think?"

"That you're a genius. I could have sworn the carpet was real. And the table. Everything." Even while she complimented them, Ali's mind reeled. She'd known Marty had gifts, but this went beyond the norm. What had she gotten herself into?

"Stars, don't tell him that. We won't be able to get his big head through a door for a month," Joey laughed. "Marty likes to have his fun, so we let him think he's a big man every now and then. I hope you don't mind."

Ali struggled to take in the change but shook her head good-naturedly. "As long as you don't tell me you're all fakes too."

Marty leaned over and pinched Joey. She yelped and slapped him on the head as he laughed. "Nope. We're real, all right. Now, let's get to work."

"Good evening, Miss Matthews," a deep bass voice spoke from the walls.

"Good evening, Zeus. And please, call me Ali."

"Thank you, Ali. I have a message for you from Posi."

"You've been in contact with my AI?" Ali asked. "How? Last I checked, my ship hadn't been fully repaired yet."

"I have not been in contact with her. Sami has, but he asked me to relay the message to you. Posi says repairs to the ship are moving along well, and she misses you. When you return, you will find her much changed."

"In what way? I like her persona."

"Her persona remains unchanged. Sami did some tweaking to her programs while there. He didn't think you'd mind. She now has more personality and more abilities, like Sami and myself. Is this a problem?"

"Um, no. Thanks. And thank you for the message, Zeus."

"Anytime, Ali."

Ali's mind whirled with everything that had happened in the past few minutes, and she had the strangest sense the surprises weren't over yet. She looked at Jason. What did she really know about him? He had a ship with more power than many ships twice its size, an AI beyond anything she'd ever known, and friends who could manipulate reality to suit their tastes. The entire situation had become too bizarre. What kind of an agency did he work for anyway? Yes, he worked special ops for Fleet, but this went beyond any special ops she had ever heard of.

Jason had been waiting for the questions he knew were coming. Joey, Marty, and he had talked about the situation, and they'd contacted headquarters for him. They all agreed Ali was ready and more than able to join them. And if she did, they'd be better able to ensure her safety. But would she? That was the big question. He glanced at and got a slight nod from Joey, so he knew Ali had been cleared.

"I guess you've got some questions for us." Jason stared at her a little too strongly, as if he expected her to run or something.

Ali smiled. "A few, but I think they'll have to wait."

"To some extent. Remember I asked you about your oath and what you believed?" Jason asked.

"Yes."

"Then consider yourself on active duty and recruited as a member of the Special Ops section of the Secret Service Police. We showed you a small part of our setup in Marty's basement. We have quite an extensive operation in this area and have been building up our forces for the past month."

Ali frowned. "I understand you're members of a special branch, but how can you recruit me so easily? I thought getting accepted entailed a lot more."

"There is. Marty did the first part of the clearance earlier. Joey finished up while we were busy on the station. Acceptance takes three recommendations from command personnel to get clearance. That's been taken care of and approval has been given. As for swearing you in, as an admiral in SSP, I have the privilege. That is, if you agree."

Ali's jaw opened and closed with an audible click. "You're the head?"

Red tinged Jason's face. "Um, not quite. I do have a boss over me."

Marty chuckled. "Ulric is the boss only when you let him be."

"Gee, if I don't join, does that mean you'll have to kill me now?" Ali joked.

"That depends. We were hoping you'd join us."

Ali choked on the sip of coffee she'd taken. When she'd regained her composure, she stared at him—eyes wide in shock. "Me? Why?"

She'd imagined a lot of scenarios for her future, but something like this had never entered her head. This was all happening so fast. SSP? She'd heard rumors in the academy about an elite group of operatives who watched out for money, energy, and other crimes, but nobody had ever been able to confirm the rumors.

"Yes, you," Jason stated. "Because you're good. Because we checked you out so thoroughly, we know more about you than you do. Because we need people like you."

"And if I decide not to join you?"

"We'll part as friends after this mission is over, and this conversation will never have happened," Marty spoke up.

"Meaning I'll never speak of this, or you'll have me reconditioned?"

"That's your choice," Jason said.

Ali chewed her lower lip while she thought. She'd planned on going back to the service after she'd finished with the pirates. This meant she'd be paid for going after them. In addition, it would mean she'd get to spend more time with Jason. She searched her beliefs. There would be no going back. She nodded her head. "I agree. What do I have to do?"

Jason nodded once. "Nothing. When you reaffirmed your loyalty to the oath earlier, you did everything you need for now. Later, after we're done with the pirates, we'll talk about the rest. Now, back to business." He looked at Joey.

"Ali, welcome to the group." She gave Ali a quick hug and then turned to the table. "Jason, you asked me to look for patterns." Joey touched a pad on the table. The tabletop transformed into a series of charts, most of which Ali recognized.

"As Ali pointed out, they're concentrating on crystal miners. The few others that have been hit, I suspect are either for cover, or, in the case of the polymer, for supplies they need. It also looks like you were right in looking at the northern section of the city. Many of the properties in that area have been bought up by a conglomeration with so many blinds, I'm still trying to find the beginning. Oh, by the way, good tag on the miner at my place. Somehow, he won an all-expense paid trip to the Abboo system, and his claim is safe. Wish we could do the same for them all," Joey said.

"Hopefully, we won't have too much longer," Jason agreed as he studied the charts and the data before turning to Marty. "Do you still have the information I asked you for?"

"Right here." The asteroid charts dissolved, replaced by topographical maps of the surface.

Ali studied the maps. Her focus narrowed down to the area north of town.

"Marty, can you enlarge this portion of the chart?" she asked. When he did, she studied the image. The others gave her the time she needed.

"Jason, look at this section here. These cliffs by the river could be riddled with caves."

Jason looked at the charts. "Even if they were, they'd be too small. You couldn't fit a sled in there let alone a fleet. You'd need a pretty large opening for the ships. We didn't see anything like that on our fly-overs."

"How old are these charts?" Ali asked Marty.

"They were drawn up when they first built the town. Nothing's been done since then. Sami did a pass for us but didn't come up with anything new."

Ali looked around the room, an idea forming in her mind. "What if the opening is disguised?"

"It would have to be an awfully good one," Marty pointed out.

"And just a short time ago, this room didn't hold an elegant table and have plush carpeting?"

Joey laughed. "She's got you there. If these guys are bankrolling something on this large of a scale, a hologram wouldn't be too hard to do. Marty, I think we'd better give this girl what she wants. How soon can she get a set of echo charts overlaid with Sami's new topographical ones?"

"I assume you don't want anyone knowing I'm doing this, so give me a couple of days."

"Thank you," Ali said and yawned. "Oh, I'm sorry."

"Jason, I think you'd better get our newest member to bed," Marty said, and then leered at them. "Why don't you stay here tonight? The inn has an empty room. I'm sure you know the one."

Jason glanced at the ceiling but shook his head. "Thanks, but no thanks. I'd rather use our site. We're well hidden and safe and have the added benefit nobody knows we're there. Hell, I didn't even know about the caverns until Ali showed me."

"Marty, Joey, this has been an interesting evening." Ali yawned again, fatigue catching up to her. A few minutes later, she climbed into the sled and strapped into her seat, adjusting it so she could sleep.

Chapter Eighteen

The next day, while Jason tended to some things in town, Ali took the opportunity to explore the cavern farther. To her delight, she found a second entrance and ledges large enough for a camp higher up on the mountain, harder to get to, but out of the water. She spent the time moving their things closer to the second entrance, and by the time Jason returned, Ali had the cots set up and dinner cooking.

"You're going to spoil me," Jason said when he returned. He looked around the new site and nodded his approval. "This is better than having to take a shower every time we want to come and go. And the entrance is still hidden."

They ate their meal on a narrow ledge outside the higher cave, their legs dangling over the edge. The first two moons were visible above the horizon with the third not yet in sight. A cold breeze blew from the woods, bringing the scent of rich earth, and Ali relished the warmth of the heavy jacket she'd thrown on over her jumpsuit. A night bird called from the trees, answered in kind from across the grove. Ali knew peace here in this beautiful place. Danger surrounded them every day, and any minute could be their last, but here, she felt happy and safe.

The next afternoon, Ali and Jason, in disguise, roamed through the northern section of town. In one bar, Ali put her hand on Jason's arm in mute warning. Three men and two women were making a lot of noise in the back corner of the bar, arguing over a card game. A gruff looking bartender frowned at Jason and Ali while he served several rough-looking patrons at the bar. As quickly as they entered, Jason got Ali back outside as a shot exploded the wall next to the door. A chorus of raucous laughter followed them.

"Jason, I recognize three of them. I'm not sure about the other two."

Jason judged the situation. There were too many for him and Ali to take, and there were the other people to consider. "We may have to let them go. It's too dangerous for us to do anything in there." He tapped behind his ear as they left the place. "Sami?"

"Here, Boss."

"I need Zeus to put a watch on a place called *Pete's Bar* on Omega Street."

"Not a problem, Boss." He paused, then came back. "Zeus says to tell you he already has a bug in there. Seems like that's not a nice place to go."

"Thanks. Tell Zeus to record any comings and goings from here for the next few days, and if he has anything from the last couple, pipe them to you." He turned to Ali. "That's the best we can do for now. We'll keep an eye on them and go from there."

"I'm glad you took me up on my offer to join me, Jason. You're the best thing that ever happened to me."

"Right back at you," he said as he gave her a quick kiss.

The next day, a violent storm kept them confined to the caverns. After having grown up mostly living in space, watching the raw power of the storm fascinated

Ali. At one point, she ventured out onto the ledge, quickly getting drenched by the deluge of rain.

Jason yanked her back into the cavern. "Stars, woman, don't you know how dangerous that is?"

He winced as a bright flash lit the entrance followed by a rumble of thunder that shook the mountain.

Ali laughed as she shook the rain out of her hair. "But Jason, this is so exciting."

"And deadly. Didn't you have any planetary training in the fleet?"

"Yes. They stuck me on an ice planet so I can tell you all about surviving in frigid conditions. But I've never seen anything like this."

"You've never seen a storm? Let me give you some details that might save your life." He proceeded to enlighten Ali about the danger of lightning and mudslides and flash floods.

By the time he finished, Ali had a new respect for the gales, but still loved them. She did, however, watch the storm's fury from the safety of the cavern. The wind captured the trees, tossing the branches as if nature wanted to tear them from the sturdy trunks. The torrential downpour limited visibility to a narrow band of blurry landscape. As Ali watched, a flash of lightning struck a tree near the opening, followed instantly by a deafening clap of thunder. Ali yelped and scurried back into the deeper regions of the cave while Jason chuckled.

"I told you it could be nasty. Welcome to the wet season in Nova Territory. This storm will probably last a few hours, then peter out to just rain."

"How long will this last?" Ali asked as she tried to

stop the ringing in her ears.

"Eight months."

"What?" She couldn't have heard him right. "You can't be serious."

"Oh, the downpour will let up to a light drizzle for a couple of hours each day, but for the most part, that's right. Storms like this will rumble through a couple times a week, but usually it's just rain."

"So what do we do until this dies down?"

"I could think of something," Jason suggested.

"You're insatiable," Ali countered as he moved to join her at the cots.

"And you're not?" He stalked her as she backed away, keeping the camping equipment between them.

"If I am, it's because you made me that way," she teased. She feinted right, then ducked left but was brought up short by a sharp tug on her shirt.

Ali stepped backward, obeying the slow tug on her blouse while at the same time undoing the buttons. She backed into him as the last button popped open.

Slowly, Jason turned her around.

She shifted in his embrace, wrapping her arms around his shoulders. The storm outside seemed to reflect the raging passion flowing through her. She trembled as Jason slipped off her slacks, letting them fall in a puddle at her feet. The remaining clothes quickly followed.

Thunder vibrated through the tunnels, as if urging them to match its own fury. The sound seemed to flow around them and through them. The heat of their bodies increased as they reached for fulfillment. Lightning flashed but only served to send them higher in their blissful search. When the crest arrived, they clung together, riding down the fury of the storm.

When Ali could breathe normally again, she grinned and remarked, "Well, what else do we need to do today?"

Jason laughed, his deep chuckles echoing off the rock walls. "How 'bout if we explore some of the tunnels leading off this cave?"

Ali shook her head. "That can be dangerous. I may not know storms, but I do know caves. From what you told me, flash floods happen often with rains like this. Well, that can happen in a cave too. Many good people have been lost because they didn't watch the signs."

She leaned on one elbow and pointed at a couple of the more likely openings. Narrow streams of water flowed from the previously dry tunnels. The streams met to form a small pool in a lower corner of the cave, the site of their previous camp.

"See those streams? They can change from those innocent little streams to a dangerous torrent in minutes, and in a tunnel, you have no place to go. It's one of the first things a spelunker learns. Never take anything for granted."

"What about this site?"

"It's high enough and with enough lower areas to keep us dry. The only way this will get wet is if the entire cave floods, and I don't see that as a possibility with us as high as we are and with other openings below us."

"Okay, so that's out. Let's work on some training exercises. This would be a good place to practice working in the dark."

"Done."

They spent the rest of the day stalking each other in

the total darkness of the cave. Jason held the edge over Ali, but she caught on quickly to his techniques. Late into the day, she managed to catch him off guard.

"I win," she declared as she forced him over onto the hard ground.

Jason chuckled when she straddled him. "You're getting too good at this."

"I want to collect my prize." She ran a finger down his jaw, stopping at the fastening to his shirt.

"And what would that be?"

"Be quiet and find out."

****

The next day, the storms died down, leaving behind a steady light rain and rivers of mud everywhere. Jason climbed out to the sled to contact Marty, but couldn't raise him, nor could Sami. Even Zeus didn't answer their summons.

"Something's wrong," he told Ali. "I want to go see what's happened."

Ali donned her clothes. "Ready when you are."

When they got there, nothing remained to be seen. The entire building had been reduced to smoldering ruins.

"Sami? See if you can raise Joey," Jason ordered as he backed the sled away from the site.

"I've been trying, Boss. All I get is static. Someone's jamming the planet."

"Damn." Jason looked at Ali. "I need to get out to the belt and see if Joey's okay. I'll drop you off at the cave. You have enough supplies for a couple of days. I'll be back by then."

"Uh-uh. Not this time. I'm coming with you, and don't bother arguing."

Jason did try, but the effort didn't do him any good. A short time later Sami picked them up, and they were in the ship speeding for Joey's place.

When they reached the asteroid, Jason turned to Ali. "Ali, listen to me. I want you to stay here, on the ship." He held a finger against her lips. "Please, don't argue. I will be back shortly. Besides, that's an order from your commander." With a quick kiss, he left.

As the lock closed behind him, Ali kicked the door. She understood his need to keep her safe, but that didn't help. She let out a long loud scream.

"Ali?"

Sami's worried voice broke through her frustration. "Relax, Sami. I'm all right." She sighed and leaned against the door. "I'm worried about Marty and Joey, and I just needed to vent."

"You humans do seem to have an unusual penchant for doing so. Is there anything I can do to help?"

"No. Thanks, Sami. What about the jamming? Any luck breaking through?"

"While we are beyond the planetary jamming, I'm still not able to raise either Marty or Joey. I'm sorry."

"Not your fault." Somewhat calmer, Ali decided to make use of the time by getting cleaned up. In the mirror, she got her first good look at herself and shook her head in dismay. Her hair had grown out every which way, and her clothes looked as rumpled and dirty as she felt. Muddy streaks marred her face and hair, looking like some kind of bizarre makeup. She thought about the beautiful hotel in ruins, not to mention the special rooms and underground facilities. She refused to think of the big man as dead.

She stripped out of her dirty things and stepped

into the shower, letting the heat soothe away the stresses of the past few weeks.

Ali was drying off when she heard a pounding coming from the lock.

"Sami? Is that Jason?" She waited several seconds before he answered her.

"No."

"Then who is it?" Puzzled by his hesitation, Ali activated the monitor.

"JC?" A decidedly female voice combined with a very feminine form stood outside the lock. She didn't recognize the woman, but her curiosity got the better of her.

"May I help you?" Ali asked through the monitor.

The woman stared at the exterior monitor, confusion on her face. "I, ah, I'm sorry," she stammered. "I thought I recognized the ship but when JC didn't check in, I came here."

Ali relaxed, but only a little. "I'm with my partner. We're stopping for the night then moving on. We got in a little bit ago."

The woman looked confused. "Then that's a double puzzle. The reason I came by is because I recognized JC's ship. I assumed he would be here."

A sick sensation developed in the pit of Ali's stomach. "Describe this JC to me."

"I can do better." The woman reached into her breast covering and removed a photo cube. She activated the display and called up a holographic picture and held it for the monitor to capture. The image flickered and wavered, but Ali saw Jason, his arms wrapped around the woman as they lay on a bed draped like the one in Marty's hotel.

Ali's heart refused to beat. A red haze descended over her, and she fought to stay civil. "Looks similar. But my partner…um…he…"

The woman laughed. "I'll bet he did. Or didn't. When he gets back, tell JC that Tommi stopped by. Sorry to have bothered you."

"No problem." Ali turned the monitor off and strode down the short corridor, her feet wearing a circular path as she paced. The man in the picture looked very much like Jason, though the poor image made it hard to be certain. It appeared rather recent as well. Maybe too recent. Just what had he been doing while she'd been stuck on the ship?

****

After Jason left the ship, he accessed Joey's central command room and sat down to check her records. As soon as he did, a program activated, and Joey's image appeared on the wall.

"Jason, if you're seeing this, then you already know something has happened to Marty. If one of us hasn't contacted you in twenty-four hours, get your butt out of here and go someplace safe—preferably to Ulric at Orion. Don't stay here and don't trust anyone in Fleet Security around here or at the station. Don't worry about me. One of us will contact you as soon as it's safe. There are two data wafers for you in the locker. Check them out. Good luck, Jason."

Jason retrieved the wafers and scanned them. The first one held the updated scans Ali had asked for. The second one required his security code to open. He scanned the second wafer, his eyes widening with each line he read. He had to follow up on this immediately. He pocketed them, intending to give them to Ali later.

After he left, he went to the bar to see what he could find out. He overheard a few snippets of conversation, but nothing of any value. He heard a loud commotion in one of the private rooms and turned as a familiar figure came staggering out of the doorway.

"Leo," Tommi called to the bartender. "Give me another tray." She turned and saw Jason.

"Hey, JC. It's been a long time. Of course, with a partner like you got, I can see why you haven't been around." She picked up the full tray and sashayed back to the party leaving Jason to wonder about her comment.

He returned to the ship gratified to see Ali had done as he asked. He found her sitting in the galley scanning the hotel brochures.

"Hello, Jason." Space atmosphere felt warmer than her tone. "Did you find out anything?"

A sharp pain went through Jason's gut as he thought about Tommi's comment. "I'll tell you later. We need to get moving. We're not safe here anymore. Did anything happen while I was out?"

"What could happen?" Ali as asked while she secured the galley. "Where to now?"

Jason knew something had happened, and he had the sinking suspicion what. Tommi's comment in the bar came roaring back to him. "The station. I need Sami to check on some things. Are you ready?" He reached out to take her hand, and she shrugged him off. He took his seat in the bridge, and she strode back to her cabin.

"Sami, what the devil happened while I was gone?" He listened in growing dismay as Sami gave him an abbreviated description of the talk Ali had with Tommi. "Take over, Sami. I'll be in the back trying to mend a fence or two."

He walked back to the cabin and found Ali sitting in the middle of her bed staring at the wall. "I think we need to talk."

"About what?"

Jason paused inside the door. "About me. You talked with Tommi?"

Ali picked at the blanket, refusing to look up at Jason. "Would it make a difference?"

"It obviously has." Jason sighed.

Ali nodded, tears sparkling in her golden eyes.

"I'm sure she told you some other things too. Now, let me tell you some things. First of all, I actually am an agent for Fleet Security. I didn't lie to you. And I am a registered bounty hunter. In my line of work, I often take on different personas, one of which is JC Draper, the person in the picture with Tommi. Draper is a real person and we look enough alike I can pass for him, especially with people who don't know him really well. It's a fluke the initials are the same. I'm sorry I didn't tell you everything, but I didn't think you'd ever meet Tommi. JC has a reputation on record as a loner and a rebel. As JC, I'm allowed a certain measure of notoriety Hunter Cole can't get away with. I can go places he can't and find out things people will only say to another criminal."

She took a deep breath and blew it out. "I understand, Jason, but it hit hard."

"I know. And I'm sorry, Ali."

"Are there any outstanding warrants for you in any guise?"

"No. However, that doesn't mean there aren't people looking for me. Once in a while someone shows up hoping to bring in Draper. What they don't know is, I took him in, legally, a long time ago. He went through recon and is living on Ki Three, employed as a hydroponics engineer."

It seemed to Jason that Ali accepted his story and decided to drop the subject, but he could see in her face that doubts remained "So why do we need to go to the station?"

"I need Sami to hook up with the station records and find out who's been purchasing large shares of stock in crystal."

"I take it Joey couldn't help you?"

"Joey's gone."

Ali gasped, and he hurried to explain. "I'm sure she and Marty are safe. They're just laying low. She did leave this for you." He tossed Ali a data wafer. "Maybe you can take a look while we're in transit."

"What are you going to do when you get to the station?"

"Sami's going to search the station records. We know Fleet Security is involved. I want to check out some personnel."

"Jason, I doubt very much if what you're looking for is going to be in any areas Sami can find."

"I resent that," Sami's voice interrupted them.

"Sorry, Sami. I meant no offense. However, these pirates aren't stupid. If they have any records, they're going to be somewhere inaccessible—like on separate data wafers. They're not going to keep them in station files."

"Then I'll look for them."

"Where? Jason, you don't know the station like I do."

"Then teach me. You can't show up there with me."

"I can if I hitched a ride from Delphi. I returned from the retreat early and found out what had happened at the hotel and decided I'd better get home and let people know I'm alive."

"Why didn't you call?"

"I was too upset. I wanted to get home. I saw you at the port and begged a ride."

"How are you going to convince the commander to let you leave with me when it's time?"

Ali cocked her head. "I'll think of something. Jason, you know I'm right. I'll have far easier access than you will, and I know places to look—and how to get into them."

Reluctantly Jason agreed. "Okay. Sami will take care of the electronics. I'll take the commander's quarters and you have the office. Keep him occupied for about an hour. Sami?"

"Yes?"

"I want a trace on her at all times. If there's even a hint of trouble, you call me."

"I'm one ahead of you, Boss. Check out the container in my out box."

Puzzled, Jason went into his cabin, followed by Ali. He accessed a compartment under the monitor, where he found a small white box. Inside rested a pair of topaz and gold earrings similar to the ones Ali's uncle had given her, as well as a green and gold pin in the shape of a star within a circle. He picked up the jewelry and studied the pieces. "They're nice, Sami, but not quite my style."

"Jeeze, do I have to tell you humans everything?

Ali, please put the earrings on and whisper the words *hunter green*." Ali did as instructed and felt a slight tingling in her lobes.

"What are they, Sami?"

"Jason, you have the com-unit, but this is extra since we haven't fitted one on Ali yet. The code word for you is *Topaz*."

Jason pinned the piece to his collar and whispered the word.

"Okay, now I have you both. Ali, I can track the earrings like I do Jason's com-unit. If you want to talk to me, all you have to do is tug on your right ear. You'll hear me as a faint sound in the background. You're also linked to each other. Jason, all you have to do is touch the center of the star. That will give Ali a faint tingling in her ear. Ali, for you to get Jason, touch your left ear."

"Sami, you're a genius," Ali said.

"I thank you, but I can't take full credit. While you were in the shower, a special courier I'm authorized to recognize delivered them. They were Joey's idea."

Jason shook his head and smiled. "Thank you, Joey, wherever you are. Thanks, Sami. Well, I guess we're about ready."

He sobered and studied Ali. "Ali, this is going to be hardest on you. You're going to have to deceive your uncle and make sure he doesn't suspect anything. You may also have to deal with Dimitri. Can you handle it?"

Ali took a deep breath and nodded. "If it will bring this to an end, I'll manage."

Chapter Nineteen

As Ali walked through the corridors of the station, people stared at her. She got the impression she had two heads or some such anomaly. The closer she drew to her uncle's office, the more nervous she became—and angry. Angry that events had forced her to go on the run. Angry she had been forced to make a decision that should never have even come up. Angry members of her own family might somehow be involved in this nightmare.

Her uncle had been a comfort after the death of her parents, and his concern and help had touched her, but that had changed. His concern had turned possessive and confining and frightening, especially when he confused her with her mother. She didn't know what she'd think when she saw him—or Dimitri. Truth be told, she didn't want to see either one of them. Unfortunately, she had no choice in the matter.

She tugged on her ear. "Sami?" she whispered. "You there?"

"Yes, Ali. You're doing fine."

"Thanks, Sami." The sound, more like a low murmur she felt rather than heard, reassured her. She wondered about Jason but didn't want to buzz him. She missed having him by her side and looked forward to rejoining him when they were done.

Ali approached the door to the office. The outer

room was empty, but she heard voices from the inner one. She paused and gathered her courage. *I don't know if I can take it if he touches me*. She peeked around the corner of the door into the inner office. Her uncle had his back to her, talking to someone on the vid. Fortunately, she didn't see Dimitri anywhere. She retreated and took a deep breath to calm her pounding heart.

"I can do this," she whispered. She looked down at her outfit. She'd selected it especially because she knew her uncle liked it. The emerald green, close-fitting tunic split almost to her hip, revealing matching shorts underneath. With a steady hand, she reached up and undid the neckline fastenings, opening it down to the swell of her breasts. She swallowed hard and strolled into the room. "Uncle Rod? I'm back."

Rod Matthews spun around in his chair, almost falling off. He stared at Ali in shock. "Lynn." He jumped up, grabbed her, and swung her around. "Where have you been? I've been crazy with worry about you, and those idiots at Delphi wouldn't tell me if you were on retreat or dead. How did you get here? The shuttle's not due until tomorrow. Why didn't you call?"

Ali forced a laugh. "Put me down and I'll explain everything."

Her resolve threatened to dissolve in the wake of his obvious concern—and his calling her by her mother's name. She disengaged his arms from hers and dragged out a chair with more force than necessary. "First of all, I just found out about the hotel. The rules for retreat are very strict—no outside contact at all. After I found out what happened, I didn't want to get in touch with you in case the pirates were still after me, so

I hitched a ride with the man I met here before I left—Hunter Cole. He had some business here on the station and agreed to bring me along—for a fee."

"I'm not surprised. He seemed the greedy type. He didn't try anything, did he?"

"He didn't have a chance. He showed me to my cabin, and I locked the door and slept the whole way here."

"I've missed you so much, Lynn. I knew you weren't dead." He reached over to kiss her. "You're wearing my earrings. I'm so glad you like them. I had Dimitri pick them up."

Ali fingered the earrings and swallowed the bile rising in her throat. Dimitri had picked them up? Had he been the one who'd put the tracers in? Not her uncle? A part of her felt relief, but a larger part felt extremely worried. Uncle Rod thought she was her mother. He didn't recognize her at all. She studied him. He had a day's worth of beard growing—something he'd never done before—and his eyes were bloodshot. She glanced at his wrist unit. The strap glowed green, but something looked different. It didn't look like a standard issue. There was something off about the strap and face. But now she had a bigger problem. She had to pretend to be her mother. "They are beautiful, Rod."

Her uncle stared at the earrings. "Yes. They look lovely on you." He drew her into his arms and covered her face and neck with kisses. "I want you so much, Lynn. Will you marry me now? My brother can't love you the way I do. We'll be happy together, I promise. Once the new troops from Fleet get here next week, we can leave. We'll be able to go anywhere we want, and nobody will find us."

Ali fought to keep her emotions in control. She'd have to tell Jason about her uncle so Fleet could get a new commander in. Her uncle couldn't continue to run the station, or anything else. He needed help. He seemed to know current happenings, but not who she truly was. She forced down the guilt as she went along with his delusion, using it to her advantage.

"I can't right now, Rod. You see, I've agreed to work with Hunter Cole in finding the pirates." She drew away from him.

"You what? You're not trained for that kind of work, Lynn. It's too dangerous."

Ali smiled. She'd caught the stunned look on his face. She hated this, but necessity demanded the ruse.

"Rod, don't be angry with me. This is something I have to do. Those rooms in the hotel were destroyed because of me. As long as those pirates know I'm alive, I'm putting everyone at risk. It's because of them I can't marry you. We'd never be safe, no matter where we went. They're in control, and I want to change that."

Ali leaned back in her seat and looked around the room to see where something could be hidden. Unlike his quarters, the office was uncluttered and clean. The space seemed smaller than the last time she'd been there. Ready to dismiss her suspicion as ridiculous, she changed her mind when she saw a crack between the floor and wall, like something not put together quite right.

"You'd be safe with me, Lynn. Nobody will hurt you as long as you're with me. I won't let them. I won't let *him*." He twisted the band on his wrist.

Ali thought she caught a glimpse of red on the band but when she looked, the indicator had turned green again. "But nobody else would be safe. This is something I have to do."

"But you'll be with the bounty hunter." He spat out the word like he'd eaten something distasteful.

Ali reached up and caressed Rod's chin. "Oh, Rod, you're sweet to worry so. Hunter Cole could never be the type of man I'm interested in. I need someone who's ready to settle down, like you." Her words caught in her throat, but she forced herself to say them.

Her uncle studied her. She looked back at him, schooling her features to look as honest as possible.

"Does this mean you'll marry me?"

"When it's safe. From what I've heard, some of the pirates have been caught. They're getting careless. That means they'll be easier to track down."

"Then let me help you. We can finish this up quickly and get married even sooner. I know things." He clamped his lips and shook his head as if stopping himself from something.

Ali shook her head for him but wondered at his words. "No. You're needed here. Besides, you're too well known around this station. If you're seen with us, they'll know we're after them, and that would be dangerous for all of us. We have to be careful about this. Come on, Rod. Don't worry so much. You know I can take care of myself, and Cole is an Orion Hunter. We'll be safe."

"That's ridiculous. Where did you ever come up with such an idea in the first place? You don't even know who you're looking for or where to look."

"It's not hard. Look at the raids. They're after Ki crystals. Whoever's behind this is cornering the market. In addition, the pirates are getting careless. They're showing up in public places where they can be recognized."

She and Jason had talked about what and how much she could say. So far, she hadn't said anything security didn't already know.

"That's because they won't listen. They're getting too cocky."

Ali strained to make out her uncle's mumbled words. "What did you say, Rod?"

Her uncle shook his head. "Nothing. I still don't like this. What happens if you do locate them? What will you do then? Go in with weapons firing? You'll get yourself killed and then where would I be? I don't want a dead bride."

"I'm not stupid, Un...Rod. Whoever their leader is, he's the one giving the orders. If we can find him, then the others will be easy for you and the other security forces to gather up."

"But how can you tell who's involved?"

Ali knew she had to be careful. "I'm sorry, but I can't tell you." She reached out to stop him from interrupting. She had to get him off the subject. "Has anything happened around here since I left?"

"Yes, but we aren't done discussing the pirates."

"What happened?" she asked, ignoring his comment.

He shook his head again as if to clear it, then looked at her in confusion. "Leksi? They told us you were dead. Dimitri's been going over our family holdings for me. He's notified your advocates and started the probate proceedings."

Ali gripped the arms of the chair until she thought she'd leave imprints in the metal. "He what? You'll have to notify him that won't be necessary since I am most certainly not dead."

"I'll do that later. Right now…Oh, I'm making some special modifications to the ship. Do you remember where your father hid the red crystals?"

"Red crystals? What are you talking about?"

"The red crystals. He had them hidden all over the ship. I know he had to. That's the only reason Lynn would stay with him. They have to be there somewhere."

"There are no red crystals. Any crystal we had belonged to miners. We turned everything over to the assay office."

Rod frowned and twisted the wristband. "No, not those. I know there were more. There had to be. Red ones." He turned and stared at the wall behind her. "There had to be." He swung back around. "But you're here, aren't you, Lynn? That means you love me."

Ali forced tight muscles to relax. She rose and kissed her uncle lightly on the cheek. "Yes, Rod, I love you." She smiled at him, fighting the tears threatening to spill from her eyes. The band blinked red, then green. She knew she'd seen the change this time. "Will you help me?"

"Help you? By letting you go off with the hunter?"

"Oh, come on. He's not so bad. He's good at what he does. I can assure you, all he wants from me is my money. I'm using him the same as he's using me, as a means to an end."

"Leksi, I can't stand the thought of you being with him. Stay here, please. Don't go with him."

Ali shook her head. She was having trouble keeping up with his changes from her to her mother.

"No. I owe it to my parents and Sean and to all those others who've been killed in these raids. I need to get my life in order, and this is the only way to do that. I'm going to do what I have to do, and nothing you say will stop me. If you can't accept that, then let me know now and I'll gather my things from storage and leave for good."

Rod's shoulders sank. "Don't say that, Leksi. I can't control them anymore. You'll be safe here. You need to stay here." He shook his head. "What about your ship?"

Ali didn't think she'd heard him correctly. Who couldn't he control? A cold chill clamped around her heart. "If the repairs are done, I'll set her in a stationary parking orbit. I'll figure out what to do about her when I get back. I'd like to find out why the pirates didn't destroy her like they did everything else."

"She's a good ship. Maybe they intended to use her."

"Then why not take her with them when they left? It doesn't make sense. That's something else I intend to find out."

"If you won't listen to reason, then there's something I need to tell you about Cole. I've been doing some checking on him."

Suspecting his revelation, Ali decided to head her uncle off. "You found out he's known as JC Draper. I know. I know what kind of man I'm dealing with, Uncle Rod."

Rod looked disappointed. "And you still want to go with him?"

"He knows if anything happens to me, he doesn't get paid, and all those credits are a great incentive. I'm probably safer with him than anywhere else. Delphi proved that."

"Where is he now?"

"He said something about getting supplies and visiting a Magdalene or two. We'll be leaving tomorrow."

"Will you keep in touch with me and let me know you're safe? I'll feel better if I know where you are."

"As often as possible. What can you tell me about the bombing at Delphi?"

"Nothing important. Will you at least spend the night with me?"

At this point Ali didn't know who she should be. The constant switching of names had grown very confusing. "I'm too beat, and I've got a lot to do. But," she tempered when she looked at his face, "I've rented a temporary room. How 'bout if you join me for dinner? Say around eight?"

"I'm going to keep trying to convince you to stay here," he warned.

"You can try," Ali laughingly countered.

Ali left her uncle and went shopping. Very much aware of the guard tailing her, she decided to have a little fun with him. Never one to spend much time searching for clothes or other necessities, Ali developed a sudden interest in trying on every outfit she could find and spending an inordinate amount of time picking out a simple pin. While trying on an outlandishly gaudy gown, she felt a tingle in her earlobe.

"Yes, Sami?" she whispered as she slipped the gown over her head.

"That gown doesn't suit you at all."

Jason chuckled in her ear and she quickly tugged

the gown into place. "Jason, where are you?" she hissed.

"On the ship. I didn't find anything in his quarters. How 'bout you?"

"Not much I could do with him there the whole time. There's something funny about the office though. The space looked smaller and one wall didn't quite fit."

"I'll check it out while you're at dinner with the commander."

Ali blushed. "You heard?"

"Yes. Ali? I'm sorry about your uncle. He actually didn't seem like a bad guy. I've sent a notice on to Fleet. He'll get the help he needs. I promise."

Ali swallowed around the sudden lump in her throat. "Thanks, Jason. I'd better go. My escort is getting restless. I'll talk to you later."

She stripped out of the gown and left the shop, her arms full of the things she did purchase, and headed for the park in the center of the station. The area consisted of a few potted plants scattered among benches and tables in the center of the shopping district. She dropped her purchases on a table and accessed the net to get her messages. Most of them were routine, but one in particular caught her eye—a general message from the family advocates concerning the distribution of the family holdings. All assets would be transferred to her uncle's power in thirty standard days if she didn't reply.

"Computer, put in a return call immediately," Ali demanded. She tapped her fingers on the table as she waited for the call to go through. A few minutes later, the face of her father's best friend and advocate appeared on the monitor.

"Aleksia? Is it really you? We'd been informed

you were dead."

"Hi, Mike. The reports of my demise were premature. I assure you I'm perfectly well and in one piece. I was on retreat at Delphi." She hated lying to him, but the line wasn't secure, so she had to keep up the ruse. "I didn't know about the problem until very recently."

"It's a good thing you got back to me. Rod is insisting we turn everything over to him. Of course, now that you're back, it won't be necessary, unless you want to?"

"Not on your life. I'm not giving him a single credit." She ignored the shocked look on his face. "I'm sorry, Mike. Can you handle this for a couple more weeks until I get some things settled here? I promise I'll come see you then."

"No problem, Ali. If you need anything, let me know."

"Thanks, Mike." She signed off. That took care of one problem. Dimitri would find her not quite as easy a mark now. She ordered a light snack and settled down to answer some of the other less important notes. On a whim, she ordered a drink sent to her shadow.

**\*\*\*\***

Dimitri strolled into Rod's office and locked the door behind him. Rod in his chair, muttered something about Lynn. Dimitri ignored him and touched a unique sequence on his desk pad. The wall behind the desk slid out of sight, revealing a bank of monitors. He activated a special code and waited for the call to go through. If he wanted to see his plans come to fulfillment, he had to get rid of Cole. Soon, he'd be rich and powerful beyond imagination, and Leksi would be his again.

First, he had to get rid of her uncle. The old man had become a definite hindrance.

He'd had the Matthews' ship spared because he knew Leksi would need a way to get to safety. The men had been ordered not to harm her. The idiots had almost blown everything when she'd floated away from them. Fortunately, she'd been found alive.

He also knew she hadn't been in the hotel at Delphi, or on retreat. The plan had been for Rod to rescue her, but she'd disappeared, and he hadn't been able to find out where she'd gone. He needed to warn his men to be more careful, though. He wouldn't miss the few who'd been killed. In fact, if anything, the person or people who'd killed them had done him a favor by getting rid of some chaff. Right now, though, he had to get rid of Cole.

"Dimitri? What's up?" A man's high-pitched voice broke into his thoughts.

"We have a problem. Leksi's back, but she's leaving with the hunter. How far away are you?"

"I'm on my way from Joey's. We came up empty there. She and the hotel owner must have gone to ground. I'll be there in a couple of hours."

"Remember, I don't want Leksi hurt."

"Not a problem, boss."

Dimitri smiled as he signed off. His men would be here soon, and he'd be rid of the Hunter and have Leksi all to himself.

****

Back in her room, Ali packed her things, trying to figure out how to get out of dinner with her uncle when her ear tingled.

"Yes?"

"Ali, get back to the ship as soon as you can. We need to leave," Jason said.

"Problems?" She crammed her remaining things into a bag.

"I'll explain once you're here. Be careful."

"What about my shadow?"

"Sami's taking care of that. In a minute you'll hear the emergency klaxons. Use the diversion to get here."

As he finished talking, Ali heard the emergency signals going off. She grabbed her bag and ran for the corridor. Sure enough, her shadow was running for his station, so she headed for the ship. The containment shields were slamming down into place, so she picked up her pace, but getting there was like swimming upstream against a waterfall. Hundreds of people ran in many directions in a panic. In the twenty years the station had been in service, the signals had never gone off. Nobody knew what to do.

Ali finally made her way to an empty corridor, only to find the shields already down. She stopped in frustration. She could see the docking bays but had no way to get to them.

"Sami." She pulled her ear. "I'm in Corridor C, Level Twelve. Can you open the shield?" The shield slid open, and she slipped through and ran for the ship. Once there, Jason cycled her in.

"Hurry!" Jason rushed toward the bridge. "She's in, Sami. Go!"

Ali barely had time to fall into her seat before Sami took off with a burst of acceleration that would have left her pinned to the hull if she'd been standing. Ali watched Jason maneuver the ship. He and Sami melded seamlessly, as though they were one. She sat quietly, letting them do their work without distraction. She used the time to study more schematics and work on ideas for attacking the pirates. She glanced up as Jason sat back and stretched. "Is everything all right?"

"It is now. We cut it pretty close, though." He sighed and ran his hand through his short hair. "You did a good job back there. I know what you did hurt, but you came through with flying colors."

"So why the sudden departure?"

"An old problem is about to deposit itself on our doorstep, and I thought it in our best interest we get out of there."

"Are you going to tell me about that problem?"

"JC Draper."

Ali sat up. "I thought you…I mean, I thought he… Isn't he on Ki Three?"

"He's supposed to be. Sami found out he disappeared about a year ago in a shuttle accident, presumed dead."

"So why is that a problem for us?"

Jason handed her the data wafer he'd picked up at Joey's Place. "Take a look at this and tell me."

Ali stared at the data, her breath nearly stopping as she looked at the face of the man who tortured and killed Sean. "That's JC Draper?" she whispered. Why had she thought he looked like Jason in Tommi's images? Yes, she saw a passing resemblance, but nobody who knew Jason would mistake one for the other. For one thing, Draper had a nasty scar going from his left temple across his face to his right ear. And he was much heavier than Jason. And…she knew him.

"Yes. Why?"

"I thought they reconditioned him."

"So did we. You look like you know him."

"I do. You saw the data wafer. The man with his back to you the entire time?"

Jason's grip on the edge of the table tightened, turning his knuckles white. She knew the feeling. "Yes?"

"I saw him from a different angle before I left the ship. He killed my brother. That man is him."

"Damn. You don't have another wafer do you?"

"No. I could only get the one before I escaped, and by the time I got back, everything else had been destroyed except the data I showed you. But I know he's the same man."

"I believe you. And I'm sorry. We'll catch him. I promise, Ali. We'll catch him."

Ali nodded and raised her chin, determined to go on. "When do we land? And where?"

"Sami is dropping us into the clearing now. Feel like a swim?"

Ali gathered her resolve and nodded. "Is it still raining?" She stripped out of her station clothes and picked up her thermal suit.

Jason chuckled. "Of course. That's why we were able to evade our tail." He nodded at her surprised expression. "Oh, yes. They tried. Unfortunately, they were busy with several other ships also heading for the planet. I'm afraid the station will have a hard time explaining to their various owners how they all malfunctioned at the same time."

Ali laughed and hugged him. "Partner, I'm sure glad you're on my side."

\*\*\*\*

Rod Matthews downed the cold ale like water and

placed the glass alongside the others. He'd spent the past several hours clearing up the mess from the false alarms only to find out Lynn had left. Nobody knew where or when, but he did. He knew she'd gone with the bounty hunter. But where? He'd checked the bases on the planet and moons, but nobody had seen them, and there were no traces of them in the belt. He'd find her, though. And when he did, he'd deal with Cole himself. Lynn belonged to him.

Chapter Twenty

"Jason?" Sami stopped Jason as he and Ali headed to the airlock.

"What?"

"I don't think you and Ali should do that. It's not safe. Take a look." Sami activated a monitor near the lock.

What Ali saw made her shudder. The clearing had become a quagmire of mud and uprooted trees. From looking, it seemed Sami had landed in the second pond, the only open area left. What had been a gentle stream and calm waters a short time ago had turned into a raging torrent. She and Jason could not survive in that kind of maelstrom.

"In fact, I'm having trouble keeping the ship on an even keel now."

"Why didn't you tell me this earlier?" Jason asked as he resealed the lock.

"Um, you two didn't look like you wanted to be disturbed."

"Oh. Okay. Suggestions?" Jason ran his hands through his hair.

"Scans show there's no place to set up camp. I suggest you stay on the ship and I move to a position closer to town."

"If I remember correctly, there's not much south of town that won't be a swamp by now."

"Correct. There is, however, a place north of town Zeus told me about before he went offline. It's the original landing site for the colonists and has been abandoned for years. We first thought the pirates were operating from there, but we've had the area under constant surveillance and never saw anything."

"Is there someplace where you can hide?"

"Yep. Place comes complete with a hangar large enough to hold me. In addition, you'll be closer to town—five hundred meters away. And we've checked the spot so many times, even a sand flea can't move without us knowing."

"Go."

Ali changed into a comfortable jumpsuit and sat down to work. She studied the maps and charts from the data wafer while Jason took care of routine maintenance. She kept coming back to one area in particular. She sensed something about the site. Her instincts told her there was more there than what met the eye.

"Sami? Can you enhance the second quadrant on this chart?" she asked. The image on the screen enlarged. She traced a thin line from one corner to the opposite, growing more excited. "Sami, follow this line to the fourth quadrant. Is there an outlet?"

The image scrolled. "Yes, Ali."

"Yes. Sami, we've found it!" She jumped up as Jason entered the cabin and hugged him.

"What's all the shouting?" he asked as he returned the embrace.

"Look at this! I found the base! We were right. It's underground—in the caves. They've been enlarged. Look here." She pointed at the charts. "Here's the main cavern. It's large enough to hold a small fleet."

Jason studied the screen. "Where's the entrance?"

"I can't be certain, but I think here," she pointed at the spot where Sami had traced the tunnel.

"Where is the area in relationship to the town?"

"Several kilometers to the north."

"That's too far for easy access. If you had people coming and going out that far, someone would be bound to notice." He pointed to one of the lines leading away from the cavern. "What's this line?"

"Another tunnel. Why?"

"Where does this lead?" He tapped his lips with his finger. "Sami, overlay the current chart with a chart of the town." The display changed, red lines from the town merging with the black ones of the tunnels. The tunnel Jason pointed out wound around under several blocks of the town.

"I can't believe they built those buildings over the tunnels. With these rains, the ground can't be safe," Ali said.

"I don't think they did," Jason said. "Sami, overlay these charts with the original geologic surveys." The image changed again, but this time, the tunnels ended well outside the town limits.

"That's what I thought. Looks like our friends have been busy. Sami, give me the names of the establishments those tunnels run under."

The information flashed on the screen. "Got you!" Jason said triumphantly. "I'm a little thirsty, partner. How about you?"

"Parched." Ali grinned.

A short time later, they were both clad in black outfits. Ali covered her hair with a close-fitting cap then checked to make sure her laser pistol and knife were in her boot holsters. Like Jason, she also wore a pistol on a belt and carried a second knife strapped to her wrist.

"Sami, what are the current weather conditions?" Jason asked when they were ready.

"Thick cloud cover, no moons, light drizzle, visibility less than one hundred meters, temperature a comfortable seven degrees Celsius."

Ali shuddered. "Well, at least the temp's above freezing."

"You don't have to do this," Jason pointed out.

"Oh no you don't. You're not leaving me behind this time."

He grinned. "I figured as much. Sami will monitor us the entire time. You still have your earrings on?"

Ali fingered the jewelry and nodded as Jason gave her a kiss for luck. They cycled through the airlock into the night.

Sami had chosen his hiding spot well. They were close enough to town for quick access, but far enough out to discourage casual visitors. Jason set a quick pace, and they reached the first buildings without even breathing hard. Even though late enough for the streets to be deserted, they stayed to the shadows. A few weak lights lit the streets, their feeble attempts to brighten the thoroughfares swallowed by the dismal rain. Three blocks from the outskirts, Jason drew Ali to a stop in a dark alley across from the bar.

"Give me three minutes to get around to the back and then go in the front." He handed her a small black box. "Hold this against the lock. It will disable the lock and any alarms." He disappeared into the night.

Ali counted off the minutes, grateful for all the

exercises they'd done in the dark. At the right time, she slipped across the street and held the device against the lock. A few seconds later, she pressed through the door. The dim light allowed her to see where things were. She gasped when a strong arm encircled her throat from behind, and she felt the prick of a knife at her throat.

"Be still and be quiet, bitch, or you're dead," a deep voice warned her. His arm tightened, cutting off her breath. "You're going to do exactly as I say. Understand?"

Cautiously Ali lowered her head a notch. She struggled to breathe against the strangle hold on her throat.

"Call the bounty hunter in here." The man relaxed his hold, but the tip of the knife remained at her neck.

"What do you want?" she gasped. She had to think fast. Jason would be through the back entrance by now. If she called a warning, she'd be dead. She sensed a tingling at her ear. Of course. The earrings. Sami. She had to let him know what was going on.

"Your friend has made some people rather unhappy, and they're paying me a lot of credits to make them happy again," he said, his voice cold and flat. "Whether I kill you or him, or both of you, it's his choice."

She had to give Jason time. "Why?"

"Who knows? Unlike you, I don't ask too many questions. Now call him."

A sharp jab at her throat caused a warm trickle down her neck. "Hunter? I'm in." she called.

\*\*\*\*

Jason pushed through the back door. Thanks to Sami, he'd heard the entire conversation. He'd been studying the situation for the past minute but couldn't see any way out that didn't involve Ali getting hurt—or worse. The assassin stood with his back to the wall so he couldn't get behind him. Coming at him from the front seemed the only option, but the man used Ali's body as a shield. He came up with—and discarded—several ideas. Finally, he had no options left so he stepped into view.

"Lose the hardware, Hunter," the assassin growled. "Any tricks and she dies. I know you're fast, but before you can get me, I'll kill her."

For an eternity, Jason stood there and then removed his pistol from his belt and placed the weapon on the bar. He dared not do anything with Ali standing there. The man stood in the shadows so Jason couldn't see his face, but he knew the voice. Quick and smart, and right now he held all the winning cards.

"What do you want, Draper?"

Draper laughed. "I'd have thought that would be obvious. All of the hardware, Hunter. I know you've got more than that little pistol." He nicked Ali's neck with the tip of the knife just enough to hurt her.

Jason blanched as Ali let out a small gasp of pain. Even in the dim light, he could see a thin dark line trickle down her neck. He swore Draper would pay for every drop of blood.

"I can carve her up a little at a time, Hunter. Your choice."

Jason removed his other pistol and knife. A tiny laser finger pistol lay against his left wrist. The piece could only be used for one shot at close range, but if he got the chance, that's all he'd need.

"Very good. Now move away from them. Sit on

that chair over there." He motioned with his head to a nearby chair.

Jason did as ordered, cursing the man and the situation. He mastered his fury and cleared his mind. His eyes never left Ali.

Draper backed toward the bar, keeping Ali between himself and Jason. "A few questions, Hunter. First of all, how did you find us?"

"Go to hell." He winced as Ali gasped and a second line of blood trickled down her neck.

"I'll ask one more time. How did you find us?" He reached the bar. "Move at all, bitch, and you're dead." He released his hold on Ali and reached for Jason's discarded pistol. The knife didn't waver an iota.

"Let her go, and I'll tell you everything you want to know." Jason countered.

Draper snorted. "I'm not stupid."

As Jason watched, Draper picked up the pistol. It disappeared between him and Ali, and Jason assumed the barrel now pointed at the middle of her back. The knife joined the others on the bar.

"Take these over to your boyfriend and bind him." Draper handed Ali a set of binders. "And no funny moves. You stay between him and me and you might live."

Jason caught a motion in Ali's eyes. He blinked once to let her know he understood. They were only going to get one chance. Ali moved slowly away from Draper. She appeared to stumble, but the move gave Jason what he needed. He dived off the chair and brought his hand up and fired at the same time Draper did.

A surprised look crossed Draper's face as he stared

at the spot of red blossoming across the front of his shirt. He raised his pistol to fire again at Jason, but the shot never came as he crumpled to the ground.

Jason got up from his position. "Ali? You can get up now." He looked at her lying face down on the floor. She was so still. "Ali?"

A touch of panic tinged his voice. He turned her over. Draper's beam had grazed her head, leaving a small wound that bled profusely. He tore a strip off his shirt and bound the wound. "Sami, I could use some help."

"I can tell she's alive. How badly is she hurt?"

"She's out cold. I can't risk carrying her out into the street. There are probably other unfriendlies around."

"Can you get her to the alley behind the bar?"

"Yes."

"All right. I'll have the sled waiting there for you."

Jason picked up his weapons and returned them to their holders. Without a second glance at Draper, he picked up Ali and carried her to the back door. "Bless you, Sami."

The sled hovered outside the door. He opened the cargo door and laid her inside as the lights came on in the bar. He jumped in behind her. "Sami, get us out of here," he yelled as the door to the bar opened and several men came pouring out, weapons pulsing. The sled took off at high speed, flattening him against the floor.

When he managed to get up, he checked on Ali. She still lay unconscious, but she had a strong pulse and was breathing normally. He strapped her down as well as he could and climbed to the front seat. The sled seesawed while Sami tried to evade their pursuers. Finally, he slid into his seat and strapped in.

"Sami, I've got control." He flinched as a powerful beam flashed against the shielding, momentarily blinding him. "What the hell was that?" He concentrated on the controls.

"They're using some kind of crystal-based weapon," Sami said. "The shields won't take much of that."

Jason maneuvered the little sled swiftly, not giving them anything constant to lock on to. "Sami, can you tell me how many there are?" He didn't want to lose his concentration to check the scanners.

"Two on your tail. The others have dropped out. I assume they're going to try to flank you."

"They can try," Jason muttered as he considered his options. "How far back are my tails?"

"About fifty meters and closing fast. What would you like me to do, Jason?"

"Pray," he said as he executed a full loop-the-loop, bringing him up behind the pirates. A few well-placed shots later, he got free—at least for the moment. He stopped in a clear spot behind some rocks to get his bearings.

"Okay, Sami, I have a minute of breathing space. Where am I and where do I need to be?" A lighted grid appeared on a panel in front of him.

"You're here," Sami said as a red dot lit up on the grid. "The flanking pirates are here and here, and I'm here." Several black spots showed the pirates' positions, closing rapidly on him, Sami just beyond them. He studied the grid.

"Sami, what's this here?" He traced a narrow line

running roughly parallel to his position.

"A narrow gully."

"Wide enough for you?"

"Negative. And the bottom is flooded. Can you get to the road?"

"Not my first choice. Too open." Jason looked over the terrain. "Only an idiot would take the gully. The road it is. It'll be close." He gunned the little sled and took off. As soon as he did, a shot sparkled against his shields followed closely by several others.

"Sami, I need you now!" Jason did everything he could think of, but the shots grew closer and more frequent. Jason checked his read-outs.

"Sami, shields are gone. Open the bay but keep dark. I'll go to night vision." He looked up in time to see Sami's welcome outline looming in the dark ahead of him. He could see the green glow of the bay opening and scooted in as another shot hit his tail. He regained control in time to avoid crashing into the bay wall. "We're in, Sami. Go!"

He waited for the acceleration to lessen before trying to move. "Go back to your hiding place and give me some lights." He strode around to the back of the sled. He saw a small hole in the canopy and a large blackened area. He winced. They'd been lucky. The sled had been built of some of the strongest known materials. Nothing had damaged the craft before this. He shook his head. First things first.

Ali looked so pale and still, but he knew she was alive. He carried her to the med-unit and gently laid her on the bunk. He grabbed the first aid kit and tended to her. The wound wasn't large, a graze across her temple, but it had bled a lot. He cleaned up the blood and sprayed a sealant over the wound and then gave her a hypo spray of painkiller and antibiotics. When he finished, he saw to his own minor cuts and cleaned up. He fixed a cup of tea for her and a glass of ale for himself and went to sit next to Ali.

Her color looked better already, and according to Sami, her vitals were all within acceptable ranges, but he knew he wouldn't relax until she woke up.

"Who are you, Aleksia Matthews?" he whispered. "And what have you done to me?" Somehow over the weeks, she'd become more important to him than his quest.

A few minutes later, Ali moaned and opened her eyes. As her wits returned, she sat bolt upright and then grimaced.

"I wouldn't do that if I were you," Jason said as he handed her the tea. "You've got a mild concussion from the blast. I've given you an analgesic, but you're going to be sore."

Ali looked around the cabin. "What happened? Where's Draper?"

"Dead."

"Are you all right?"

"Yes, thanks to you."

"We've lost our edge now that they know we're here and that we suspect something."

"Maybe—maybe not," Jason said.

Ali yawned. "What did you put in my drink?"

"You need sleep." Jason took the cup, placed it on the console, and drew the cover over her now reclining body. "Don't worry, love, I'll be right here. Sami, keep an eye on things, please." He settled on the next bunk and fell asleep.

\*\*\*\*

"Ali, would you stop worrying? I'll be fine," Jason assured Ali, as he strapped on his weapons. "We know the entrance is near here. I'm just going to go out for a little look see." He was tired of playing cat and mouse games and tired of waiting for something to happen. He'd awakened that morning determined to take matters into his own hands. The pirates had held the high ground for far too long.

"At least let me go with you. Two sets of eyes are always better than one."

"No. And that's final. You're still recovering. Besides, I need you to go over those charts some more. Maybe you can find some way in that doesn't go through town. I'll be back before lunch. Sami, make sure she stays put."

"Yes, sir," the AI said as Jason cycled through the lock.

Ali waited a few minutes, then strapped on her hardware.

"Ali, what are you doing?" Sami asked.

"After last night, if you think I'm going to let him out of my sight, you're sadly mistaken. Now, are you going to let me out or do I have to get tough?" She relaxed when the lock popped open. "Thank you, Sami. Can you tell me which direction he went?"

"I can do better than that. Go to the galley and in the second cabinet on the left, third drawer down, get one of the wrist units there."

Ali did as Sami directed and strapped the unit to her arm. "Okay, now what?"

"Check the screen."

Ali looked at the tiny screen. A small white light

pulsed in one corner of the screen. A few centimeters away, a red light pulsed. As she watched, the red one changed position while the white remained stationary.

"The interface is tied to your jewelry. The white is you and the red is Jason. I show up as a blue blip."

"Thank you, Sami. If you weren't a computer, I'd hug you."

"Aw, shucks. Be careful, Ali."

"I will." She stepped through the lock and out into the rain, grateful for the insulating warmth of the thermal suit she wore. The special material shed the rain like water off a duck's back and kept her comfortable in any weather. She set a moderate pace, following Jason's trail. She didn't want to catch up to him, just trail him. A short time later, from the safety of a high hill, near where they thought the entrance to the pirates' cave was, she spied him creeping through a rocky outcropping. She also saw something else—a group of men moving to surround Jason. She only saw one way out for him.

"Sami. We've got a problem," she murmured. "Jason's practically surrounded. He has one chance to get out. He has to move to the southeast as soon as possible. Can you do something with the sled?"

"Not soon enough. I've told him about the ambush. I'm sending the sled to you."

Ali watched, her heart pounding, as Jason moved to a narrow break in the rocks he could slip through. She maneuvered her way around the rocks until she lay in front of the spot he'd have to go through. A minute after she reached her position, Jason came rushing through, followed closely by the pirates. From her location, she took out three of them before they ran for cover. Jason scrambled into her position as the rock next to them exploded in a shower of shards. Ali took aim and winged another pirate.

"I thought I told you to stay on the ship," Jason groused as he took down a pirate.

"You're welcome." Ali grinned as a shower of pebbles fell on them.

"Ali," Sami's voice whispered in her ear. "The sled is directly below your position, approximately twenty meters."

Ali looked down the hill. "Jason, Sami sent the sled."

He nodded at her. "You first. Go. Now." He watched as Ali dodged from rock to rock and made her way to the sled. A minute later he joined her, and they made their escape. Jason maneuvered the sled through the rocky area, evading any pursuit. By the time the pirates had their own sleds in the air, Jason and Ali were hidden back at the ship.

"That's one I owe you," Jason said as they sat in the galley eating a light lunch.

"Maybe now you'll stop trying to leave me behind." Ali ducked as he flicked a forkful of fruit her way.

"Oh no, you didn't!" She flicked her own fruit back at him, and a full-fledged food-fight ensued that ended with them both on the floor licking the damage off each other.

Chapter Twenty-One

As Dimitri re-read the note, an impotent rage came over him. He was still alive! Those incompetent fools he'd hired hadn't even been able to find Cole, let alone get rid of him. The man had more lives than a Super Soldier from Earth. Dimitri looked around his cramped apartment. If not for Cole, he'd be enjoying a first-class cabin, where he belonged, instead of this working berth. He'd been a little unhappy when he'd thought Leksi had died. He'd given orders not to kill her unless absolutely necessary, but those idiots he had working for him kept messing up. The others had been unfortunate, but then he'd found out about the money—that she'd stopped the transfer of funds to her uncle.

Leksi owed him, and this time he'd collect in person—with interest. After he finished with her, she'd gladly turn over the ship and its hidden rare red crystal to him. That imbecilic uncle of hers kept assuring him the crystal still existed, but they hadn't been able to find any. He needed to get rid of the uncle and get Leksi back. Maybe, if she behaved, he'd let her live—under his care, of course. He lay back in his bunk and smiled as he thought of the various ways he'd use Aleksia Matthews and all her lovely money.

He grinned as he grudgingly admired her courage and daring. Aleksia was a rare object. She had spirit, and he intended to be her master. Once she'd been properly disciplined, she'd never refuse him again. Hell, after he tired of her, he'd be able to make some money offering her to select clientele.

Naked images of her filled his mind—images of her with him, and with other men while he watched. Drugs—carefully administered—would have her begging for him. Restraints and other devices would have her just begging. Once he had control of Leksi and the money, he'd have everything he ever wanted. The new fleet would be the icing on the cake. He'd have the entire quadrant at his feet.

\*\*\*\*

Jason and Ali spent the rest of the day going over the charts of the area. Their first guess at the entrance had been wrong. Jason's aborted *look-see* had proven that.

"Why do you keep going back to that spot? There're no entrances there. What are you looking at?"

"A hunch. Look at this tunnel leading away from this spot."

"Yeah? What about it?"

Ali traced the line, scrolling it further from the base. "Guess where this leads?"

Jason looked at the confusing web of tunnels and cross tunnels. Except for the ones under the town, he didn't see anything of significance. He looked at Ali and shrugged.

Ali grinned. "This particular tunnel leads to a certain cave hidden behind a waterfall."

"Our cave? But that's kilometers away."

"Overland, yes, because you have to either climb over the mountain or go around. However, underground, you go through the same space, cutting the distance in half. Do you want to see what's in those caverns?"

Jason looked at the lines on the charts. "How do you know we could get through?"

"I won't know for sure until I try, but from the looks of these charts, there are only one or two tight spots."

"What about the water?"

Ali pointed to several side tunnels. "These run deeper. If there's any water, it'll be there. To be safe, we'll wear environmental suits and carry breathing tubes. That way if we do run into anything, we'll be safe. Any more objections?"

Jason rubbed his hand through his hair. "Sami, what're the chances of you being able to set down in the second pond?"

"No can do, Jason. However, if I understand Ali correctly, you won't need me there. I can take you there and drop you and the sled at the base. I'll come back here and track you the entire way."

"Okay. We'll leave in the morning." He turned to Ali. "Since you're the expert, I'll leave everything to you." Jason abruptly left the cabin.

Ali could hear Jason puttering around in the cargo bay. "What was that all about?" she wondered aloud. "Sami, I need a hard copy of these charts to take with us. Can you give me that?"

"Do you still have the wrist unit on?"

"Yes. Why?"

"Look at the screen."

A few seconds later the unit beeped, and Ali looked down at the tiny screen. There, in detail, were the charts. "This is great, Sami, but I can barely see this."

"Press the second button on the left."

Ali did as directed and watched in amazement as a readable hologram appeared centimeters above the unit. A light blip flashed at the pond end of the tunnel. "I assume that will be us?"

"Yes. Right now, this is a simulation. Once you're moving, I'll track you on the screen the same way I did earlier."

**\*\*\*\***

The next morning, Sami set Ali and Jason down in the clearing as close to the ponds as he could get. "Watch yourselves. There's a little storm brewing," he warned as they prepared to leave.

As she stepped out into the raging gale, she gasped and yanked her mask down, trying to catch her breath as the downpour engulfed her. Jason grasped her arm and motioned for her to follow him. She nodded and leaned into the wind. An eternity later, they reached the cave and ducked into its shelter.

Ali removed her mask. "Stars, if that's Sami's idea of a little storm, I'd hate to see what he considers a big one." She looked around the cave. The lower portion where they'd originally camped had flooded, and streams now flowed from several tunnels.

"Please don't tell me we're going into one of those." Jason pointed as he watched the water pour through one crack.

"No. The one we want is up there." Ali pointed to a rough crack in the rock face several meters above them. She switched on her headlamp. "Are you ready?"

"Yes," he said and lit his lamp.

Ali looked at Jason. He'd grown extremely quiet,

though she didn't know why, but she gave him the time he needed to come to terms with whatever bothered him. Perhaps, she reasoned, he had trouble accepting what had happened at the bar. After all, he had an abundance of pride—not one to give in lightly, and he'd had to do that in order to save her life. And then she'd had to rescue him from the ambush.

She scrambled up the steep slope to the tunnel, followed by Jason. She slipped through the slot into the narrow opening. The floor of the tunnel was wet, making walking treacherous. They slipped and slid their way through until they had to crawl. A short time later the space opened back up, and Ali called for a break. She pulled two drinks and energy bars from her pack.

"How far do we have to go like this?" Jason asked. He was sweating and his breathing labored.

Ali watched Jason and finally understood the problem.

"Jason. Look at me." She took his head in her hands, forcing him to face her. "You're suffering from claustrophobia. Take a deep breath and try to calm yourself. Think of something else."

"That's ridiculous. I've never had a problem with small spaces before. Sami isn't all that big, and I spend a lot of time in the ship."

"True. However, this is different. Not everyone can handle caves. It's a different feeling. Now, relax your breathing." She activated the screen on her wrist unit. A white flash showed her their current position. "We're about halfway through. Can you handle this?"

"I guess I have to. You do this for fun?" he asked as he sipped at a drink. Ali nodded, and he chuckled. "You are certifiable."

Ali laughed. She studied him. His breathing had steadied, and the tension had left his voice. "I've been called worse. Are you ready?"

Jason nodded, and she moved out. Their lights picked out bands of Ki crystals and other minerals as they made their way through the narrow space. Ali couldn't help but think about the wealth of energy surrounding them. The entire mountain seemed to be an incredible source of crystal—enough to supply the entire Amalgamated system and still have some left over. She concentrated on that as they crawled, sometimes on their stomachs, through the stygian darkness. The last half kilometer put them almost completely through water as they followed a stream. Finally, Ali drew Jason to a stop.

They were at the top of a precipice, standing on a narrow ledge over which the stream flowed, dropping to an underground pool. The pool took up one end of a huge cavern. Mist swirled around the roof of the cavern, clinging wetly to the formations. Artificial lights gave the cave an ethereal quality. Suddenly, Jason yanked Ali down. He pointed toward the opposite end of the cavern where a group of people emerged from a large ship unlike anything they'd ever seen. Although shaped like any other ship, the exterior was a dull black in color—and more, as if the surface absorbed the spotlights shining down.

"I think we found the base," Ali murmured.

"That must be what they built with the polymers," Jason whispered. He counted ten small ships in addition to the larger one. While they watched, a group of pirates climbed into the largest ship.

Ali clasped her hands over her ears as the ship

powered up, waiting for the blast that would lift the ship. A few seconds later, she took them down in puzzlement as the ship moved silently out of the cavern.

"They have a red crystal drive," Jason whispered. "It's the only thing that explains that much power. We need to get back. It's time to call in the troops."

"Sami, do you have the position of this cave?"

"Yes, Boss."

****

Jason glanced at the time, noting the late hour before he finished composing and sending several messages. To Special Ops, he sent the location of the base and what he'd seen there. He glanced over at Ali asleep in his bunk and smiled. She'd been instrumental in finding the base and the pirates. He added another note, this one to Joey and Marty. If anything happened to him, he wanted to be sure she'd be taken care of.

She'd been the one person who'd seen through his shell and captured his heart. Her hair fell gently over her forehead, and he ached with longing for her. From the beginning, she had accepted him, and he admired her strength and intelligence. She had proven—several times—she would be there for him, and that's what was so damning. His love for her could get them both killed. He had to get her someplace safe before the war broke out—and war it would be. He'd seen the number of ships and knew how many men each one held. The few pirates they'd managed to take out were nothing to a group this size.

"Sami?"

"Yes?"

"Set course for Joey's. I need to use her room. Then we'll be coming back here."

"Done, Jason. Sleep well."

"Thanks."

\*\*\*\*

Jason slipped into the hotel, Ali close by his side. There were several people in the corridor, so he hauled her into a hearty embrace until the others left. Finally, the corridor cleared and he accessed the opening. Once inside the room, he activated a special program.

"What are you doing?" Ali asked.

"Leaving messages for Joey or Marty. No matter where they are, they'll get them, but retrieval won't reveal their position to anyone." He touched a few more pads, and Joey appeared on the wall monitor in front of them. She held Me-too on her lap.

"Hi, Jason. Thought I'd send this to let you know Marty and I are safe. We have a party to get ready for. There're going to be lots of guests. I hope you and Ali can come. Oh, and tell Ali Me-too is doing great and she's expecting. We'll see you on the other side."

Although the message said very little, Jason read the deeper meaning. HQ had received the messages he'd sent from the ship, and the troops were underway. That was good news, but having Joey and Marty safe mattered more to him. When they finished the mission, he'd see them again. The two old friends were the closest things to parents he'd ever had, and he'd hate to see anything happen to them.

Ali wrapped her arms around him. "I'm glad they're safe. So why did we need to come here? Couldn't you have sent these messages through Sami?"

"No. This room and this equipment have a lot more scramblers than Sami. It's one of the few places where it really is safe to send these messages."

"Got it. Is there anywhere around here where a girl can freshen up a bit before we head back to the planet?"

"Yeah." Jason touched a pad, and a door at the far end of the room swung open, revealing a small, neat bedroom and adjoining bathroom. "Joey has this here for anyone who doesn't want to be in the public rooms. You might even find some clean jumpsuits in there."

"Smart woman."

While she showered and freshened up, Jason continued to send missives to various people, updating them all on the latest information he had. When his stomach rumbled, he grabbed a couple ration meals from Joey's stores and warmed them up. He didn't want to go out into the public areas any more than he had to so they'd do for now.

"Everything all right?" Ali asked when she emerged, wearing a clean jumpsuit.

"Yes. Just leaving a few more messages. I heated a ration for you." He pointed with his chin. "I'll be done here in a sec."

****

Back on the planet, Jason and Ali prepared to re-enter the cave at the entrance above the pools. They planned to make their way to the base in order to get a closer look at the pirates' operations.

As Sami took off for his hiding place, Jason looked around the clearing. Something didn't seem right, but he didn't know what.

"What's wrong?" Ali asked, looking around the peaceful clearing. The rain had tapered off to a light drizzle.

Jason wasn't surprised she noticed his tension. They were uniquely attuned to each other—as if each had become an extension of the other. "I'm not sure. Something doesn't feel right. Get into the cave, now. I'll be right behind you."

She scrambled for the cave as Jason scanned the surrounding area. He turned to follow her when a band of pirates swooped in, riding on silent sleds. They surrounded Jason, leaving no avenue for escape. He glanced at the cave entrance. Thankfully, he didn't see Ali. She'd be safe. This time, he didn't see any way out, and if he tried to fight, he'd end up dead. He prayed Ali wouldn't do something foolish like try to rescue him. There were too many.

"Where's the woman, Hunter?"

Jason shrugged. He had no illusions about what the men were going to do to him, but he'd never let them get Ali. He'd slipped the wrist unit and collar pin off with his weapons and ground them under his heel so they couldn't track her. "I haven't seen her."

A geyser of stone and mud exploded next to his foot, but he held his ground.

"You've been showing an awful lot of interest in town. Why?"

"My business, not yours." Another geyser of ground erupted. He had to get them away from here.

"We're making it our business." The leader directed two of his gang to bind Jason and haul him onto one of the sleds. "You're so interested in things, we'll give you a grand tour. Bring his sled."

\*\*\*\*

Ali looked at the grim faces and the weapons the men held and swallowed against the sudden lump in her throat. One man, riding the biggest sled, looked familiar, but she couldn't place him. She had the suspicion she knew him and hated him. Then her mind cleared, as if a door opened, and she recognized the second man from her nightmares.

She had to let Sami know their situation. She reached for her earrings and blanched. They were gone. Where were they? The last place she'd seen them had been at Joey's. Damn. She remembered taking them off to shower and must have forgotten to put them back on.

As she watched, the gang buzzed around Jason like a swarm of angry bees. Every now and then one would swoop in closer, forcing him to dive for the ground. Finally, the leader called a halt, and Ali strained her ears to hear what they were saying.

Ali watched as they bound Jason and threw him into one of the sleds. She couldn't follow them, and she had no way to contact Sami. "Think, Ali. Where would they be taking him?" She snapped her fingers. "Of course. The base." She prayed she'd remember all the twists and turns in the caverns. She didn't have much to take with her. Beyond her environmental suit, she just had her light and a few weapons. She climbed into the tunnel and began the long trek to the base.

****

Jason shifted in the sled to find a more comfortable position and received a vicious kick in the ribs for his efforts. They had to be taking him to the base. He hoped Ali had called Sami and they'd get to safety. Not seeing any other options, he began a series of mental exercises to get him through what he figured was coming.

Inside the base, the leader and three of his men taunted Jason. They'd secured his arms to a rock above his head, stretching them to the limit, his feet barely touching the floor. Other shackles clamped his feet in place. The leader directed one of his men to strip Jason's shirt off, leaving him exposed to the chill, damp air.

"Ever experienced real pain, Hunter? I wonder how much it will take before you break?" He tapped a very solid-looking bar along his leg. "Did you know that for all our advances as a society, the ancients were actually the experts on pain? Their practices are a special interest of mine. I've made a study of various techniques. For instance," he swung the bar against Jason's ribs, and he gasped at the pain. "I can choose to beat you, but such a tactic lacks finesse. So do drugs. Much too easy. I prefer my subjects to be aware of what they're telling me."

Jason gasped as the bar struck him again. Several ribs cracked, and he tried to blank his mind against the pain. He knew this was only the beginning.

"I can see you're going to be an interesting study. I hoped you would be." The man grinned. "Tell me where she is, and this will end."

"Safe from your clutches."

Jason clamped his mouth shut as the man attached wires to various spots on his body and hooked them to a small black box.

"Tell me what you know and who you notified."

"Everything and everyone." Sweat broke out as a jolt hit him that felt as if his muscles were being torn apart.

"How do you like my little box? That was the first setting. There are a total of ten, but I've never tested this beyond five. I wonder how long you'll last."

Jason had heard about people who enjoyed

inflicting pain for fun. He'd never understood such depravity. He clenched his jaw as another jolt hit him.

For an hour, the man worked on Jason, but he held silent. It took all his willpower not to cry out, but he wouldn't give the man the satisfaction. His last thoughts before blessed darkness overtook him focused on Ali.

## Chapter Twenty-Two

Ali emerged from the tunnel, careful to stay low so anyone glancing her way wouldn't spot her. Most of the smaller ships were gone, but the big one sat there in the center, like royalty upon its throne. She could see a group of men to one side of the entrance, but she couldn't make out what they were doing. As quietly as possible, she crept around the ledge, getting as close as she could. When she ran out of ledge, she still remained too far away to hear anything, but she could see and what she saw sickened her.

The pirates had a man hanging by his arms from a rock. His head hung down, so she couldn't see his face, but she had a bad sense. The pirates moved away from their sport and Ali got her first good look at their victim. Her worst fears were confirmed as she recognized tight black pants and high boots. Her mind screamed a denial, but her voice remained silent. Cold calm came over her as she looked at the body of her love.

She vowed to exact a price for every mark on his body. As she watched, they cut him down and dragged him into a dark opening. When they returned alone, she feared the worst. She crawled back to the tunnel behind her to think—to plan. No matter what, she would go after Jason. Even if he hadn't been her love, you didn't leave a man behind.

There weren't many people around, but she didn't know how much longer that would last. She needed to move fast. She risked a glance over the ledge. So far luck had been with her. The pirates were vicious, but not particularly intelligent. All their warning systems were toward the front of the cavern. And where all the guards were posted.

The way down looked easy enough, but what to do with Jason once she got him. She couldn't carry him up the cliff. The open sleds the pirates used sat close to the entrance, between the guards and the side cavern. Fortunately, Jason's sled sat there also. If she could get him to it, they had a chance. With patience she didn't know she had, Ali bided her time, waiting until the pirates settled down for the night.

****

When Jason woke, he seemed to be lying on a rock-filled ground. Shackles bound his wrists and ankles, but at least he no longer hung from the bar. Here, he had a chance. He had trouble seeing anything, and he hoped the problem came from a lack of light and not any damage to his eyes. He tried to sit up and gasped in pain.

"Ah, you're awake."

Jason peered into the darkness. He could make out a figure in the gloom. "Where?" His voice came out as a dry croak.

"Where are you? Welcome to Hell, my friend. Here, this will help."

Jason heard the sound of chains moving and something being pushed toward him. He flinched when the edge of a bowl touched his face. He eased to a sitting position, picked up the bowl, and took a tentative sip. The liquid tasted like water—slightly brackish—but most welcome. He drank his fill, not caring if it contained any drugs. Basic survival said drink, so he did.

"Thanks." He nudged the bowl back in the direction of the other voice. "Please tell me it's dark in here."

"As dark as the back side of space. How are you feeling?"

The other voice coughed, and Jason thought he heard a stifled groan. He knew the sensation. "Like I've been worked over by an expert. How long have I been here?"

"Not long. Afraid I can't be more specific. I seem to have misplaced my watch." The chains rattled. "So, what did you do to get them so mad at you they want you to live?" The man's voice sounded weak and raspy, but he still had a good sense of humor.

"Refused to tell them what they wanted." Though grateful for the water, and even the conversation, Jason wasn't about to tell anyone—especially someone he couldn't see—about Ali.

"Must have been something extremely important. I've never known them to let anyone else live."

"What about you?" Jason asked. He heard the chain and figured the guy must have shrugged.

"I'm not sure. They keep asking inane questions about my ship. Don't know why. There's nothing left of her. They occasionally take me to a lab where I do some tests for them, but nothing any half-brained lab tech couldn't do."

Jason chuckled, then stopped as pain slashed through his chest. "That's the problem then. Gather them all together and they haven't got a half a brain among them."

The other man laughed, briefly. "By the way, I'm Sean Matthews. I don't think I caught your name."

Jason caught his breath. Could the other man be Ali's brother? "Sean Matthews? Do you by any chance have a sister Aleksia?"

"I did. She's dead. Who the hell are you and how do you know about Ali?"

Jason could hear the despair in the man's voice. That kind of deep emotion couldn't be faked. He decided to take a chance. "My name's Jason Cole, and I've got some news for you. Your sister isn't dead. In fact, she's the most alive person I've ever met."

"Met? I don't recognize your name. How did you meet?"

"She hired me to help her find the pirate gang who destroyed your ship. We've been working together for the last few weeks."

The man growled. "Now, I know you're lying. Ali wouldn't willingly take up with anyone—especially a strange man—and go gallivanting around the cosmos with them."

"I think you'll find Ali a much-changed person. Let's see—how to convince you. She has short, white-blonde hair in a mess of riotous curls and the most incredible golden eyes I've ever seen. She's also smart, tough as nails, and stubborn as a team of Terran mules."

The other man gave a weak chuckle. "That's Ali." His laughter turned to a sob. "Oh, gods, she's alive. She must be the one they've been talking about. I never knew. Oh, gods, I didn't know."

Jason swallowed a sudden lump. "What do you

mean you didn't know?"

"The last time they let me out, they had me work on some sort of weapon they were going to use on some woman. It's like a stunner in that the beam immobilizes the victim but lets him stay awake. The power pack is black crystal based. More powerful but smaller."

Jason shook his head. "You couldn't have known. Besides, what could you have done? They'd have killed you if you hadn't helped them."

"I wish they had. There were times when I begged them to kill me. I hate what I've become."

"Sean, there are things no man can be expected to hold out against. These animals enjoy pain and torture. The fact you couldn't handle what they did shows you are more civilized than they are. How badly are you hurt?"

"It's not good. I'm not sure how much longer I can last. What about Ali? Is she safe? Don't tell me where she is, just if she's okay."

"She was the last time I saw her."

"Thank you." The man's voice faded. "Jason? I think I'll sleep now."

Jason listened to the man's labored breathing. He needed to figure out how to get out of this mess—and get Ali's brother out before his time ran out. He went to work on his chains.

****

Ali slipped down the face of the cliff. Using every available hiding place, she made her way toward the sleds. When she reached the closest one, she checked the controls and grinned. They had advanced power systems, but they were still sleds and easily sabotaged. She checked on the positions of the guards and went to work, making her way one sled at a time closer to Jason. With a deft twist in a certain area under the control panel, she disabled all the sleds except hers. She risked a quick look. They hadn't done anything with hers—thank the stars. She said a silent prayer the sled would work. She was a still short distance from the side tunnel when she ran out of things to hide behind.

Ali waited until the guards all had their backs toward her and dashed for the tunnel. Luck stayed with her, and she slipped through without being seen. She paused inside the entrance to allow her eyes time to adjust to the gloom. She didn't want to switch on a glowstick in case the light could be seen from outside. The glow from the outer cavern gave her enough light to see a tiny cave—actually, not more than a space between huge slabs of rock. There were several dark shapes on the ground, but what was rock and what was human, she couldn't be certain without actually touching them.

"Who's there?"

Ali heard a gravelly voice from the rear of the space. The man's voice sounded familiar, but she couldn't place the rough sound. She figured him to be a miner she'd met somewhere.

"Who are you?" she whispered. "Jason?" Her voice sounded unnaturally loud in the surrounding silence.

"Ali? Woman, what the hell are you doing here?"

Ali moved cautiously toward the voice. "I've come to get you out. Where are you?"

"To your left. Be careful. There's another man here. I'm afraid he's out cold." He paused. "Ali, it's Sean."

Ali stopped, her heart beating so fast, she thought it

would burst. "Sean?"

"Yes. Can you get to me?"

Ali swallowed her nerves and crept to her left. Her toe bumped into something soft, and she stopped. "Jason?"

"Yes. You found me."

"Are you okay?"

"I've been better. They have chains on us. I've gotten the leg irons off, but I can't manage the wrists. They're too close together."

"What can I do?"

"I have a lock pick, but I dropped it, somewhere near my left foot. You can use it to spring the locks. They're pretty old-fashioned."

Ali felt her way around until she found the pick in the dirt. After several false tries, she finally got the manacle open, sweat making her palms slick and her job more difficult. She paused as she heard a noise at the entrance, ducking behind a large boulder as a light shone into the opening.

"What'd I tell you, Gene? They're both out cold," a disembodied voice said from the entrance.

"I tell you, I heard something."

Something large and furry ran over Ali's foot, and she struggled not to scream. She swatted at the vermin, relieved when it scrambled around the boulder toward the light. A second later, she heard the ominous hiss of a laser pistol.

"See? Nothing more than a damned cave rat. Come on. Let's get something to eat. I'm starving."

The light left, and Ali let out the breath she'd been holding and crawled back around the boulder. "That was close. Give me your other hand." A minute later she had Jason free. "Can you walk?"

"I'll manage. But there's no way Sean can."

"Can you handle him?" She wanted nothing more than to go to her brother, but she needed to concentrate.

"Maybe. But not far."

"Understood. You get him while I check outside."

Ali slipped up to the entrance. She lay down on the ground and glanced out the opening. One man stood between her and the sleds and one at the entrance to the cave. She figured the others were all either eating or asleep. Stars, how was she going to get two injured men out of there? She crawled back to Jason.

"There's the two guards here and at the entrance. We have to get to the sled—about ten meters. Can you make it?"

"Not with Sean, and you can't carry him and protect us. Can you get the sled here?"

Ali bit her lip. "I'll manage something. Give me five minutes."

"We're not going anywhere."

Ali crept from the hole. She reached for the knife in her boot and hesitated. Then she thought about Jason. She gripped the knife and let it fly across the open space. The guard dropped silently to the ground. Ali dashed across the space and dragged the man to a pile of crates out of sight of the other guards. She looked down at his face and clenched her jaw. He'd been one of the ones who'd beaten Sean so badly on the ship. Instead of satisfaction, all she felt was disgust.

"Hey, Carl!" The other guard called. "Carl? Where are you?"

Ali held her breath as the man checked around and then looked down and saw the blood on the rock. He followed the trail to her position where he faced a very large pistol in a very steady hand.

"Gene?" One of the other guards called from the ship. "Everything okay?"

Ali mouthed an answer for the man.

"Yeah. Carl needed to take a leak."

She motioned for him to sit down next to his dead partner. He did as she directed, and she slipped behind him and cold-cocked him, and then trussed him with binders she found on his partner. She searched around for a gag and settled for a rag she found in one of his pockets. That evened the odds a little more in her favor.

She powered up the sled. The engine sounded like a fanfare in the cavern, and she knew it would only be a matter of seconds before their time—and luck—ran out. After Ali maneuvered the sled to the slot, Jason dumped a body in the rear hatch and fell in on top of him.

"Go."

Ali heard his grunt. She gunned the engine as several guards ran down the ramp. "Sit tight, partner. We're not out of this yet. Now comes the hard part," she whispered. She maneuvered the machine until she had a clear shot at the entrance. "Here goes nothing."

The other two guards spied her and raised the alarm.

Ali flew straight for the men. They dashed for cover when she sped past them toward the opening. She ducked as an energy beam scorched the air above her head. The shields had never been repaired from the last time. They'd need a miracle to get them out of this alive.

The sled burst through the cavern entrance, and Ali banked sharply to the right, heading along the ridge.

The air sizzled with fire from the pirates, and she did what she could to make the sled a difficult target to hit. She needed her lights to see the path, but with them on, it also gave the pirates something to aim at. Though not exactly sure of her position, she knew the general direction of Sami's hiding place. Disabling the other sleds gave her a small advantage, but a very slight one. Hopefully, she'd be out of the hand weapons range in a few seconds.

The sled lurched as a shot caught the port side, and Ali struggled to maintain equilibrium. The pirates lit up the night with their shots, but most fell short as she forced the engine into the red. The ridge next to her exploded with the power of a laser canon, and she heard the pinging of pebbles and dirt as they rained down.

"Sami? Are you there?" Ali yelled. The sled rocked as another canon blast hit them.

"Yes, Ali."

"Where am I? I need an escape route now!"

"You need to turn right. You're headed for a gorge."

"Why can't I hide there?" There were now several sleds behind her.

"It's flooded."

She risked a glance at Jason and the other man. They were both out cold. "That's it, then. We go by water."

"Ali, it's too dangerous," Sami protested as a laser flare lit up the area in front of the rocks. "The sled's been damaged."

"I don't have much of a choice, Sami. They haven't seen me yet, but they will soon, and I don't think this baby can take too many of those crystal hits, can it?"

A very reluctant "no" issued from the speaker.

"Keep a fix on me, Sami. I'm going to be busy, and I'm going to need your help. Activate night vision."

"Ali, you can't be serious. The odds of you surviving in such turbulence are beyond my capabilities to compute."

"Sami, either help me or shut up." She lifted the sled out of the rocks and took a perpendicular line to the river. A minute after she left the safety of the rocks, a flare lit them up, and she blinked against the sudden glare—momentarily blinded. The sled bounced as she scraped against a low rise, staying on course by instinct alone. As she reached the river, another flare burst, lighting her for the pirates to see.

"I've been spotted, Sami." Ali killed the night vision and turned on her running lights as a beam whizzed by her port side. She gulped at the sight of the raging torrent but headed into the dubious safety of the water. Hopefully, the roiling water would dissipate some of the power of the beams.

"Baby, I sure hope you're watertight." Ali crossed her fingers as she dropped the sled into the water. The flood caught the little ship, tossing them around like litter in a hurricane. Ali risked a quick glance at Jason and the other man and almost wished she was the one lying there unconscious. She sank the ship just beneath the top of the water.

"Sami? Can you hear me?"

"Barely, Ali." Sami's voice crackled over the speaker.

"How long do I need to stay here?" She fought for control as the ship bounced and swirled in the flood.

She tried to ignore the water streaming in from one corner of the canopy. "Make it as short as possible. I'm taking on water."

"Given your current rate of speed, three minutes from my mark." A second's pause. "Mark."

"You had to say *current,* didn't you?" Ali muttered as she gripped the controls. With all the mud and debris, she couldn't see anything beyond the dome. A couple of times, the only thing keeping them from certain disaster couldn't be attributed to her skill, but pure luck. The stretch of time became the longest three minutes of her life. At Sami's beep, she attempted to raise the ship from the water, but the power of the flood proved to be too great.

"Sami, I can't break free," she called.

"Ali, according to my scans, there's a natural dam building up on your port side. The water on the other side is calmer. See if you can aim for there."

Ali gulped when she saw the huge mass. She scraped by one side, praying to whatever gods were listening. Slowly, but steadily, the small ship drew free of the flood, finally reaching calmer water. Ali rose from the gorge and headed for their base.

A black shape loomed in front of her, and she swerved to miss it before she recognized Jason's ship. As Ali powered back the sled, the bay doors opened, and she flew into the welcoming space.

"We're in, Sami. Go," Ali instructed. The doors slammed shut, and she leaned her head back against her seat as the force of Sami's lift-off hit her.

What seemed like an eternity later, the pressure lifted, and Ali climbed out of the sled. "Sami, is there an anti-grav cart on board? I need to get Jason and Sean to sick bay."

"Maybe I can help."

Ali looked up as Joey came through the hatch with a cart. She was never so glad to see anyone in her life. "Joey? You're here? But how? Wait. Don't answer. Help me with Jason." With Joey's help, Ali managed to drag Jason onto the cart, and then she turned to Sean. He was on his face, so she gently turned him over. "Oh my God." The strength went out of her legs, and she collapsed to the floor.

"Ali? What's wrong? Are you hurt?" Joey checked her pulse and eyes.

Tears streamed unheeded down Ali's face. "He's my brother. Sean. But what have they done to him?" she whispered as she took in the cuts, bruises, and other evidence of torture

Joey looked in the back at Sean. "Come on, Ali, pull yourself together. I can't get him out of there by myself, and he needs help. Now."

Ali responded to the order in Joey's voice and helped get Sean to a cart. She traced his jaw line, swollen and bruised beyond recognition. "Sean," she whispered. "Oh, Sean."

Joey took over and gently, but firmly urged Ali aside. "You leave them to me. Why don't you go clean up? You're a mess. Marty's waiting for you in the galley."

Though reluctant to leave Jason and Sean, she did as directed. When she saw her face in Jason's mirror, she gasped. Drying blood mixed with dirt covered her face, and she winced as she cleaned myriad small cuts from her quick traverse of the tunnels and cliff. She applied dressings and changed into a fresh outfit, then went to join Marty. She found him pouring out two cups of coffee in the small galley.

"You look like hell," he said as he pushed one cup toward her. Before she could drink, he pulled the mug back, took a small flask from a compartment on his chair, and tipped a healthy portion of amber liquid into both cups. "Looks like you could use this."

"Yeah, it's nice to see you too." Ali tasted the fiery brew.

"Relax, Ali. Joey knows what she's doing. She's a bona fide medical doctor. They're in good hands. Now, tell me what you found down there that got those men so riled. And who's the extra body you brought along?"

Ali brought her attention back to Marty. "I thought Jason sent you messages about all this. But I'll tell you only if you'll tell me how you got there at the right moment. Not that I'm complaining, but the timing does seem odd."

"Not at all," Sami's voice interrupted. "Can I tell her, Sir?"

Ali looked at Marty. "Sir?" she said and grinned when he blushed to the top of his bald pate. "And here I thought only Zeus called you that."

"Say something, Sami," Marty said. He sighed and sipped at his drink.

"After I dropped you off at the clearing, I came here and found Joey and Marty waiting for us. I had a track on Jason, but not you, Ali."

"I believe you misplaced these," Marty interrupted as he dropped the earrings into her hand. She chuckled and clipped them to her earlobes.

"Took them off to shower and forgot to put them back on."

"That's your story?" Marty asked with a raised eyebrow and a twinkle in his eyes.

"It's the truth."

"Anyway," Sami continued, "When the wrist unit went dead, I switched over to Jason's implant and heard everything. Since you were gone, I assumed you would go after Jason. Marty, Joey, and I planned what to do from there."

"Thank you, Sami," Ali said. "You arrived just in time. So now what?"

Marty held up a hand. "Are we there yet, Sami?"

"Another hour, Sir. I had a little trouble shaking our tail. Oh, and I'm supposed to tell you local clean-up is done, and a certain party is on the station."

"Thank you, Sami. Change course for the station."

"Aye, Sir."

Ali looked at Marty, one eyebrow raised. "Do you want to tell me now, or is this something I'll find out later?"

Marty chuckled. "I wondered how long that curiosity of yours would stay reined in." He poured another cup of coffee.

## Chapter Twenty-Three

"After we picked you and Jason up, our forces went in and are taking care of the pirates. They also took command of that rather unique ship. As the others return, we'll deal with them also."

Ali experienced a sense of let-down. She'd wanted to be there when the pirates were caught. She knew she ought to feel good because they'd been stopped, but missing the end still bothered her.

"I know you wanted to be there," Marty pointed out as if reading her mind. "But those people were the peons. We still don't have the head. I think you know who he probably is."

"My uncle."

Marty shook his head. "Maybe at one time, but not any longer. Dimitri is controlling the strings. Posi has been monitoring him for us, and we learned some very interesting things about Mr. Kolanka. I thought you'd like to be the one to bring them in."

"Can I do that?"

"You're one of us, especially after this rescue. Do you think you can handle this?"

Ali thought about her parents and all the families destroyed by the pirates and knew only one way this could end. She nodded. "Yes. When do we get there?"

"We're docking now," Sami said. "Your uncle is on your ship. I'm not sure about Dimitri. I'll let you know as soon as I do."

"Thank you, Sami." Ali turned around as Joey came into the galley. "Joey? How are Jason and Sean?"

"They'll be fine. They're sleeping right now. Now, about you, how's your face?" She took Ali's chin in a surprisingly strong hand and assessed the damage with a critical eye. "Looks like you cleaned up pretty good. You might have a few bruises, but that's easily taken care of." She turned to Marty. "Sami kept me apprised of events."

"Are you ready, Ali?" Marty asked.

Ali nodded. "I am. Where's my ship docked?" She would meet him on her turf, not his. It gave her the advantage.

"Your ship is one level up and two slips to the right," Sami relayed.

"Thanks. I'll see you shortly." She smiled a determined smile. She thought it somehow fitting the former leader of the pirates would end his reign of terror on the ship where he'd caused her so much heartbreak. She strapped on her knives and pistols.

# Chapter Twenty-Four

"What are you doing here?" Rod asked Dimitri. "And where is Lynn? You're going to ruin everything."

Dimitri lounged back in a bunk. He could see the confusion on Rod's face. The old fool disgusted him. He'd have to get Carl to take care of the old man. He'd served his purpose. Besides with Matthews gone, he'd get the entire fortune to himself. "I'm seeing to things for Leksi."

"Leksi? Oh. That's okay then. She'll be back soon."

Dimitri yawned. Soon everything would be ready, and he would have the entire quadrant under his control. The new commander would have to be someone he could buy. It would take some doing, but with the Ki crystals under his control, he had the power. Soon he'd have sweet Leksi again. He and his friends would have a good time with her.

"Why that's wonderful news, Rod. I can't wait to see her. I'd like to renew our relationship. If you don't mind, I'll wait here for her. Why don't you go back to your office in case she goes there?"

Rod turned to go, then looked back at Dimitri. "You shouldn't have killed Lynn." He twisted the band on his wrist. "You shouldn't have done that."

\*\*\*\*

Ali sneaked onto the ship. She didn't want to alert

her uncle to her presence. A noise from her cabin sent her in that direction. When she got there, she stepped in and took a deep breath and exhaled slowly. A man stood at the back wall. He'd removed several of the panels and worked at another. She watched a minute while he pried and tugged at the panel. She smiled grimly. He had his back to her, but she'd recognize his form anywhere.

"Dimitri."

Dimitri spun around, his eyes wide. Then he smiled at her with a look that sent a shiver through her. "Leksi? What a wonderful surprise. I knew you'd come back to me. Welcome home."

"What are you doing on my ship?" Ali kept her back to the bulkhead, leaving plenty of room between her and Dimitri.

"Why, dearest Aleksia, waiting for you of course. I heard about your untimely demise—and return from the dead. You can't imagine how glad I am to see you alive."

"Are you? I'd think you'd have been happier to see me dead. After all, then you'd have everything." She watched him as he crept nearer her. She felt a little like a mouse being stalked by a snake. He'd find out, though, that this mouse had teeth. She was no longer the naïve young woman he'd once taken advantage of.

"Leksi. How could you think such a thing?"

"Easily. You're a pig, Dimitri. I've come to take you in." She sidestepped as he stalked her. Her training and agility gave her the upper hand, but she wanted room to maneuver. She backed away down the corridor, and he followed. If he hadn't been so pathetic, she'd have laughed at him.

"Aw, come on, Leksi. We're friends. Friends shouldn't fight."

"Friends don't kill their friends' family. My parents died when your men killed them. My brother nearly died. You're nothing to me except an arrest to be made." Ali flexed her wrist, and her knife dropped into her palm. She kept the blade hidden. "Tell me, what did you do to my uncle? What kind of drugs did you use on him?"

"A new one being tested for those with mental problems. It puts the person in a type of dream world and leaves them susceptible to suggestion. It's quite effective, but short lived."

"You're an ass, Dimitri. An evil, conniving, disgusting ass. And you're under arrest."

Dimitri surprised her by producing a pistol. "You're a bitch, Leksi. You've always been one. I'm going to enjoy taming you," he taunted as he held the gun on her. "Your roommate was too weak. You were much stronger—much more enjoyable."

Ali's heart lodged somewhere in the region of her throat. "You were the one."

"Of course."

"Why?"

"Why? Because your uncle owed me, and you were the payment. Your roommate became extra collateral. But you surprised me. How did you ever manage to get away? I'd really like to know."

"Screw you."

Ali heard a loud noise from the direction of the docking bay, and the ship lurched. She lunged for Dimitri as the gun went off. Searing pain tore through her shoulder.

She stumbled slightly when Dimitri leapt for her. For such a large man, he moved fast. Ali bit her lip against the pain and feinted right as Dimitri grabbed for her arm, and they both went sprawling, the gun sliding out of reach. They struggled in the corridor, each one trying to control the knife Ali had palmed. Dimitri fell on top of Ali, knocking the breath from her. The knife lay trapped between them.

As she watched, his face went pale. His body stiffened then went limp. She struggled to roll his body off her and saw the knife sticking from his chest. She knelt on the floor, trying to get her breath, and looked at the body. She should have felt something, but she didn't. No remorse. No regret. Not even satisfaction. Nothing. The nightmare had finally ended.

"One down, one to go," she murmured. The pain pulsed through her shoulder. She had to find a first aid kit. The ship lurched to the port side, and the lights went out, leaving only the emergency lights shining. The bulkhead doors slammed into place.

"Posi?" Ali called. The faithful AI didn't answer but Sami did, through her earrings.

"Ali? Where are you? My sensors don't pick you up on the station and Posi isn't answering."

Ali scrambled to her feet and ran toward the bridge. "That's because I'm not on the station. I'm on my ship. What's happening?"

A second shudder hit the ship, and she struggled to maintain her balance. Her arm ached, sending waves of pain through her entire body. The loss of blood had her head swimming. Another shudder sent her reeling into the wall, and she fought to remain conscious.

"Sami?"

"Ali, can you get to a suit? The back half of your ship is gone." Sami's voice brought some semblance of reason to her whirling head. She stumbled to the control panel and accessed the emergency closet. She grabbed the first aid kit, slapped a bandage on her shoulder, and then struggled into the suit. As she tightened the helmet, another shock hit the ship, and the hull next to her gave way in a shower of fire and debris. The vacuum of space sucked Ali out.

## Chapter Twenty-Five

Jason struggled to wake up. Gingerly he tested his muscles, relieved to find only a slight stiffness and soreness. He looked around and recognized his cabin. How had he gotten here? And where was Ali? He climbed out of the bunk and leaned against the wall, waiting for the room to stop spinning.

"Sami?" he croaked. His throat felt parched, so he stumbled from the cabin toward the galley in search of a drink.

"Jason? What are you doing up?" Joey shook her head at him and led him to a seat.

Jason sank into the chair and gratefully accepted a mug from her. "Joey? Marty? What are you doing here? And where is Ali?" He sipped at his drink as Marty filled him in on events.

"Did you get all the pirates?" He didn't remember anything beyond the cave. He must have been working on automatic.

"Most of them. The team is rounding up the last of the ships now. Ali went after Rod," Marty said.

"She what?" Jason jumped, spilling his drink.

Joey put her hand on his shoulder. "She'll be fine. He's on her ship with Dimitri. She's going to wait for him to leave and then capture him."

"Dimitri's on her ship? Oh gods. Does Ali know?"

"No," Marty said. "She was going to confront Rod,

and we just found out about Dimitri a minute ago. Why?"

Jason rushed back to his cabin, his head clear, and tugged on his clothes. "Sami, where is Rod now? And Ali?"

"Rod's in his office. Um, Boss, we have a problem. I can't find Ali, and Posi isn't answering my hail."

"Where's the ship?" Jason asked as he strapped on his guns.

"My sensors don't show her as docked." Sami's voice sounded a little too frantic for Jason's comfort. "All I'm getting is static, boss. Someone's jamming me from the office. I can't get any readings anywhere. I'm trying to break through, but they must have upgraded the system. It's slow going."

Joey strode into the room. "Jason, you're in no shape to get into a fight."

"Then get out of my way," he growled and then softened. "Joey, I owe her my life three times over. And a lot more. I can't let that madman have her."

Joey moved aside. "Then go to the commander first. He the one jamming the signals. Once the signal's clear, we can find her. Marty and I will work from here. We'll find her, Jason."

Jason nodded and took off for Rod's office. As he ran, the emergency klaxons sounded, and people scrambled for shelter before the bulkheads closed. Jason slipped through the last one a second before the barrier slammed shut.

Rod emerged from his office and saw Jason. A look of pure hatred marred his fair features as he faced him. "How many lives do you have, Andrew?"

Andrew? That was Ali's father. "More than

enough," Jason said as he assessed the situation. The commander had totally lost all sense of reality. He needed to play along with him. Thanks to the shields, they were alone. Rod had a small pistol, but so did Jason. The odds looked about even.

Rod glared at Jason. "You! You ruined it all!"

Jason shook his head. "Give it up, Commander. Your fleet has been impounded or destroyed, your men captured. Everything is gone."

Rod reached for his weapon, but Jason was faster.

The commander fell to the ground, a large red stain growing on his shirt. "I found the red crystal. It's mine now. It's all mine now. Dimitri thought he would win, but I'll show him. He'll pay for everything."

Jason walked over and kicked the gun out of the way before he knelt down. "Where's Ali?" he demanded. Before Jason could stop him, Rod hit a button on the back of his wrist unit and Jason felt a shudder go through the station. "Where's Ali?"

Rod looked up at Jason, puzzlement and pain in his eyes. "She's with you."

"She was last seen heading for her ship to meet you." Jason watched Rod's face. He could swear from the shocked look the man knew nothing about Ali.

"She was coming for me?" A brief smile lit his face and then dissolved into despair. "Oh my God," he whispered. "I've killed her. Lynn? Forgive me." The light went out of his eyes as he sighed his final breath.

Jason dragged the body into the office where he wouldn't be seen by anyone and accessed the station control panel. He reset all the controls, relieved when the sirens stopped and the shields lifted. "Sami? Are you clear now?"

"Yes. Uh-oh. We have major trouble. Get your ass back here."

Startled at Sami's tone, Jason sprinted back to the ship, ignoring the shocked cries of people emerging from their shelters. The airlock cycled shut as he squeezed through and dashed for the bridge, settling in his seat as Sami took off for the far side of the station. Marty and Joey were already strapped in, running scans of the area.

"Where is she?" Jason murmured as Joey joined him. "Sami, do you have her?"

"I've got her signal, boss. She's on the far side. I can't raise her, though. And her movements indicate a random drift."

"Get us there, Sami. Joey, I'm going out. Get your med-kit ready."

Jason yanked on his suit and cycled through the air lock. He floated out into the vastness of space. A field of debris surrounded him, and he had to move carefully in case a stray piece hit him and punctured his suit. He looked around but didn't see Ali anywhere. "Sami? Where is she? I don't see her."

"Twenty meters on the Z axis."

Jason looked down and thought he could make out her shape. He powered his jetpack and dived. When he reached Ali, he gathered her into his arms and headed back for the ship. Her features, what he could see through the helmet, were so pale. Drops of blood floated between her face and the view plate. Except for the blood, this reminded him of how they'd met. He'd be damned if this would be the way he'd say goodbye to her.

"Come on, Ali. Don't you leave me. I need you. I

love you." He stepped into the lock with Ali as the shock wave from another explosion hit them. He braced his feet against the walls and clung to Ali as the ship rocked. A minute later, the inner door slid open and Jason stumbled out with Ali.

Joey waited with a grav-cart. Jason yanked off his helmet and gloves. "How is she?"

"I can't tell you through her suit. I'll let you know as soon as I do. Now, go up to Marty and let me do my job." She muttered something about déjà vu as Jason backed away.

A short time later, Joey joined Jason and Marty in the galley. "Marty, if you haven't wasted all your hooch, I could sure use a shot."

She held out her mug, and Marty poured a generous amount in. "Ali is fine. She lost a lot of blood, but the shot didn't hit anything major. She needs rest. So, are we done now?"

Marty chuckled. "I think so. Let's see—" He held up his fingers one at a time. "—One, we collected all the pirates. Two, we captured a fleet of rather special ships our experts are going to have a field day with. Three, we found an incredible source of Ki crystals easily accessible, including red—oh, by the way, Jason, you are now an extremely rich man. I took the liberty of filing mineral rights for you. Four, we cleaned up a rat's nest of bad guys for the locals. They were associated with the pirates, but not part of them. Five, um, let's see, is there a five?"

"We got a new agent to work with us, and she's a babe." Sami chimed in.

"Sami," Joey scolded.

"Anyway," Marty continued, "all in all, I'd say we

had a pretty successful run. What do you say we go home? Sami?"

"Already on our way, Sir. The clean-up team is sweeping the station. They say everything's under control."

Jason stood and wandered back to his cabin. After everything that had happened, he felt slightly let down. All he wanted now was a few years' worth of sleep. Ali's brother, Sean, slept in her cabin. He would be okay, but recovery would take some time and a stretch at a reconstruction clinic. Jason paused when he got to his cabin. There, curled up in his bunk, lay Ali. As quietly as he could, he stripped out of his clothes and lay down beside her. Her eyes opened, and he gazed into them.

"Hello, Hunter," Ali murmured. "What took you so long?"

"I had a few loose ends to tie up. How are you feeling?" he asked as he ran his hand down her leg.

"Like I've been shot. How 'bout you?".

"Like I've been beaten by an expert." He caressed her cheek with his lips, enjoying the little sounds of pleasure she made.

"Then I guess we shouldn't do anything," Ali murmured as she turned toward him.

"I guess we shouldn't," Jason agreed as he continued his assault.

"What about the others?" Ali gasped.

"What others? There's just you and me. Let the rest of the universe take care of itself." Jason moved on top of her and gasped as his abused ribs sent him a painful signal.

Ali bit back a giggle. "What do you say I do the

flying this time?" She shifted position so he could lie down. She leaned forward, her breasts touching his chest, and settled her hips over his. "Feel better?"

Jason proceeded to show her how good he felt.

Later, curled up in the curve of Jason's arm, Ali glanced at him. "So what do we do now?"

He ran his hand up and down her arm. "Much as I'd love a repeat performance, I don't think my ribs will let me."

"That's not what I meant. I meant, what about us? Where do we go from here?"

Jason struggled to sit and looked at her. "Now, we take time to recover. And go home."

"And where is home?"

"Anywhere you want, but I kind of thought a little house near a series of ponds backed by a system of caves would be nice."

"Sounds like heaven to me. A good place to go back to when we're not on the job."

"You still want to be an agent?"

Ali sat up and stared at him. "Of course, I do. But only if we work together as a team."

"You got it, Ali. Together, we can do anything."

"Yes, we can."

****

"Do you think we need to do anything?" Marty asked as he plugged the data wafer Joey handed him into the console. Me-too purred from her spot in Joey's lap as Joey petted her.

"Like what, dearest? Don't you remember what it's like to be young and in love? Is she there, Sami?"

"Yep. I'm glad she told me about this program. May I introduce you two to Posi?"

"Hello, Posi," Marty and Joey said in unison.

"Hello, Joey, Marty. It's nice to finally meet you. Sami and Zeus have told me so much about you."

"Isn't she wonderful?" Sami cooed as soft music emanated from the speakers.

Joey nudged Marty and winked. "Marty, I do believe our Sami is smitten."

"Humph. Next thing you know there'll be little AI robots running all over the place," Marty complained as he grinned at Joey. "Sami, I am experiencing a need to test my navigating skills. How 'bout if you let me fly for a while?"

"Yes, sir. Thank you, sir."

Marty grinned as Joey took the seat next to him. "Guess we old folks should let the youngsters have their time."

Joey raised her eyebrows. "I don't know about you, old man, but as soon as they make an appearance, I plan on doing some disappearing of my own."

"By yourself?"

"Not if I have anything to say." She grinned and kissed him soundly, making him blush to the top of his bald head.

Me-too continued to purr.

**A word about the author…**

Vicky has been married forever to the one person who accepts that she lives in a fantasy world most of the time. She's even been seen at the beach building worlds for her stories. In addition to creating fun characters, fantasy worlds, and suspenseful situations, she also enjoys and is very good at things like writing policy and procedures manuals and setting up continuity and organizational spreadsheets, both of which she has actually earned money doing.

She has a master's degree in library science, so likes things organized. Okay, so her family thinks having the spice rack alphabetized is a bit much, but she has no trouble finding what she needs when she needs it. And just because her extensive library is cataloged and organized, that doesn't mean she's obsessive. Honest.

When not writing, Vicky can be found in the kitchen whipping up gluten-free, lactose-free, and other allergy-free meals. Or watching the world go by from her front porch swing.

http://burkholv.wordpress.com

Thank you for purchasing
this publication of The Wild Rose Press, Inc.

For questions or more information
contact us at
info@thewildrosepress.com.

The Wild Rose Press, Inc.
www.thewildrosepress.com

To visit with authors of
The Wild Rose Press, Inc.
join our yahoo loop at
http://groups.yahoo.com/group/thewildrosepress/